Where Drowned Things Live

Where Drowned Things Live

A Kristin Ginelli Mystery

SUSAN THISTLETHWAITE

RESOURCE *Publications* · Eugene, Oregon

WHERE DROWNED THINGS LIVE
A Kristin Ginelli Mystery

Resource Publications
An Imprint of Wipf and Stock Publishers
199 W. 8th Ave., Suite 3
Eugene, OR 97401

www.wipfandstock.com

PAPERBACK ISBN: 978-1-5326-1363-0
HARDCOVER ISBN: 978-1-5326-1365-4
EBOOK ISBN: 978-1-5326-1364-7

Manufactured in the U.S.A.

Your silence today is a pond where drowned things live
I want to see raised dripping and brought into the sun.

ADRIENNE RICH, "TWENTY-ONE LOVE POEMS"
THE DREAM OF A COMMON LANGUAGE

Acknowledgments

The University of Chicago is, of course, an actual place but all the people, buildings, departments and events in this novel are fictional. I regret I cannot actually gift this fine university with these buildings and academic departments. I am glad, however, that the events portrayed here are completely without basis in fact and are wholly a creation of my own imagination.

Regrettably, however, violence against women is all too real, and the widespread failure of individuals and institutions to prevent this viciousness and to quickly and competently identify and prosecute the offenders is all too common.

This must change.

This volume, fictional though it may be, is dedicated to the women and men who have suffered many forms of violence at educational institutions and been denied justice.

Contents

1

All these things, Socrates, my dear friend, so many and so great, which they say about virtue and vice, and how both gods and men respect them—how do they think they will work on the souls of young people when they hear them?

PLATO, *THE REPUBLIC*, BOOK II

She was terrified.

From the top of her smooth cap of black hair to the tips of her shiny little black pumps with their fixed bows, her body was rigid. I'd heard the expression "scared stiff" many times. I'd never given any thought to the fact that it could be taken literally. She was practically catatonic and I was pretty sure the cause was fear.

Well, she should be afraid. Because above the rim of her prim, white, Peter Pan collared blouse was a purpling ring of bruises clearly made by someone's fingers. Her name was Kim, Ah-seong, Kim being what Westerners would call her last name. She was a sophomore at the University of Chicago. Ay-seong was probably fulfilling her Korean parents' dream of an expensive American education. I'd bet they were not aware that someone at this famous university was putting bruises on their daughter, or worse. And I had been asked to find out who and why.

This was Monday afternoon. On Saturday night, Ah-seong's roommate had noticed that she had returned to their dorm room bruised and upset. She had refused to talk about it to the pleading roommate, to the concerned dorm resident, to the Dean of Students, Margaret Lester, and now she was refusing to talk about it to me. Apparently this was not the first time Ah-seong had come back to her dorm room with some bruises and the roommate was guessing it was somebody she was dating who was making these bruises on her. Date battering. Great.

"Just talk to her, Kristin," Margaret had pleaded.

She had more confidence than I did that because I'd been a cop before I became a university instructor I'd be able to figure out who was beating on this kid. Well, I'd seen my share of domestic violence calls, one reason, among many, that I was no longer a cop.

"Ah-seong."

Her head moved stiffly, slowly to look up. But she didn't look directly at me. Her dark eyes were flattened and her gaze glassy. She directed that unseeing gaze at the ersatz medieval turrets outside the window. The main quadrangle of the university was built of grey stone in a gothic style—it had its own grim beauty, unlike the spread of disconcerting and disjointed modern that now made up the majority of the rest of the campus. Yes, I might be a lowly instructor, but I did rate a window that gave on to ivy-covered buildings in faux medieval style. But she was not admiring the view.

I decided not to come at her directly about the events of Saturday night, or even about the bruises. I thought I'd start with something safer, her friendships at school.

"Ah-seong, Dean Lester tells me you belong to a student group. Right? In fact, you spend a lot of time with them."

The face in profile nodded, the cap of ebony hair falling forward.

"Well, that's good. Have you many friends in the group?"

A nod.

Well, this wasn't moving swiftly along, that's for sure. Especially when you've been hurt, trusting anyone often came very slowly.

"What student group is it?"

I already knew. I had her student profile in front of me. But anything to get her talking.

"Students—Korean Students. Korean Students Christian Association."

Her voice was faint, whispery. Her head was down again and she spoke directly to her hands gripping her backpack on her lap. She hadn't even trusted me enough to put her books down when she had reluctantly sat in my one office chair.

I wondered how much pressure those fingers on her neck had applied. Whether she had actual damage to her larynx. Margaret had told me she had refused to be seen at student health. Typical.

I decided to go with the Christian affiliation.

"That's good. Really good, Ah-seong. And as a Christian, I know you know it's not right for one person to hurt another person. "

I went in for the kill.

"That's not what Jesus would want, is it?"

For the first time, eye contact. Her head in its little Peter Pan collar with the circle of bruises right above it lifted and sad, drowned eyes met mine. I almost hated myself for pushing that button, especially when I saw the hurt and what seemed to be confusion in her eyes.

"No . . . Professor Ginelli."

Barely a whisper.

"But someone did hurt you. I can see the bruises, there, around your neck."

She lifted a hand to her neck to re-adjust the scarf that I guess she had arranged to try to hide the neck bruises, but it had slipped. As she raised her hand, her sleeve dropped back, revealing a bracelet of bruises to match her necklace. She followed my eyes and made a tiny sound of distress. Her head dropped down again and her hair swung forward, nearly hiding her face.

She was ashamed. Ashamed that someone would hurt her and ashamed that someone else would see it.

My stomach clenched with rage, and, God help me, some of my own remembered fear. I had to put all that aside for Ah-seong's sake.

"Someone put their hands on you too hard and left bruises on you. It must have hurt. Why don't you tell me about it?"

Nothing. Just another glance out the window.

Okay, so back to manipulating her about her Christian faith. I knew a lot about the Christian faith as I taught in the Philosophy and Religion department here at the U. of C., though I supposed by Ah-seong's standards I was an atheist. By my standards, maybe not an atheist. More like an agnostic. I made a religion out of doubt.

Long ago I had rejected my parents' brand of white, upper class, self-congratulatory Lutheranism, though their god was not technically the God of Martin Luther. They were really idol worshippers; they worshipped money and greed was their daily ritual.

Their worship of their own wealth and their conviction it made them superior human beings whose judgment was correct in all things, and certainly correct for my life, had gradually alienated me. I'd rebelled and left home after high school. My Great-Aunt, who lived part of the time in Denmark and part of the time in the U.S., was equally alienated from the family and their single-minded devotion to the acquisition of money. She'd set up a trust fund for me so I could be independent. I adored her. She was the only person in my family I knew who was remotely like me. I'd used the money for college and then I'd decided to become a cop, frankly just to continue to annoy my parents. But I'd liked it.

At first.

When I was a newbie cop I'd adopted the functional belief system all cops seem to have. 'Somebody upstairs' is watching over me. It's a blend of faith and fatalism. But after my policeman husband was killed in the line of duty, killed because his backup had not gotten out of the car, I'd become a dedicated doubter, but a reformed variety. I worshipped ideas.

But Christianity wasn't an idea to Ah-seong. Her faith was obviously personal and important to her. I felt like a rat using her faith to manipulate her.

I'd be a rat, though, if being a rat could save her life. Choking is often a signal that a future attack will be fatal, and the bruises on her wrist, bruises that seemed a little more faded than the livid marks on her throat, meant she'd likely been bruised more than once. Really dangerous pattern.

"Alright, Ah-seong, you know that Christians believe hurting another person is wrong and that Jesus would not like that. So the person who is doing this to you is doing something wrong. You need to tell me who that is so we can help him. Help him stop sinning in this way."

I tried out the pronoun; pretty sure it was the right one.

Women who get hit by boyfriends or husbands many times won't get help for themselves, because at some level they think they deserve the abuse, but they'll respond to a plea to get help for their batterer.

Ah-seong was no different. She sat up, straightened her narrow shoulders and turned directly toward me.

"He does not mean it to hurt me. He is sad if he hurts me. He has much affection for me—it is only if he is frustrated for his grades and to be on team at the same time."

She trailed off, perhaps aware that she had just revealed that the boyfriend who was making bruises on her was on a college team and had to keep his grades up—to keep a scholarship?

The University of Chicago long ago gave up its powerhouse football team, the original "Monsters of the Midway," the midway being the large grassy mall that bisected the campus. The Chicago Bears became the "Monsters of the Midway." But even the rigid, scholarly President Edward Hastings, who dismantled the university's athletic program because he deemed too much concentration on sports was incompatible with true dedication to intellectual pursuits, had been unable to take all the scholarship money from football. A few named scholarships had remained. The best Hastings had been able to do was tie them to high grade point averages, a 3.5 or even 3.8 I thought.

"Does he play football, Ah-seong?" I asked.

Her hair swung across her face, as she vigorously shook her head no.

I wasn't buying it.

"I think he does play football, if he has a scholarship and hopes to keep it. I'd like to help him."

I knew exactly how I'd like to help him.

"I pray for him. They pray for him."

Barely a whisper escaped her rigid lips.

"Who prays for him, Ah-seong?"

"We all do." Her eyes met mine. She felt on solid ground here.

"All the Koreans in your group?"

"Yes." Almost inaudible.

So the student group knows this is going on? Not good.

"Ah-seong, prayer is good, but we must help him in other ways too. He must get counseling. You need counseling too."

"No!" She rose slightly out of the chair and fear coursed into her eyes, driving out the brief look of trust. Her knuckles grabbing the backpack were white. She lowered jerkily back down but her thin frame was vibrating with anxiety. What was going on here?

"No, I do not wish counseling. I do not wish to talk to anyone about this. No one."

She let the backpack slide to the floor unnoticed and she wrapped her arms around herself and shivered. She was self-comforting and trying to make herself even smaller at the same time. I felt a wave of pity.

Yet, I literally had no idea what was going on in her mind at that moment. One thing was clear though, whomever this guy was he needed to be identified and stopped. But first I needed to reduce her terror.

"Okay, okay. Nobody will force you into counseling. Take a few breaths. We'll figure this out."

I thought for a minute and then decided to try something. Maybe this guy who was hurting her was a member of the prayer group. I decided to try it out.

"Ah-seong, you know Jesus does not think anyone should hurt another person, but especially Christians should not hurt each other. Is he in the prayer group with you all when you are praying for him?"

"We pray for him."

Not clear.

"Yes, okay, praying for him is good, but perhaps you should try not to see him, you know, give him some time to repent and change."

Wow, was I blowing this. I knew that wouldn't happen. I opened my mouth to retract what I had just said, but Ah-seong spoke first.

"It is not right I do not see him. Our prayers will help him."

So what? Had the prayer group convinced her she could convert this battering boyfriend if she sticks with prayer? That is the kind of 'hit me again' idea of Jesus and sacrifice that is responsible for so much pain and suffering among conservative Christian women.

I hoped Ah-seong could not see the steam coming out of my ears. I was really furious. But I needed to control my own anger and focus on this hurting person in front of me. I took a breath. Jesus help me. Literally.

"Ah-seong, it is never right for someone to hurt another person. You are God's child and Jesus loves you. You must get some help for yourself, for him, so that he stops doing this."

She shook her head from side to side again, but so slowly, so sadly I felt a prickle behind my eyes. I'm not a prayer person myself but I did send an urgent message out into the universe, 'Let this person seek help.'

"I will pray about what you say."

She bent and picked up her backpack and then neatly gathered her coat and disappeared around the divider that made one office into two cubicles.

She left so quietly I barely heard the door open and shut.

I hoped if she wouldn't talk to me she'd seek professional help elsewhere in the university and not just go running to the prayer group. So far they seemed to be enabling more than helping.

Christ Almighty, what a mess. So to speak.

Well, now it was Margaret Lester's problem. I picked up the phone and called her, expecting to speak to her secretary, or even more likely a recorded voice telling me to leave a message. Well, I wouldn't leave a detailed message, that's for sure.

I was surprised that Margaret herself answered.

"Kristin," she said.

I was startled for a minute and then realized our names displayed on the phone in the campus system. Margaret must have been waiting for my call.

"Margaret. I talked to Ah-seong Kim. She just left. I think you'd better look into this student group she belongs to."

"The Korean Students Christian Association?" Margaret sounded surprised.

"Yes. My best guess is that she's got a boyfriend who is knocking her around, or worse, and the student group is encouraging her to keep dating him so that her turn-the-other-cheek Christianity will convert his rotten little heart."

"Wait a minute." Margaret's disbelief come through loud and clear. "Run that by me again. You're saying a student group knows she's being hit and is encouraging it?"

"No, not exactly, and look, she really didn't tell me all that much. I'm guessing here, but my best guess is that a guy she is dating, probably not a member of the group, is being rough with her. Date battering is not uncommon you know, Margaret. Another guess is that he's a scholarship student on the football team, at least she admitted that he has one of the few sports scholarships, and I think he's hitting her to let off steam, feel manly, who knows? Maybe she got the most recent bruises because she was trying to break it off. Anyway, the student group is praying for him and I think that adds up to a lot of secondary gain for them. Do they think he's a guy in need of salvation? I really don't know, but I don't like the sound of what I think I heard."

"Slow down, slow down. How do you know whosever hitting her is a football player?"

Margaret's voice was sharp. How administrators hate to go after the athletes, even here.

"Ah-seong told me whoever made the bruises on her is frustrated by keeping his grades up so he can stay on the team. I think that sounds like someone who needs to keep his scholarship, and practically no sport here has scholarship money for players except football."

"Well, perhaps."

Margaret's voice was toneless. Bad sign. She was going to fob me off. It was so damned irritating. I hadn't asked to talk to this student. She'd begged me to do it.

"Now, what's this about the KSCA being involved? I find that very hard to believe. I know Professor Lee, their advisor, and I can't believe he'd condone something like this."

I could almost understand why Margaret was so anxious to play down these unpleasant facts. Almost. Sports were always politically important because the alums liked them and that caused them to open their pockets and donate. And the Korean student group was another politically hot item. The University needed intelligent students whose families could afford the more than $50,000 in yearly tuition (not counting room and board). Parents could spend more than a quarter of a million dollars sending one child to college for four years. Yes, a lot went into debt and there were scholarships, but the university needed the cash flow of tuition. There was active recruitment around the world in fast-growing economies, including Asian economies. And wealthy graduates became wealthy donors.

I tried for patience.

"Listen, Margaret, Lee might not necessarily know about these special prayers. Or, he could know they were praying for someone without knowing the specifics of what was going on."

But my patience goes only so far.

"This student group, though. Isn't it a little, well, narrow for a university group?"

Margaret sighed.

"Kristin, come off it. There are nearly 400 student groups and many of them are racially, ethnically and religiously specific. That's what students want."

"Yeah, it's what students want, Margaret, but didn't I just see a idiotic memo about the fact that we don't do 'safe spaces' here any more?"

She paused.

I waited. That memo was a bunch of legal malarkey and Margaret knew it and I knew it too.

"I think you probably misunderstood Ah-seong, that's all. You said she spoke very little. I think it's likely there's no connection here with the student group and that she's having some trouble with someone she's dating."

Okay. Patience gone, waiting over. I sharpened my voice.

"Look, Margaret. What is going on here is dangerous. Very dangerous. What I know for sure is that it is best to assume the worst. I have seen the bruises around her neck, so has the roommate and the RA. Are you really going to brush this aside as 'boyfriend troubles'? She has certainly been physically assaulted. That we can see with our own eyes. Keep that in mind. I think there's a good chance she's been sexually assaulted as well. Remember what the roommate said about the torn clothing."

There was a sharp intake of breath on the other end of the phone, but Margaret didn't speak.

My voice rose.

"You twisted my arm to look into this thing. I didn't volunteer. And now when I tell you what I think is going on, you're trying to minimize it."

I gripped the phone hard.

"Assume the worst, Margaret. You must assume the worst and you have to do that even if it pisses off some alumni or faculty or students or recruiters or coaches or whatever.

"It will accelerate, you know. If there's no intervention the odds are she'll be assaulted again. Probably hurt even worse. That's the normal trajectory of these things. They. Get. Worse."

I waited. When she didn't respond, I changed tactics. If a frightened and abused woman student didn't move her, investigations and lawsuits might. And no memo about the purity of intellectual freedom would protect us from that.

"Margaret, don't you realize there are now nearly 100 pending Title IX investigations of colleges for mishandling sexual assault and sexual misconduct pending? Our university is currently not on that list. Do you want it to be? Anti-rape activism is on the rise on college campuses. Remember earlier this year when that guy, you know the one who was after Clinton for so long, Starr, got fired at Baylor? He and the football coach were axed because they failed to help victims of sexual assault. And don't count on a misogynist climate in Washington D.C. to slow down the campus protests. Women's activism is increasing, not decreasing.

"Just get off the dime and start the administrative wheels rolling. We have enough for an initial complaint. I'll make it, for Christ's sake. I talked to her. I saw the bruises. I heard enough to alarm me as to her safety and well being.

"In fact, consider this phone call the initial complaint. I'll follow up in writing and have it to you by tomorrow."

I was breathing heavily. There was silence on the other end of the phone. This time I would wait.

Margaret finally spoke.

"Thanks for talking to her, Kristin. I'll talk to her again myself."

And she hung up.

Great. The full administrative brush-off. Well, Margaret would soon realize that not only would I summarize my conversation with Ah-seong Kim in the complaint, I would summarize this conversation as well. If she didn't shape up and do her job right, she could end up needing legal counsel.

But I realized I couldn't write a complaint feeling like this. I had to get a grip first. I was vibrating with anger. This was far too close to what police work had been like for me. The kind of work I thought I'd left behind when I quit the force. Well, not all that close since now I was bringing up Jesus every second sentence, but I felt an all too familiar cold knot of frustration in my stomach, the frustration at all the kinds of violence that are covered up, pushed away, and that I was powerless to do anything about.

I turned my chair and gazed for a moment out the window at the same view that Ah-seong had focused on such a short while ago. Grey stone. Lots of very depressing grey stone. Bad choice for buildings in a metropolis nicknamed "The Grey City" for its constant leaden skies. Here it was October and what we had was pale yellow leaves and overcast skies instead of the brilliant hues of the trees and the blue skies of my native New England. Why did I stay in this walk-in refrigerator of a city with all its bad weather and bad memories?

I gave myself a little shake and turned to my computer. I opened a file and started summarizing the conversations I'd had that afternoon.

Then I stopped. It was no good. I needed more distance. I saved the few sentences I'd written and sent it to myself to work on later at home.

Besides distance, I realized, I would need to write this up using whatever was the university's recommended format. I logged on to the section on University Policies and Procedures. I started to read about the published procedures for filing a complaint on sexual misconduct. There was an additional link for faculty, but when I clicked on it, I realized I needed an additional password.

I also needed more time to process my emotions before I wrote anything that would become part of an official complaint.

I looked out the window again, not seeing the grey this time, but other experiences with administrative duck and cover on Chicago's police force and their endless, deliberate refusal to deal justly with police misconduct that only sent a clear signal to cops that they could continue to do what they wanted to whomever they wanted, whenever they wanted.

Until some lawsuit caught up with a few. No wonder Chicago was so broke, having to pay out millions and millions of dollars to victims of cops who should have been kicked off the force years before—shooting unarmed civilians, making false arrests, torturing suspects, raping and battering women, and persecuting whistleblowers on the bad cops.

Law and order. That's what I'd wanted when I'd chosen the police academy. Law and order that would stand for the victims of injustice. Right out of the academy at twenty-four, I'd married a detective, Marco Ginelli, who believed the same as I did. Marco was as Italian as his name with thick, full dark hair always in need of a haircut, framing a face with deep brown eyes, a face full of passion and mischief and intelligence. A face that was fortunately reproduced in our twin boys, Sam and Mike, now aged six.

All that warmth and passion had entered my cold Scandinavian bloodstream and thawed my ice-queen defenses erected against the lovelessness of my childhood and the isolation from peers that my height had caused. When I'd been nearly six feet tall at age fourteen, my parents had actually taken me to a doctor to see if 'something could be done about it'. Unconditional acceptance was not my parents' strong suit. Besides, it was their families' genes that made me so tall. But they'd made me feel like the ugly duckling come to life.

A huge bear of a man, Marco had enveloped my height and my defenses and I had started to melt into a human being. And yes, I was still in love with Marco, only he had been dead five years now, killed when he'd stopped a car containing suspected drug dealers on this same south side of Chicago, shot in the line of duty because his partner hadn't gotten out of the car to give him back-up. Nobody really investigated. The failure of police procedure, if that was all it was, was brushed under the carpet with the old administrative two-step. Marco's death only gave me the final excuse for leaving the force.

My own disillusionment with so-called law enforcement had begun much earlier, when I was still a rookie. Getting along, going along, doing what it took to get by and being punished, not even too subtly, by colleagues threatened by anyone who cared too much, who tried too hard or who wouldn't look the other way when a few bucks changed hands, and most of all by men who were threatened by a blond Viking.

It was not whether I'd been sexually harassed by my fellow officers, it had only been how much and how often. It isn't the sex. It's about controlling women. It's about power. It's about letting women know you don't belong here.

But the unwritten rule about police work was never, ever complain about another officer. I had finally complained—about the guy who was assigned to be Marco's temporary partner the day he'd been killed.

Was it deliberate, a set up to send a message to both Marco and me? A set up that had gone lethally wrong, or was it meant to be lethal all along? I'd always believed the latter, but even the lawyer I'd hired hadn't been able to make a case that stuck. My grief at Marco's death and my leaden despair over my inability to do anything about it pushed me nearly to the brink. If I hadn't had my baby boys to think about, I don't honestly know what I would have done.

Put up. Shut up. No law and order here.

And now I was finding that my attempt to find refuge in academics was a joke. This was no refuge at all. It was the same human violence met with the same inadequate, even corrupt, tools of bureaucracy.

The grey stone came back into focus. I had to shake this off and do right by Ah-seong Kim. And, I realized with a jolt, actually do my academic job.

I was late for a faculty meeting. I didn't exactly jump up and rush to the meeting, however.

You'd think at $50,000 per student for tuition that there would be enough money to hire faculty. Wasn't that the point of a university, teaching students?

If you thought so you were decades out of date.

Universities and colleges are engaged in an orgy of budget cutting. But only in faculty positions and faculty salaries. Administrator's salaries and huge outlays for new and fancier buildings just keep growing like some hideous cancer.

Humanities departments, like my own, were especially vulnerable. We had no huge grants like the sciences. We had no wealthy alumni like the economics department and business school. We were, in short, budget canon-fodder.

I shut down my computer and rose. There was no need to rush to a meeting where so little would be said so slowly and repeated so often.

I grabbed my coat. I'd leave right after the faculty meeting. I passed the divider that separated my part of this shared office from my officemate, Henry Haruchi.

Henry was Japanese on his father's side and Welch on his mother's side. He taught Buddhism, though also comparative religion and he had an interest in religion and science. He was a terrifically interesting guy and when we were in the office together we often talked to the detriment of actually getting work done, though as I thought about it he'd been gone from the office a lot this fall quarter. I wished he were around. I assumed he was at the meeting. I'd have loved to run my conversation with Ah-seong by him.

I had to just shelve this onslaught of feelings and get on with it. Just get on with it. I opened the door to my office.

Directly across the hall, Mary Frost, the departmental secretary, was rooting around in her desk. I wondered why. She should have been taking notes at the meeting.

She glanced up and frowned deeply at me. The students called that 'being Frosted.' Too bad. I asked her for the password to the faculty link to Policies and Procedures.

She just continued to glare at me without responding.

Just perfect.

2

When I was fifteen years old I saw the University of Chicago for the first time and somehow sensed that I had discovered my life. I had never before seen, or at least had not noticed, buildings that were evidently dedicated to a higher purpose, not to necessity or utility, not merely to shelter or manufacture or grade, but to something that might be an end in itself.

ALLAN BLOOM, *THE CLOSING OF THE AMERICAN MIND*

I turned and stomped down the hall. The flagstone floor of these fake gothic buildings made a satisfyingly loud sound as I trudged on down the long hall toward the conference room at the end of the hall. On this floor of the Myerson Humanities building, we in Philosophy and Religion occupied one side and History had the other. A big staircase bisected the building in the front. There was one creaky old elevator somewhere. Not really ADA compliant and I'd never consider riding in it.

One side of our hallway had faculty offices arranged from smallest to largest, Henry's and mine being the smallest. The Department Chair, Dr. Harold Grimes, of course, occupied the very largest. On the other side, the department secretary occupied an equally small office, the mirror of my shared office, and then there were two empty offices, now used for very small classes, and a large conference room at the end where the meeting was taking place. Grimes had the showcase office, a semi-circular room with stained glass at the top that was inside one of the four turrets that anchored the corners of the building.

I clunked along, thinking that if the university really did attack us with more drastic budget cuts we could always defend ourselves by shooting arrows out of the narrow slits in our turrets. With the water in the water cooler and the snack machines in the basement, we could hold out for weeks.

Even as slowly as I was walking, I finally reached the conference room. Though the meeting had started at 3:30 and it was now nearly 4, I could not bring myself to open the door right away. As I lingered in the hall, I could hear the raised voices inside probably making points that had been made several times before, and surely would be again.

This was another area where I had discovered to my dismay that being a cop and being an academic did not differ substantially. Squad meetings were also endlessly repetitive. Of course, at squad meetings we'd had donuts to keep us going. No donuts at faculty meetings, or none that I had ever seen.

I finally pushed the heavy oak door open and shards of afternoon light spilled through the mullioned windows that lined the conference room on the west wall. The light shot directly into my eyes and poked at the headache that had been building since I'd first met with Ah-seong. It had been a long afternoon and it was going to get a lot longer.

Seated around an oak table fully thirty feet in length were the remaining full-time members of the Department of Philosophy and Religion. Many chairs lined the walls, but there were three empty chairs still at the table. One because I was not yet seated in it, and the two others for the two tenured positions we had lost in the last two years.

Yes, of course, those courses were still taught, but just by underpaid adjuncts, the fast-food workers of the university whose ranks of cheap labor were growing even as full-time positions were cut or moved to more lucrative departments. I thought it was rather like playing at the ghost in *Hamlet* to keep the empty chairs pulled up to the table. Were they meant to echo a mute cry for revenge from those whose jobs had been murdered?

The head of our department, Harold Grimes, was standing at the head of the table, the filtered light behind him glinting off of his full head of white hair. This was an effect intended by Harold, as was keeping his suspiciously tanned face out of direct light, the better to hide the network of wrinkles direct light would reveal. He thought he was handsome and affected the clichéd horn-rimmed glasses, tweed jacket, leather patch elbows, pipe in pocket look so beloved of his generation of academic men. He really didn't look too bad. Stereotypes are stereotypes for a reason.

Harold was tall, probably now just a little over six feet as age took its toll on his height and contributed to his increasing girth around the stomach. His veneer of absent-minded professor covered a power player of some skill. He had survived to his nearly sixty years of age having published very little, and none of it of note, in a university where that should have finished him long ago. That it had not, and that he was, in fact, a tenured senior professor, was strong testimony to his palpable personal charm and to his ability to know and be known in the labyrinthine ways of power in the university.

Harold's field was Ethics, a fact I tried not to dwell on because I found it made me laugh. It's not wise to find your boss too funny. Harold was not a person to underestimate. Yet, in a weird way I was glad he was our department head. If anybody could protect us from the accounting sharks that ruled academic budgets today, Harold could. That is, if it suited his own purposes. I glanced at the two empty chairs. He hadn't been able to save the ghosts. And an untenured professor like my lowly self who has not completed her dissertation is very vulnerable at budget-cutting time.

"Ms. Ginelli, so glad you could join us," said Grimes, pausing to underline my peon status by not even using the customary faculty honorific of "professor." He then waited, underlining my tardy status, until I had crossed the large room to take my seat.

Well, given my height I am not able to insinuate myself into a room in any case. I paused behind my chair for a minute and looked at him. I'm about an inch taller than he is and he really didn't like the fact that I could look down on him. He was used to looking down on women (literally and figuratively) and on most men for that matter.

"Take your seat," he barked out, having been pushed too far.

I could feel my job sway under me and decided I'd really better sit down.

Henry, my office-mate, swiveled his pseudo-Tudor conference chair in my direction as I took my seat, and with his back to Grimes crossed his eyes at me. Wow, this meeting must be excruciating for Henry to mug in front of Grimes, even discretely. Henry desperately needed his job. This must really be bad.

Grimes seemed to decide he had punished me enough and began pacing at the head of the table.

"As I was saying, at the Department Chairs meeting, Dean Wooster emphasized that the self-study is a way for all departments to have access to the creation of a curricular structure that befits the intellectual demands this twenty-first century have laid upon us."

He paused for emphasis, not for comment. At least not from me. Anything I could truthfully have said would have further imperiled my job.

Hercules Abraham, Professor of Judaism, the most senior member of the department and the kindest man I have ever met, nodded his small, neat, white head from his position directly to Grimes' left. I wondered what he was doing here. At more than seventy years of age, he was semi-retired and only taught a few seminars and tutorials. He had no committee assignments and was not expected to have to attend faculty meetings. He must be here voluntarily. I was stunned. I would have used any excuse not to be here.

Hercules spoke, his still prominent French accent making the words seem to flow.

"This is necessary, I believe, for in these changing times we have to adjust ourselves."

As he spoke, his blue eyes peeked out from his wrinkled face radiating good will. He leaned his thin frame back against the high-backed chair and smiled at all of us, confident that he, Hercules, had helped our leader make an important point.

It would probably never occur to Hercules that this was bureaucratic claptrap. To him, it would mean we would all pull together and in the spirit of self-sacrifice and devotion to learning make this university a new Garden of Eden.

Hercules combined the innocence of a child with the wisdom of Solomon. He had been a four-year-old Jew in France when the Vichy government, far from trying to hinder the Nazi round up of Jews to send to concentration camps, was being positively helpful to their occupiers. Hercules and his mother (his father had fought and died in the French Resistance) had been hidden in the French village of LeChambon, the tiny mountain town in France where literally hundreds of Jews were saved by French Protestant farmers who became expert forgers and smugglers to fool the French government officials and Nazis in order to save Jewish lives.

Maybe Hercules believed in goodness because he had seen it. He just made me feel like I wanted to protect him, but in many ways he was also like a tough little French rooster, too thin and wiry to be eaten. And sometimes there was a suspicion in my mind that Hercules saw right through Grimes, but felt that by not directly challenging him Grimes could be brought to see what was right. If you grew up hiding from Nazis, you probably had a good idea how to hide what you were thinking.

I was too new to this academic culture to read it accurately.

But before Grimes could get his mouth open, Adelaide Winters jumped in with her customary bluntness.

"Is it a raid, Harold or can we ride it out?"

Adelaide Winters was Professor of Women and Religion and no innocent and nobody's fool. At fifty, with slate-grey hair, an extra hundred pounds, and a laser-like brain, she was a formidable presence in any meeting. She gave off strong "take it or leave it" vibes. A former student in Philosophy and Religion had told me last year that when Adelaide had entered the lecture hall and approached the lectern, he had at first thought a "cleaning lady" had taken leave of her senses. He said, like he was proud of himself, that it had taken him only "three seconds" to realize his mistake. I doubted that he realized he was both a sexist and a classist for making that particular error. So I'd told him. He didn't seem to appreciate it.

Adelaide was one of the few people I'd ever met who when they spoke, I was tempted to write it down. She always cut directly to the heart of any topic and her terse, laconic approach boded ill for academic claptrap. She and Grimes seemed to be long-time enemies, though I did not know if there had been something specific that caused that, or whether it was because they were so completely opposite in virtually everything they approached. You couldn't miss the antipathy and it seemed like years in the making. And it had been, what, over twenty years?

Grimes, of course, was furious that the shadowy, intricate tunnels of rhetoric where he'd planned to lead us had been rudely exposed to the light of day by Adelaide. But he hardly showed it. His eyes, hidden behind his horn-rims and his face shadowed by the backlight, only swiveled to glance at Adelaide sitting well down the conference table, a ghost chair on either side of her. Perhaps she had chosen that seat to convey that she preferred the company of the dear departed. Or maybe she just liked the elbowroom.

Grimes drew himself erect and looked directly at her.

"There is absolutely no question of a raid. What we have here is an opening to explore the kinds of issues that you yourself deem so important. What constitutes knowledge? How is the content of the curriculum to be determined and what content is necessary for the well-educated, twenty-first century graduate."

Now, I might be a new academic, but I knew baloney when it was being fed to me, in fact, to the whole group, in one large serving. Adelaide was right. What was going down was more cuts in the humanities areas. More faculty positions being given to economics and to the "hard sciences," computer, math, physics.

Unless we could, by some miracle, come up with a coherent reason for our existence.

And there, we in Philosophy and Religion were publicly, embarrassingly split. And, as we knew only too well, the backlash against diversity, against women's studies, black studies, against multi-culturalism, was being fueled by theatric political challenges to what was again being labeled "political correctness." One of the two faculty members whose position had been eliminated had been a promising young African American guy whose scholarly specialty was African and African Diaspora Religion, including African American religion. There were no black studies offerings at all being taught this quarter. Would they ever be taught again? We had one cross-referenced class in Islam actually taught by a Muslim Scholar in another department. I was the "Christianist," and heaven help the Christians if that were to continue as our only perspective on one of the world's major religions. Adelaide held firm on teaching a very diverse array of women thinkers in religion, but when she retired? What then?

This was nothing new for the University of Chicago. Decades before, this territory had been staked out with the fierce intellectual fire of Allan Bloom, arch nemesis of all things not mentioned in Plato or Aristotle. According to Bloom, when we had starting teaching anything but the "classics," we had abandoned American society to such ills as divorce and abortion and a host of other supposed moral decay. Those who felt that the idea that the "classics" represented disinterested "truth" in Western culture were countered by those who pointed out how these classics valorized slavery, the oppression of women and LGBTQ people and greased the skids for colonial exploitation for millions around the world. They were in turn dismissed as "hopelessly PC." Adelaide brushed that aside as so much nonsense and kept on questioning. Grimes was sure truth was objective and he had the lock on it. I'd seen the reading list for his introductory class on Ethics. No women, minorities or "third world" authors need apply. And certainly no Queer theory ever crossed his mind.

Adelaide looked impassively at Grimes, but I noticed her hands on the table were clenching and unclenching, a sure sign of agitation in her. Grimes noticed too, but he plowed on.

"Why, I wouldn't be surprised if this self-study enabled us to enlarge our department, given the kinds of substantive classes we teach."

"Who?" Adelaide's sharp voice cut through the room. The one syllable stopped Grimes like somebody had attached a chain to his axle.

"Who? What do you mean who?" he blustered.

"Look. Harold. If it's not a raid then it will be a plant. And what gets foisted on to us depends wholly on who writes this self-study and who ultimately will determine the content. That's what this discussion is about, isn't it? You have somebody in mind to add to our department. Maybe you and the Dean together have somebody you'd like to add to this department and this self-study is the fig-leaf that will cover that maneuver."

Whoa. Made sense to me, but also made me want to crawl under the table. When mastodons clash, the calves run for cover.

But I hadn't reckoned with Donald Willie, Professor of Psychology and Religion. Donald verbally stepped between them.

"I think both of you are making good points."

Maybe we should get a sign for the conference room door that said "Counseling Session in Progress."

"I think we should do a self-assessment and I do think the whole department should have input. Can we turn this to a discussion of what subcommittees we would need here and who would be available for what? That way we can break through this impasse and move the discussion along."

Donald's voice came reasonably and softly from between his mustache and beard. He referred to himself as a "Jungian," and as far as I could tell that meant he spent a lot of time on dreams and on the unconscious. Well, since this meeting was alternately traumatizing me and threatening to render me unconscious from boredom, I thought he was our best bet for cutting through to some kind of conclusion so we could get out of here sometime this week.

Grimes looked at Donald for nearly a full minute and everybody, including Adelaide, kept quiet. Grimes started patting his pockets, eventually finding pipe, tobacco, damper and the other impedimenta of the pipe smoker. I couldn't help myself. I looked at the prominent "No Smoking" sign on the wall. Grimes didn't seem to notice, however, and the fiddling didn't result in a pipe to smoke. It resulted in a pipe with which to gesture at Willie.

"I'm sure that's a very productive suggestion Donald and thank you for making it."

With that the unlit pipe and the other equipment went back into his pockets and Donald was effectively dismissed.

"I think we're getting ahead of ourselves here. What's really needed as we begin this process is a survey of the students who take courses in our department as part of their overall humanities distribution requirement, which classes have been and continue to be the best subscribed, which group of classes produce the most majors and so forth."

Grimes tapped a stack of papers in front of him.

"This is a set of guidelines on conducting the self-study; the guidelines are also on your faculty page on the website. Self-study, we believe, means nothing less than that we study ourselves."

Adelaide snorted, but let Grimes continue.

A slight flush on Grimes' cheek betrayed he'd heard the snort, but he didn't glance in her direction.

"Let's take this back, say, at least ten years."

Grimes looked around the table expectantly, still standing, legs akimbo in his 'captain of the ship' stance. Nobody saluted the captain and nobody took him up on his suggestion, which obviously involved the most tedious kind of scut work, comparing years of online registrations and cross-referencing it with students who became majors and their cumulative class schedules.

"Can't the secretary get us that kind of information? Why do you need to put faculty on it?"

Donald was not through being helpful.

Grimes adopted a pensive look for about five seconds and then shot Willie down again.

"As you know, Professor Willie, Mrs. Frost is our one remaining secretary for the whole department. She has her hands full now—I can scarcely add to her workload."

Actually, Frost did nothing but work for Grimes, and much of the rest of the time she seemed to sit at her desk doing online crossword puzzles. She worshipped Grimes, of course, since he let her do what she wanted and gave her regular doses of his charm that he seemed to be able to turn on and off at will. I'd made the mistake of asking her to find me some pens and legal pads when I'd first joined the department and she had not even looked up from her screen. I'd had to ask Henry and he'd told me where the faculty supply closet was. The key hung on a hook by Frost's desk. I didn't ask her again; I just went in to her office and took the key off the hook without a word. Her thin shoulders, hunched over the keyboard, tensed when I did it, but she didn't look up.

"I think," Grimes continued smoothly, "that this initial research would be an excellent introduction to the workings of an academic department in relationship to the curricular needs of the university—I'm going to suggest that our two newest colleagues take this on and use it as a way to orient themselves to the whole ecology of the humanities division."

Grimes gazed at Henry and then at me, not bothering to hide his smirk.

Henry looked as stunned as I felt.

Neither of us had finished our dissertations when we had been hired, and we had received many assurances from the Dean and from Grimes himself that the university was "committed to protecting the time of junior faculty so they could complete their dissertations." Finishing what was effectively a book length research project along with coming up with six classes per year, never having taught before, was already daunting enough along with the committee work we'd already been assigned.

Basically, we made up our classes as we went along, and we often asked each other how far ahead of the students we were in the material for a course. Sometimes it was a matter of hours.

I'd managed to get off a couple of unwanted committees as a rookie cop by suggesting we spend money. Police departments always had hidden pockets of money to spend, and actually so do humanities departments. Worth a try.

"While I think that's a possibility, Dr. Grimes, I might suggest that we re-direct slightly and assign one of our graduate students to this project? We do have a budget for graduate student stipends."

I looked at Grimes with what I hoped was my most academically neutral face. Out of the corner of my eye, I could see Henry looking at me gratefully. Henry moonlighted at a convenience store in the suburbs four nights a week to help support his family, a pregnant wife and 2-year-old son. That was strictly forbidden in our contracts, supposedly because we were instructors and needed to focus on our dissertation work. Right.

Grimes brushed off my suggestion like he had dismissed Willie. Twice.

"No. That won't work. We need those few dollars for other projects, Professor Ginelli."

'Nice try,' his voice conveyed.

"We'll start with you and Professor Haruchi gathering this data by . . . ."

He bent over his IPad and scrolled over a few screens.

"Let's say, November 14."

That was less than a month away.

And Adelaide, Donald, and even Hercules just sat there and let him get away with it.

3

Q: Could you briefly outline the route which led you from your work on madness in the classical age to the study of criminality and delinquency?

M.F.: When I was studying during the early 1950's, one of the great problems that arose was that of the political status of science and the ideological functions which it could serve . . . [A] whole number of interesting questions were provoked. These can all be summed up in two words: power and knowledge. I believe I wrote *Madness and Civilization* to some extent within the horizon of these questions.

Michel Foucault, *Power/Knowledge*

The grey sky had lifted when I exited Myerson and a rarely seen setting sun tipped the gothic towers of the university with gold as though they had been heavily gilded. This display did little to lighten my mood, however, as I walked home with the rest of the academic community streaming from the campus toward the train and bus stops, or their homes in the communities surrounding the campus. There is no point in driving to work in Hyde Park, or what is called "Hyde No-Park." There are very few parking spaces on campus, and on the adjoining streets 'residents only' stickers keep commuters at bay. The university ran shuttle buses that came in especially handy in the sub-zero temperatures of the Chicago winters, but today in late October it was actually pleasant.

I live only three blocks from campus in a Prairie-style Victorian (that meant there was a reduced amount of ginger-bread as Midwesterners had altered the fanciful Victorian style to fit their more sober tastes). The tall, thin houses have only thirty feet between them, with garages opening on to alleys in the back. Lined up along the street, they always remind me of rows of teeth, kind of housing dentures.

I was often told I was lucky to have found a house that was so close to campus. This was told to me by people who had never owned a home that was 125 years old. When we moved in, there was a dead rat in the kitchen. Carol, one-half of the live-in couple who helped me take care of the boys and the house, said, "At least it's dead."

Yes. I thought that was a plus. But I wondered what it had died of.

The house needed absolutely everything—new plumbing, new wiring, storm windows, paint, and new appliances. The list was endless.

Well, we'd started the painting. The boys, Carol and I, and Carol's husband Giles were dabbing paint on from time to time. We had decided on bright yellow with green trim as an explicit insult to the grey of Chicago.

Giles was from Senegal and doing a Ph.D. in math at the university. Carol was from Iowa and at the School of Social Work. I had thought that tackling the painting would be a nice project for all of us to undertake together. But between caring for the boys, doing our various kinds of academic work and keeping up with the housekeeping, the boys would be graduating from college by the time we finished.

I will hire somebody, I thought to myself as I walked down our street and saw the expanses of beige peeling paint on my house illuminated by the setting sun. I could afford it. Unlike most instructors, I am not poor. I had that trust fund. When we'd married, Marco had wanted no part of my trust fund money, and I'd just thought we'd keep it for the boys' education (since it was likely to cost a million dollars each by the time they reached that age). When Marco had died, I didn't care. I used it to support us during my graduate school work and then, when I'd gotten the instructor job at the university, I'd plunked down the money for this over-priced piece of crumbling real estate without a qualm.

I saw the ladders from the weekend's painting were still lying along the side of the house where we had left them. Not good. I made a mental note to ask Giles to help me lock them in the garage later tonight. We have a fairly high crime rate in Hyde Park. The surrounding communities are not affluent, and some are quite poor, and in our racist country, consequently mostly black. They seemed to regard the mostly white, upscale university as a deliberate insult to their existence (it is) and a shoplifting mall (it is). Students are incredibly lax about locking, picking up after themselves or the simplest security measures. The ones who are mugged are usually those who decided to walk alone to get a pizza at 2 in the morning. They leave their rooms unlocked and are surprised when they return to find all their electronics are no longer there.

As I walked up to the sagging porch (I really needed a contractor, not just a painter), I could smell dinner. Giles does the cooking and he uses a lot of spice. My palate had certainly been expanded beyond my parents' white-bread meals.

When I opened the door, the smell became stronger. Not African, Italian.

Marco's mother, at least, must be here and probably also his father. If my parents were cold fish, Marco's parents were as far as you could get in the opposite direction. Their affection was like being wrapped in a warm, fuzzy blanket. All the time. They were overwhelming in their care of me and the boys after Marco died. In fact, they would have taken over our lives if I had let them. And I'd almost let them. It had only been in the two years or so and our move to Hyde Park that I'd tried to pull back a little and define our lives myself. It wasn't easy.

"Mom, Mom, Nonna and Nonno are here!" Two faces, two voices raised to a decibel no human voice should be able to achieve. Sam and Mike came barreling down the long center hallway and careened into me. At six, they packed quite a wallop. I dropped to my knees, both to hug them and to keep from being knocked over backwards.

"Hey, guys! Big, big hug." We all linked arms and swayed first right and then left, faster and faster until we all went tumbling onto the floor. It was our ritual greeting since the time they could walk, but it was getting tougher and tougher not to get flattened on the floor when we did it. They each weighed about fifty-five pounds and could take me down when they chose.

"Kris-tin-a?"

Mama Ginelli called from the kitchen at the back. Nonna's rolling Italian accent made my name into three syllables. You'd think Nonna had been born in Genoa, but she was a native Chicagoan. She'd grown up in the kind of closed, ethnic community that so characterized Chicago with churches, stores and clubs rooted in particular immigrant identities. That was eroding some, now, but it hadn't affected Nonna in the least. Or maybe it had, and she was clinging to it nevertheless.

"Yes, Nonna, we're coming," I called obediently.

I gathered a bunch of child under each arm and left my briefcase on the floor where it had fallen under their assault. I'd get it later.

"Let's march."

We frog-marched, arms linked, bumping into the walls of the narrow hallway and staggered into the kitchen.

Nonna turned from the stove where she'd been stirring the sauce that was the source of the intense garlic smell in the house. Marco's mother was fully a foot and a half shorter than I am, with a bosom that could double as a tray if she would ever eat in bed, a luxury, I was sure, she would never permit herself. With her steel-grey hair pulled back into a severe bun and a floral patterned dress, should could have been posing for an ad for pasta sauce. 'Tastes like Mama made it!'

"There you are. Finally. These boys have missed you so."

Yes, while Nonna was warm and basically sweet, was there a mother-in-law alive who would miss a chance to distribute a little guilt to a working daughter-in-law?

"Now Natalie. You know she keeps better hours these days."

Marco's father was behind us, seated at the built-in breakfast nook under the kitchen window. I was surprised he could still fit between the bench and the table. Since his retirement last year, Marco's father, Vincent Ginelli, had probably put on a good twenty pounds or more. And that was on top of the weight his six-foot frame had already carried. The beer bottle in front of him looked like it was almost empty.

I turned and winked at him. Vince winked back. He loved it when we shared a joke on Natalie.

Marco's father had also been a cop. He and Natalie had both been devastated by Marco's death; I was surprised he hadn't retired right after that. But he'd stuck it out—not just for the pension increase, but I thought because he had to continue or he would have been consumed by the anger as well as grief.

He had certainly approved of my leaving the force since he'd never really approved of my being on the force to begin with. Not a woman's job, though he'd also been a little proud of me. At least I hoped he had been.

Now, both he and Natalie really liked it that I was a professor. They would have preferred I stay home, of course, but they found my 'studying all the time' a source of pride and a little awe. I was in Religion (never mind the Philosophy). Very respectable. (If they only knew). Marco had seen to it that the boys had been baptized Catholic, but we didn't go to church. They knew that, but didn't nag. As long as I mourned their son, they seemed willing to forgive me anything.

"I thought you two were still in Wisconsin with Vince, Jr. and Marilyn."

Vince and Natalie had had five children, all boys. They spent their retirement now visiting the four boys and their families in turn in a large motorhome. I wondered where they had parked it.

Vince, Jr. was Marco's oldest brother. He and his wife had four kids.

"Marilyn's mother came on the weekend and we came on back," Natalie explained without turning from her sauce.

Well, that was why they were here. Daughter-in-law Marilyn was from California, and her mother Beverly, several times divorced, could not have been more different from Natalie. They were from different planets, different galaxies even. Not that Natalie would have had to share the kitchen with Beverly. Beverly knew exactly how to order take-out in any city she visited.

On the other hand, I did know somebody who minded that Natalie took over the kitchen when she came.

"Where's Giles?" I asked.

"Oh, he took that stew he was making up to their apartment."

Natalie knew she'd driven Giles out and her uncharacteristically short sentence revealed it. And she was probably still upset over Beverly's unexpected arrival at Vince, Jr.'s.

Great. I sighed inwardly. Giles took his cooking very seriously and did not like to have dinner plans changed at the drop of a hat. Now we were going to have someone in a French African funk for a few days until we ate enough Giles-cooked food to make it up to him. Fortunately, the boys would eat literally anything you put in front of them.

They were over by the stove now, behind Natalie, sniffing around like hungry puppies.

"When do we eat? When do we eat?" they chorused together.

I wondered vaguely if their simultaneous talking, something they had done since they had learned to speak, as I'd learned twins did, should continue to worry me. I'd raised it as a concern with their pediatrician several times over the years, and been waved off with 'they'll grow out of it.' Fine. But when?

"Can we eat soon, Natalie? We have Tae Kwon Do class tonight at seven and I like them to digest a little before class."

Three nights a week the boys and I took classes in Korean martial arts at the local Y. They loved it and so did I. I'd learned some self-defense techniques at the police academy, but this was different.

Taw Kwon Do meant "the art of hands and feet." It was much more graceful than Karate, emphasizing quick kicks and jump turns to get out of an assailant's way. The boys needed the structure of the class and a release for their nearly inexhaustible energy. I needed the chance to kick and punch the blue pads we used. I would imagine specific faces on the bags. I always felt like a rag doll after class, but more alive, more human.

"So, show your old Nonno what you learn in this class of yours."

Vince extracted his bulk from the banquette and stood up, mimicking a martial arts fighting stance.

With a whoop, the boys were on him, throwing kicks and punches at his knees and thighs. Their high-pitched yells, called a "kihap" by our teacher, attracted Molly, our golden retriever from outside where she'd probably been napping in the last of the sunshine. She banged through the kitchen dog door and jumped up on poor Vince's back.

"Ah, oh—coming to get me are you? Down, Molly, down. Think that will get me, huh? Oh, Sam, not so hard—Molly!"

Vince was sounding out of breath and increasingly desperate.

"Kristin! Get this . . . dog off me!"

Vince always had trouble moderating his natural swearing in front of the boys.

"Charyuht!"

I yelled that command for attention directly behind the boys. One of the first things we'd learned in class was that not to obey that command could get you thrown out of class. Since the boys would rather be deprived of all video games for a month rather than being denied Tae Kwon Do class, they had learned to respond immediately.

Commands of any kind had no effect on Molly, so I grabbed her collar and forced her to sit. Luckily she's so docile most of the time it doesn't matter.

"Say, that's, that's . . . pretty good," Vince puffed.

His face was starting to return to his normal ruddy color rather than the mottled purple it had been a minute ago. His breathing was still ragged, though. I was increasingly alarmed at how little stamina he had these days.

"Eat, eat!"

Natalie was ready to serve.

At least she no longer said, "Mange, mange."

When I first met Marco, his mother's Italianisms used to drive him crazy. I had found it sweet and harmless. Of course, I could afford to, they weren't my parents. Our own parents can get to us in ways no one else possibly can.

Natalie staggered across the kitchen with a huge platter of spaghetti and meatballs with red sauce, cheese piled high on top. She deftly elbowed past me when I tried to take the heavy platter from her. So I just cleared a path between children and the dog so she could get to the table unmolested. It was a near thing. I spotted a Matchbox car and kicked it in the direction of the counter before she stepped on it.

As we all squeezed into the breakfast nook and bowed our heads, my mind wandered to Giles and Carol. I'd better try to mend that fence before we went to class.

But by the time Natalie and Vince left, we'd barely time to climb into our uniforms and out the door to class. The speed with which the boys could get those martial arts uniforms on was a constant source of amazement to me, especially compared to their glacial pace getting dressed for school in the morning.

I grabbed my keys and shouted up the stairs to Carol and Giles we were leaving. I'd have to deal with that conversation later.

When we got back the boys fell on their beds and went immediately to sleep. I pulled off their uniforms from their slack little bodies and covered them up well. I sighed over teeth brushing, vowing to make them do more in the morning.

I went over to the door that led to Carol and Giles' apartment on the third floor. Time to face the music about the spaghetti.

"Giles? Could you come down and help me with something?"

I really did want to get those ladders locked up and couldn't do it alone. I figured carrying the ladders to the garage would give us some time to talk.

"Yes?"

Giles came slowly down the stairs, his brown eyes cloudy behind his wire-rimmed glasses. His long, narrow face was giving nothing away, but the tension in his shoulders betrayed he was still upset. He was slender, and he dressed exclusively jeans, tee shirt and flip-flops. He wore flip-flops in-doors and out until Carol wrestled them away from him in early December.

"Could you help me move those ladders into the garage?"

Giles just nodded.

Great. I'd been surrounded today either by people I wanted to talk to me who wouldn't, or by people who wanted to talk to me whom I wished would shut up.

We went out the kitchen door, Molly following us expectantly. With-out exchanging a word, we lifted the ladder on top and started to maneuver it to the garage at the back of the small, oblong yard.

As I tried to avoid tripping over Molly, who was entranced by this new game, I tried to think of how to apologize for Natalie's rudeness without further offending Giles.

We slid the first ladder into the garage, along the inside wall, and started to walk back to get the second. I had a brainstorm. I would criticize Natalie's cooking.

"Well, at least you and Carol got to have a decent meal tonight. I could hardly do class with Mama's heavy pasta and sauce in me."

We picked up the second ladder and Giles looked at me across its length.

"It was not good?"

He looked a little less grim.

"You know how she is, the more garlic the better. You can't taste anything else. It ruins the whole meal."

I put my end of the ladder down and Giles bent and slid it efficiently next to the other one inside the garage. I locked the door.

He hummed tunelessly as we walked back to the house. I sighed with my garlic breath (it really *had* been a little too strong). Another relational fire extinguished.

I opened my portable computer on the kitchen table and logged on to my email account. I opened the document I'd sent myself about my conversations with Ah-seong Kim. I'd need to add the conversations with Lester too, and I struggled over the wording. Drat. Without the complaint form guidelines in front of me, I was floundering over the formatting. Still, as I typed I realized writing it up while it was still fresh in my mind was crucial. I could cut and paste it into the online complaint form when I got the password. I sent Henry an email asking him if he knew what it was, and then I saved the file and closed the computer.

I went to put on the night bolt on the kitchen door and the smell of the garlic in the kitchen hit me again. If I didn't want to have to face that at breakfast, I'd better take the trash out tonight.

I grabbed the trash bag from under the sink and called to Molly. No woof in response. She was probably sacked out on one of the kid's beds. She'd been out with Giles and me earlier so I decided to let her be. I normally took her out one more time for a short walk down the alley and back just before bed, but we could skip that.

The night had turned cloudy and colder with very little moon. I skipped a coat, though. If you start wearing coats in October in Chicago you won't toughen up for the months to come.

Our skinny yard, fenced on each side, ended with two garages that opened on to an alley at the back. Between the garages, a walkway stretched to the alley where the trashcans were located. Our yard was floodlit from the back of the house, but it was still a little dim closer to the garages.

I reached the gate at the end of the walkway and saw that it stood open. I was furious. The kids were strictly forbidden to go in and out of the alley and the open gate meant that Molly could get out.

The alley could be dangerous for kids and unleashed dogs. It was not well lit, and kids from the high school on the south end of the alley loved to drag race up and down its narrow length. They'd careened more than once into our cans, but you couldn't relocate the cans. Sanitation workers in Chicago would refuse to take your trash if the cans were not where they were supposed to be. I'd learned that after moving the trash cans to the side of the garage after the last drag race trash can collision. My trash was still in the cans after normal pick-up day. So I'd dragged them back and let them be sitting ducks.

I didn't like that gate being opened. It meant somebody had probably cut through our yard or intended to.

I pushed the gate all the way open. There were no cars in the alley. I turned, pulled off a trash can lid and started to stuff the bag into the already overcrowded can when I heard a noise that made my heart nearly stop. Next to my right ear, somebody took a breath.

I started to turn in that direction and the next second I saw a shadow rise up. I pulled back as far as I could against the rough brick of the garage wall and a hand holding a knife came slashing down directly where I had been standing a moment before.

Reacting more than thinking, I grabbed at the arm with the knife as it rose up again and pulled with all my might to the side. My assailant rocketed into the narrow walkway and I gave him as assist with a sidekick to his ribs. I felt my foot connect and I heard a grunt. I hoped it was a grunt of pain.

I turned to run down the alley and nearly fell over the can now spilled at my feet.

I jumped over it and continued running, yelling at the top of my lungs. Behind me I heard a thud as the attacker also jumped over the can.

I hadn't disabled him with that kick.

He was following.

Damn this poorly lit alley.

I picked up my pace but the following footfalls sounded like they were gaining on me.

I zigged left and then turned as the knife came slashing down again. I chopped down hard on the arm holding the knife and used that momentum to hook my right foot behind him and flip him on to his back. I heard an "oomph" as he fell back, but it was muffled by his stocking masked face.

He had grabbed my left wrist as he fell. I twisted and wrenched away from his grip and that meant the slashing knife meant for my chest only raked down my arm from elbow to wrist. I jumped back, keeping my eyes on my assailant and cursed myself for leaving my cell phone in the kitchen.

I braced myself for another attack and I heard a noise. The revving of an engine of a car entering the alley behind me. I turned and ran toward it, yelling my head off. My attacker turned tail and ran the other way.

I kept my injured arm by my side and waved the other arm, flagging down the car. Two guys getting ready to race down the alley caught me and my bloody arm in their headlights.

They cut the engine and opened their doors.

4

"Discipline" may be identified neither with an institution nor with an apparatus; it is a type of power, a modality for its exercise, comprising a whole set of instruments, techniques, procedures, levels of application, targets: it is a "physics" or an "anatomy" of power, a technology. And it may be taken over either by "specialized" institutions (the penitentiaries or "houses of correction" of the nineteenth century), or by institutions that use it as an essential instrument for a particular end (schools, hospitals), or by preexisting authorities that find in it a means of reinforcing or reorganizing their internal mechanisms of power.

MICHEL FOUCAULT, *DISCIPLINE AND PUNISH*

I sat on the ground next to my rescuers' car with my head between my knees, a tee shirt loaned by one of them pressed to the cut on my arm. Lots of commotion around me that I struggled to sort out. I seemed to see it through gauze.

A car squealed up and braked facing the kids' dented Chevy.

I raised my head to look. The University had arrived in the person of its private police force (the second largest police force in Illinois, following the City of Chicago). The university cops had by and large seemed okay to me. Many of them were said to be moonlighters from the suburbs. I'd met a couple when we'd had a break-in at the departmental office last spring. Frost's computer had been stolen while she was out to lunch. She hadn't bothered to lock her office door. The officers pointed out this was not a good practice, though Frost had then given them such a glare they had departed without delay.

An African American woman in uniform pushed through the crowd of neighbors now gathering from other homes that backed on to the alley and maybe even a few from the pizza place on the corner. She knelt down beside me.

"I'm Officer Matthews, University Police. Do you need medical attention?" She had a short, brown fringe of hair peeking out from under the visor of her cap, large, warm brown eyes and skin the color of caramels. Her uniform trousers strained at the thigh and hip. She looked like a slightly plump kindergarten teacher, though a kindergarten teacher with a side arm. Maybe I should have stayed a cop, gotten a job policing the university rather than trying to teach at it.

"Ma'am, I asked you if you need medical attention."

I made an effort to sit up straighter, look her in the eye.

"Yes, yes I think so. Yes I do. I was cut and I think it's pretty deep. "

I stupidly lifted the arm my assailant had slashed and I felt the pain jar my whole side. I gasped and slumped back down against the car.

Matthews called over to another officer who was standing at the back of the car questioning my high school heroes.

"Mel, call for an ambulance. Now."

She turned back to me.

"Ma'am, assistance is on the way. Name?"

Out came the notebook.

"Kristin Ginelli, 6756 S. Rosemont. That house over there."

I used my head instead of my arm this time and just nodded toward my house. I realized I still had on my headband from class. I looked down. I still had on my white Tae Kwon Do uniform, though now splashes of blood were visible between the various patches on the front. I wondered what Officer Matthews though I was playing at, running around in a martial arts uniform with blood on it.

"Can you tell me what happened?"

Matthews was still squatting next to me, looking concerned. Maybe she wouldn't hold my outfit against me.

"Male, above medium height, stocking mask and knife."

I shuddered involuntarily. Matthews took off her own jacket and put it around my shoulders.

"Thanks. Anyway, I was taking some trash out to the cans and he just slashed at me. Just slashed down with the knife. He didn't say anything. Just tried to knife me."

"Is that how you sustained the injury?"

"No, not then. I . . . we struggled and I knocked him down, but he came at me again and tried to, tried to stab me, I guess, but I pulled away and the knife just got me on the arm."

I nodded toward my tee shirt covered arm but didn't move it.

"Then the kids pulled into the alley and he took off."

"Race? Age?"

I struggled to remember if I'd seen his hands. Gloves, I thought.

"No, can't get a fix on that. Gloves, dark alley. Age, I'm not sure. Not young. Older male build. Tall. About as tall as I am. Male. I'm sure of that. He was wearing a stocking mask."

"Did he speak? Ask for money? Anything?"

"He grunted twice. Once when I kicked him and once when I knocked him down but he never said a word. Not a word. One minute I'm at the cans, and the next minute this knife is swinging down at me."

Matthews stopped writing for a minute, looked me in the eyes.

"You kicked him? Knocked him down?"

"Yes."

I didn't feel up to explaining.

"But you didn't recognize him?"

"No."

I knew what she was thinking. This was not your typical bash and grab robbery attempt like most the crime in Hyde Park. It didn't even sound like an attempted sexual assault. I am not a rival gang member. What else was there? Was there a maniac running around in a stocking mask with a knife?

Running around. Running around.

Suddenly a thought so vivid, so horrible popped into my mind that I jerked backwards and hit my head on the car door.

"Are you all right?"

I struggled to get up.

"No, no. Let me go. The back door—my house—I didn't lock it. The perp. He could have gotten in. My six-year-old sons and a student couple are in there."

I literally could not complete the thought. I needed to just go to the house. I managed to get to my feet, though I swayed.

"Mel! Mel! Get over here."

Mel ran up, Matthew's tone telling him it was time to spring.

"Ms. Ginelli here lives in that house."

She pointed.

"She did not lock her back door. The perp could have gotten inside. Take two officers and go to the front and the back. There's an adult couple . . . "

She turned to me.

"Names?"

"Carol and Giles."

"And two kids in the house. Ring. If there's no answer, we'll call for back up."

"And a dog," I managed. "A dog. Friendly."

Mel sprinted away at a good clip toward the other campus cop cars that had pulled up. The city cops had not yet put in an appearance. I had to follow. I had to follow.

I started down the alley, struggling at every step, and Matthews stepped in front of me.

"You're not going to be able to help. Mel's good. He'll let us know."

She walked me toward one of the university police cars and gently took my arm to try to usher me inside. I just wearily shook my head and slumped back to the ground.

Mel had better be good.

The wait was excruciating. Matthews stood next to me. I was just struggling to my feet again when her radio crackled.

"Matthews? Billman here."

Mel?

"Just checked the Ginelli residence. A couple answered the door. They let us in and we did a thorough check. The children were sleeping and the premises are clear. They said they'd lock up behind us. Oh, and the woman wants to know if Ms. Ginelli wants her to accompany her to the emergency room or stay here."

I let out the breath I'd been holding for the last ten minutes and looked up at Matthews. She was raising a questioning eyebrow.

"No. Tell Carol, her name's Carol, to stay with her husband and the children. If the kids wake up, they'll want her there."

Matthews nodded. She must have kids, I thought.

So, I'd let them fix my arm now. If the boys had been killed like Marco, I wouldn't have wanted to go to an ER to stop the blood flow. In fact, I'd just have cut the other arm too and waited to bleed out.

* * * *

I'd been sitting for the better part of an hour in a little room that could easily double as a meat freezer. Matthews had dropped me off at the ER instead of making me wait for the ambulance, for which favor I was profoundly grateful.

A nurse had ushered me into this cubicle after making sure I passed that most important of medical tests, the valid insurance test. By coming up as a member in good standing of the university's health plan, I was ushered in and given a blanket that seemed to be made of tissue paper.

After a few minutes, a young woman who identified herself as a medical student and who seemed about twelve-years-old had come in briefly, taken my temperature and blood pressure and then lifted the tee shirt on my arm to look at the cut. She had blanched and looked away. I bet medical school was kind of a trial when you can't stand the sight of blood. She quickly had left and that had been that, for nearly an hour.

I knew the symptoms of shock well enough to know I was not in immediate danger of dying. At least I hoped not. I was still somewhat shocky, I thought, and I was having trouble regulating my body temperature. But still, I bet it was fifty degrees in this little white on white room. There was no thermostat that I could discover.

My head was beginning to clear and I was starting to get seriously annoyed. None of the other meat-lockers seemed occupied. Where were they all and when was someone older than twelve who could stand the sight of blood coming to see me? I gathered my tissue paper blanket around me and leaned out the door. The only person I could see was a woman in a flowered tunic, whom I took to be a nurse, sitting at a computer down the hall. She had a magazine open on her lap. I called out.

"Nurse!"

She turned her head toward me and amazingly enough her helmet of blond, teased hair did not seem to move with it. She looked darkly at me over pink plastic reading glasses while placing a finger in the magazine I'd so rudely interrupted her reading.

"Yes?"

This nurse could give Frost lessons in the art of freezing someone over with just a word or a glance.

"When will the doctor be here? I've been waiting nearly an hour."

I tried to keep the annoyance out my voice, but I'm pretty sure I did not succeed. I wondered if nursey would turn down the temperature even more just to punish me for wanting medical services in a hospital.

"I'll check."

She turned toward the desk the computer was sitting on and picked up an in-house phone. She dialed a number and waited. And waited. And so I waited.

Finally, without having spoken to anyone, she hung up.

"I will let you know as soon as someone is available."

And astonishingly, she turned back to her magazine.

I went back to the examining table and sat down. I thought about the assault. To be mugged for your purse or wallet is bad, but it's reasonable. You have some money, some credit cards. Your car keys. Somebody else wants them. There was a certain kind of rotten logic to that.

Sexual assault is brutal, but even sexual assault has a logic. Some guy who has trouble with women wants to control them, see their fear. That also makes terrible sense.

But to have someone try to pierce you from stem to stern at random and with no warning is disconcerting in the extreme. What possible reason could he have had to lunge at me with clearly lethal intent? There seemed to be no motive. There are plenty of drive-by shootings in Chicago, but I'd never heard of a run-by knifing. Maybe there was such a thing, but I doubted it.

I went over and over every detail of the struggle in my mind, racing through the images like running a video at triple speed. One frame racing by might contain a useable image. But nothing would stick. Possibly because I had lost blood, was exhausted, in pain and freezing to death.

I'd had enough. Walking out was no good. I needed the arm sewed up.

Just then I remembered I knew a surgeon. I served on a university committee with him, a committee that oversaw all human science research to make sure it was compliant with current ethical regulations.

What was his name?

Tom. Tom Grayson.

I picked up the in-house phone on the wall of the cubicle and asked for paging. I asked to page Dr. Grayson and even though it was nearly midnight, he was listed as 'in, on call.' I gave the page operator the extension on the wall phone.

I jumped when the phone rang almost immediately.

"This is Dr. Grayson answering a page," said the voice on the other end.

I explained in rough outline the events of the evening, ending with my current frustration and location.

"You're in the ER? What number is the examining room?"

I told Tom to hang on and I opened the door to look.

"Four."

"You just caught me cutting through the ER on my way to the parking garage. I'm just about fifty feet away from you. I'll be there in a couple of seconds."

I sat back down on the examining table and further shredded the crinkly paper I'd been sitting on for the last hour.

The door opened and Grayson came in. Followed closely by the big hair nurse who had blown me off. I felt a moment of pure satisfaction when I saw her annoyed look. She clearly did not approve of patients who procured their own doctors.

"Kristin!" Tom said, "I'm so glad I was still in the hospital."

Grayson was tall, probably 6' 4" if he would stand up straight, but he always seemed to be leaning over slightly, the better to listen. His too long, sandy colored hair was falling over his forehead and his blue eyes met mine with warmth. I'd noticed in the committee meetings that he had very long eyelashes. They were so long they brushed the inside of the lenses of his glasses and he was forever polishing them. I realized with a jolt I'd been aware of him as more than a fellow committee member. I gave myself a mental shake and decided not to go there. I'd also noticed that he almost always looked tired, and now, at midnight, he looked even more so. I felt somewhat guilty keeping him from heading home. But I was oh so glad to see him.

"Like I told you on the phone, I was mugged this evening and the assailant cut my arm."

I gestured toward the tee shirt covered arm with my other hand. It had begun to feel fairly repetitive to keep gesturing to my injury without getting any help for it.

Grayson leaned forward and lifted the shirt. We both looked down at the blood encrusted, jagged cut. It really looked awful.

"How long have you been here without someone cleaning this?" Tom asked, real anger in his voice.

I glanced over his left shoulder to where helmet hair nurse was standing, glaring at me.

"More than an hour now. I'm sorry to bother you, but I just wanted to get it taken care of."

"Nurse." Grayson's voice could have cut glass.

"Get a full set up in here. We need to wash this wound out thoroughly. It looks bad enough that I want to give Professor Ginelli a dose of IV antibiotics."

Helmet hair nurse looked a little sick when Grayson called me "Professor." One thing universities thrive on, it's hierarchy and I'd just moved up a whole bunch on that ladder.

Tom turned to the nurse and gave her further instructions in medicalese. I didn't even try to sort out what it meant. Now that he was here, I was really fading.

Tom turned back to me and seemed to see I was a little woozy.

"Let's get you lying down here, and warmer."

Blankets and pillows were obtained from a locker across the hall. Real blankets. And my head and feet were elevated slightly. Amazing how much better that felt.

Tom bent over the head of the table and shone a light in my eyes. I guess what he saw was okay.

"Kristin, I'll clean this cut out well and then we'll get it sewed up. I'll just get this IV started to get some antibiotic into you quickly and then I'll give you something oral to take home with you. You should be out of here in 30 minutes.

He turned to the sink and began washing his hands. Helmet hair nurse gave me such an angry look I thought it was quite possible I could be mugged twice in one night.

Okay. This was better. This was a lot better. I was warm and not in pain. Grayson had given me a shot of something that made me feel kind of floaty. I could feel a kind of tugging on the skin of my arm as he intently sewed his way down the cut. Didn't matter. Didn't feel much of anything.

"I'm sorry to be keeping you up, Dr. Grayson," I said to the back of his head.

"Call me Tom and don't worry about it. Who knows when I'll need an emergency 'Plato-ectomy' and you can return the favor."

His eyes never lifted from my arm, but I could see them crinkle a little at the sides of his face.

A huge jolt of guilt shot through me, so much that I inadvertently jerked my body.

"Don't move, Kristin. We're almost through here."

Tom's calm tone did anything but calm me.

I was realizing how attracted I was to this man and the sense of disloyalty to Marco was intense.

'Get a grip, Kristin,' I lectured myself. This has been a very emotional evening. You were almost killed for Christ's sake. Don't mistake adrenaline for sexual attraction.

Yeah. Right.

I hoped I was more convincing when I lectured students.

I knew I had been aware of him at the Human Experimentation Committee meetings. As junior faculty I had twice as many committee assignments as my more senior colleagues, but I'd not minded that one. And it wasn't the interesting discussions of ethics.

"There."

Tom had finished sewing.

"I'll just wrap this up for you, take out the IV, and make you a very unattractive sling from gauze that will hold the arm still."

He turned and opened a supply cabinet.

"Is someone waiting to drive you home?"

"Ah . . . no . . . no. It's okay. I'll call a cab."

"Well, I can drop you. You live on Rosemont, right? I'm only a few blocks over and one block north. No problem."

He looked over his shoulder at me and smiled.

Yeah. No problem. Right. Except my heart started to race. Oh, well. If I had a heart attack, the ER was a better place than most for that.

Tom helped me sit up and he expertly wound gauze around my arm and then fashioned a sling.

"Use this sling to keep the arm elevated. It will swell less and be less painful for you."

He handed me several little foil packets and a piece of paper.

"Here are some samples of the antibiotic that will get you started until someone can fill this prescription for you tomorrow. And here's something for pain if you need it."

More little packets handed over.

"Otherwise, I won't need to see you for ten days to two weeks. Just call my office and schedule an appointment. Of course, if there is increased redness and swelling, I'd like to see you right away."

He stood aside and took my good arm to help me get off the table. The blankets slid off to reveal my bloody martial arts uniform. I flushed with embarrassment.

"I knew you'd been a cop, but must you clean up crime in Hyde Park single handedly?"

Tom chuckled and tucked my good arm under his and headed for the door.

"Come on, Wonder Woman. It's been a long day for both of us."

I had the immense satisfaction of watching Helmet Hair's face as I was escorted out of the ER by a surgeon. And I loved the feeling of his tall frame bending solicitously toward me as we walked to his car.

I leaned back against the seat and closed my eyes. Then I snapped them open. How did he know where I lived?

Oh, for Pete's sake, Kristin. That's the kind of question you ask in junior high. I closed my eyes again and smiled a little at the memory of middle school gossip and going with boys in cars.

Good ole pain medication.

"Are you smiling or grimacing?" Tom broke into my thoughts.

Tom glanced again at me from the driver's side.

"Not a grimace. Not in pain. Thanks for asking."

And for the rest? I just needed to get home, get into my own bed and forget this day ever happened.

5

Your silence today is a pond where drowned things live
I want to see raised dripping and brought into the sun.

ADRIENNE RICH, "TWENTY-ONE LOVE POEMS,"
THE DREAM OF A COMMON LANGUAGE

The shrill ring of my cell phone jolted me out of the pain meds-induced sleep I'd had for . . . I glanced at the time displayed on the cell . . . five hours?

What the hell? Who was calling me at 6:30 in the morning on my cell?

I thought about ignoring the call, but I didn't give out my personal cell number to that many people. I picked it up and the number displayed on the screen was a university number. Better answer. I pressed 'ok' and held the phone to my ear.

"Kristin? Kristin?"

Margaret Lester's voice was tight, like she was controlling herself with effort. We did not have good news here.

She barely waited for my affirmative grunt.

"Ah-seong Kim has been found drowned in Mendel Pond. I'm there now. Could you come right over?"

The words were business-like but the tight voice was veering toward panic.

I fought my way up through the haze of the medication and too little sleep. I'm never at my best first thing in the morning anyway, at least before an infusion of caffeine. I ran my hand over my face and tried to focus. What had she said?

My lack of response shredded Margaret's fragile control.

"Kristin! Please! Students are starting to come to the Union for breakfast and the police have sealed off the west entrance of the cafeteria. They're all just hanging around, looking, talking, crying, even though the cops keep ordering them to move on."

Margaret's shrill voice drilling into my ear had the simultaneous effect of waking me and starting to give me a headache. Okay. Okay, my brain said. Now for my mouth.

"Hang on, Margaret. I'll be there as fast as I can."

I pressed end and swung my legs over the side of the bed. The movement jarred my arm. I'd slept in the sling as Grayson had advised so I'd move it less. But it hurt like stink.

Well, no pain pills for me. I tried to think. Tylenol, maybe. Then clothes. Then coffee. Then Carol and Giles. Oh, how I wished coffee was first.

I stumbled into the bathroom and managed to locate some Tylenol. I gulped three down and eased out of the sling. I used my good arm to get my clothes off. I'd not bothered with changing last night. I looked down at the bloody martial arts uniform on the bathroom floor. I lifted it and stuffed it down into the bathroom trash can. I'd get another.

I gingerly eased a loose sweater over my head and drew the sleeve carefully over the bandage. It wasn't easy to position the sling again, but with a little help from my teeth I got it pulled into about the right place. Pulling up sweatpants didn't require teeth, but it was awkward. I shuffled into slip-on low boots, got my purse and my cell and made my way to the kitchen. The blessed auto-brew coffee machine just required a one-button tap to start, and in seconds it was gurgling. I hovered over it until some had dripped into the pot. I pulled the pot out and poured some into a travel mug and took a minute to gulp it down despite the risk of scalding my tongue. I sipped more slowly and called Carol's cell phone. I didn't have the energy to troop up two flights of stairs to their apartment. She answered with her soft, kindly voice. I explained briefly, leaving out the drowning, just that there was a problem with a student on campus and the Dean of Students had asked me to come. I did ask her not to tell the boys, just that I had to go into work early. As I was finishing saying that, she walked into the kitchen and gently gave me a brief hug on my good side. Then she wordlessly took my mug, topped it off and handed it back to me. The little kindnesses in life help us get through. I leaned my cheek down and rested it for a second on her brown cap of hair. She helped me get one arm in my trench coat and belted it securely so it closed over my arm in the sling.

"Thanks, Mom," I said.

Carol didn't smile.

"Are you up to this?" she asked.

"I don't know," I said.

I picked up my coffee and my purse and headed out the door toward the part of the campus that contained Mendel Pond.

I walked the three blocks to campus. It was ridiculously tiring. As I approached the entrance to the main quadrangle, it began to rain lightly. Great. At least I had the coat wrapped around me, but where the sweater was exposed in the front was getting wet. Wet and cold. I started to shiver.

The flashing red and blue lights of four Chicago police cars and about four more university police cars around the quad reflected crazily off of the wet ivy covered pale stone of the surrounding buildings. Mendel Pond was in a cul-de-sac created from the backs of Myerson, where my office was, and the student union. Directly behind the pond to the north was one of the high walls that ran between buildings. The walls were topped with spikes, hundreds and hundreds of spikes topped with balls. They always reminded me of German Christmas ornaments.

A stone arch cut through the wall with a monumental gate, probably thirty feet high, made of elaborate bars, convincingly medieval. "Crescat scientia; vita excolatur" was spelled out in an ironwork banner arching above the gate. It was creepily reminiscent of the pictures of the ironwork banner above Auschwitz, only this didn't mean "Freedom Through Work," it translated as "Let knowledge grow from more to more, and so be human life enriched." English always has to fill in the Latin gaps. Given what that gate must have cost, even more than a century ago, it plainly enriched quite a bit.

I continued to slog along through the growing puddles toward the lights. Mendel Pond I had always assumed was named for Gregor Mendel, the famous botanist and priest. Long ago, Myerson had been the science building. Botany students had probably messed around with plants in this pond in those days. Nobody did anything scientific with it now, at least that I'd ever seen. Plants did grow in it, waving their big leaves over the surface. Now in the fall, those leaves were gold, a gold turned blue and red from the flashing lights. The flickering lights showed where a canopy of large leaves had been torn. Some were scattered on the grass.

Mendel Pond was irregular, shaped like a jigsaw puzzle piece, jutting in and out, wider at the end closest to Myerson, narrower where it came closest to the gate. It was about thirty feet across at the widest place and rimmed with a concrete wall, about two feet high. Not impossible to fall in, but how likely was that?

Police tape was strung around the whole pond. I spotted Margaret toward the gate, standing beside an ambulance. The medical team had obviously arrived, as had the city cops. I doubted any detectives had arrived yet. They'd be here, though. They'd examine the scene, and with the medical examiner's report determine if it was accident, suicide or even a homicide.

"Margaret!" I called out.

Margaret started and then hurried over to me.

"Oh, Kristin! Thank you so much for coming."

But her eyes narrowed as she took in my arm in a sling.

"Are you okay? What happened?"

"I'll tell you later. Right now, tell me what you know about what happened to Ah-seong Kim."

"Well, what I know so far is that the sanitation guys drove in here at about 5:30 in the morning and they spotted a body floating in the pond. She was out toward the middle. One guy jumped in and pulled her out, tried CPR, while the other called the University Police who must have called the EMT's. They were just over at the hospital ER and got here really quickly, they said, but it was no use. She was already dead and had been for some time. Our police called me after they got a look at the body. Guessed she might be a student. I suppose they called the city cops too. I got here just before 6. I looked at her face, saw it was Ah-seong and I called you."

Margaret glanced at the ground beside the pond nearest the ambulance. A little mound under some kind of covering was visible.

I frowned at Margaret.

"That's not right. That can't be right, Margaret. The body couldn't have been floating. She must have died sometime during the night and the water in the pond is fairly cool. She wouldn't float for a couple of days. Besides, if it was a suicide, she might have weighted her pockets. Same with murder, really. This pond's not that deep, is it? It doesn't make sense."

Margaret looked blank.

"What do you mean, she couldn't have been floating?"

I spoke slowly.

"Dead bodies don't float for several days. And that's in warm water. In cooler water they stay submerged even longer."

I needed more information. I looked around.

"Where are these sanitation guys?"

"Over there."

Margaret turned and gestured toward the rear of the student union where the cafeteria was located. I could see the sanitation truck pulled up beside the dumpsters. Two men in grey coveralls and two men in uniform were standing in the archway of the entrance to the building to get out of the rain. The overalls were talking, gesturing. The uniforms were nodding and writing.

I started to turn and walk toward them. I stopped. Not my job anymore. Not welcome. I stood there, watching. Frustrated.

I turned away. Well, police work wasn't my job any more, but meeting with students was and I'd met with Ah-seong not long before she'd died. I'd obviously be questioned. I wondered if I was the last person to talk with her. Unlikely. Still, I thought it might be helpful if I could get a look at the body.

The little mound was pitifully obvious on the ground beside the pond. I walked closer. Whatever had been used to cover her was actually pulled to the side. It did not hide her white blouse, the same one with the little Peter Pan collar she had worn to see me. Weeds from the pond clung to her hair and were scattered on the ground around the body. Some looked like they had been torn. It looked as if the guy who'd pulled her out of the pond had had some trouble getting her free of the tangle of vegetation. I wondered if the lovely long stems of the plants had, in fact, been lethal. Her feet stuck out at the bottom of the blanket. Her hose were shredded and her feet were bare. It struck me there was no coat visible.

From what I could see of her face at this distance, there wasn't much lividity. She'd not been in that pond very long.

That was a good thing. The decay of bodies in water has to be seen to be believed. Actually, has to be smelled to be believed. I remembered my first drowning call as a rookie cop almost exclusively by the smell. The body had been in Lake Michigan for at least a week. The remains of the old man had looked like a bundle of discarded clothes until you got closer. Then the smell hit. It's worse than a decaying body that's not been submerged, even in the summer. And the body isn't a body. It's a group of sinews holding bones and white, shredded flesh. I'd vomited when I'd smelled that first body and nobody ridiculed me for it. Floaters are too awful even for cop humor. I shook myself as I looked at what I could see of the ivory oval of Ah-seong's still face. Her head had lolled to the side and her eyes were open.

Her face changed from this drowning victim to the student I'd talked to yesterday. I felt a hot stinging behind my eyes. 'Why wouldn't you talk to me?' I mourned.

Yes, I'd looked at death before when I had been a cop, but I'd not just had a counseling session with the victim the day before. Though you couldn't call what I'd done 'counseling.' I hadn't touched the surface of what had been going on with her. Not all my fault. Yeah, yeah. I knew that. But some fault was mine. I grabbed a tissue out of my pocket with my good arm and wiped my face as I turned away. Not all of the moisture was rain.

The EMT's were still at the back of the ambulance, obviously waiting for someone from the Medical Examiner's office to show up and pronounce her dead at the scene. That had become standard practice after a horrible heat wave in Chicago decades before where the dead had piled up like corkwood in the emergency rooms of Chicago. Now it was legal to pronounce death at the scene and take the body directly to the city morgue.

At last there was some movement. They were getting out the gurney. The ME would probably be here any minute. I took out my cell phone and managed to get the code typed in with one hand. It was going to be trickier to take one-handed photos with a cell phone slick from rain. Nobody was paying much attention to me fumbling around. I got to the camera screen and clicked a few times. I got my thumb on the screen to get more of a close up and that little oval swam up onto my screen. I clicked. And clicked. There was no chance of sketching the scene; one-handed and no notebook made that impossible. But I had always preferred my own sketches, cell phone cameras weren't the same. Your own sketch with thorough labeling was so much better. Details were documented. Cell phones were too convenient, too fast.

I stuck my phone back in my pocket and stood there, thinking. I didn't like the floating body. It was odd.

I took out the phone again and looked at my close up photos. She was on her back, her head turned toward the pond. She didn't seem to have any bruises on her face. I could see a little of the bruises around her neck I had seen the day before. She had quite a lot of plant matter in her mouth and even her nose. That could mean she was alive when she went into the water. If you're already dead you're not going to be trying to inhale and getting leaves and weeds stuck in your mouth and nose.

Too bad the body had been moved, but of course trying to save her life had priority. Still, the position of the body in the pond could have been important. How much was she held down by the big stems and flat leaves? Where exactly in the pond had she been floating?

"Please move back, ma'am."

I'd been noticed. One of the ambulance guys gestured me to move away from the police tape. I took a step back.

"Sorry."

I turned and looked for Margaret. She'd moved further toward the archway where the gates stood open. A new car was pulling up. I bet the detectives were arriving. I started in that direction. And I stopped.

A guy got out of the passenger side and looked around. He wasn't tall. I could just see his head over the top of the parked car. Same round head, slightly more bald. The narrow eyes in the porcine face turned in my direction. Karl Kaiser. Marco's partner the day he'd been killed. The guy I'd reported for sexual harassment.

I turned away and walked toward the cafeteria in the student union.

I got myself a fill up of coffee in my mug that I'd shoved in the outer pocket of my purse when I'd been taking photos. There was no line. All the students were standing at the window looking out at the scene around Mendel Pond.

I took my coffee and stood behind them. At my height, I had little trouble seeing the scene spread out like a film set for a police drama. I took a scalding sip of the coffee and tried to calm down.

I didn't succeed. Out the window I could see Kaiser and what seemed to be his current partner, a tall, thin guy whose head bobbed forward over his narrow chest. He had a kind of Ichabod Crane look about him. The old drawings of that character, not the TV hot guy actor. They were standing just to the right of the body, talking to Margaret. The rain had continued and hatless Margaret was looking like she'd been the one in the pond.

I tried to get a read on my own emotions and failed. I felt distinctly odd. It seemed like I was both standing here in the warm cafeteria and also standing out on the wet grass, looking down at Ah-seong. I tried to focus on the scene outside and shake the doppelganger feeling.

Kaiser spoke to Margaret again and she started looking around. I bet she was looking for me. Even if she weren't, no woman should have to talk to Kaiser without a friend nearby. Not even out in the open.

I carried my mug outside.

When I walked up to them, Kaiser's partner was moving away toward the cops who'd been questioning the sanitation guys. Margaret looked relieved to see me. Kaiser did not.

The full body view of Kaiser had not improved. He'd been a wrestler in college and like so many who'd bulked up their muscles when younger, age and gravity had taken a toll. Well, actually, age, gravity and carbohydrates. His face had always had a piggy look. Now his body had caught up. Good. Maybe he'd have a coronary.

"Kristin, I was looking for you," said Margaret, glaring at me through the mist.

"This is Detective Kaiser. Detective Kaiser, this is . . . ."

"Mrs. Ginelli."

Kaiser did not extend his hand. Neither did I.

"Why're you sticking your oar in here?"

Margaret looked from Kaiser to me and seemed to decide she should be the one to answer.

"Professor Ginelli teaches here. She's the faculty member who spoke to Ms. Kim yesterday afternoon."

"Professor Ginelli???? How the hell did you pull that off, Ginelli?"

He glanced over toward where Ah-seong's body lay on the ground and then pulled his upper lip up to show some teeth in a mockery of a smile.

"Did the kid jump in the pond because you gave her a bad grade? Nice job, Professor."

Margaret looked stunned by Kaiser's hostility. I wasn't. I'd seen him far more hostile. It was his stock in trade.

He wasn't the only detective to operate that way. They seemed to think if they stirred up as much negative emotion as they could at a crime scene, a pot already simmering would boil over. Somebody would get pushed too far and maybe blurt out something they shouldn't, something they were trying to conceal. Kind of a sledgehammer technique. It actually worked, some of the time. But a lot of unrelated emotion could also boil over at the same time. It took someone with a lot more insight into the human condition than Kaiser to sift it out.

I tried for an even tone of voice.

"Dean Lester asked me to talk to this student because of some problems she was having."

"Problems? What kinda problems?"

His tone clearly implied that anyone privileged enough to go to the University of Chicago could not possibly have serious problems. I saw Margaret stiffen. She was going to stiffen a lot before she saw the last of Karl.

"The student had unexplained bruises on her neck and arms," I said. "It seemed to her roommate and her dorm resident that she had boyfriend trouble. Dean Lester thought I could help figure out what was going on."

I was almost succeeding with the patient tone of voice. Almost. My good hand holding the travel mug was shaking, though. I hoped Kaiser didn't notice. I wasn't shaking from fear, but from the effort to keep from throwing the hot coffee in his face.

"Well . . . .it doesn't seem you helped her much, does it, Ginelli?"

He stuck his thumb out in the direction of the small body on the ground. He turned from me and addressed Margaret.

"What's the kid's name again?"

"Ah-seong Kim."

"What's that? Jap?"

Margaret drew in a sharp breath. She was incensed. Well, Karl had gotten somebody to boil over.

"Ms. Ah-seong Kim is a Korean student, Detective."

"Nah," smirked Karl, actually happy with the reaction he'd gotten.

"She *was* a Korean student, Dean. Now she's a corpse. What I need to figure out is if she fell in accidentally or offed herself cause she couldn't cut it here. Lots of pressure here, right? Betcha a lot of these kids wanna take the easy way out."

Karl glanced at the surrounding buildings, perhaps expecting students to be leaping from the windows at any moment.

I couldn't help myself. I added, "Or, if she was killed by someone and put in the pond."

It was typical of Kaiser to have made up his mind to take the easy way, accident or suicide would mean he didn't have to do any more work. Not that he did a lot of work even when he was investigating murders.

Karl snapped his head around and looked at me. I moved a little closer and looked down at the male-pattern balding on top of his head. It was glistening in the rain. Kaiser had always hated it when I looked down on him. Well, it was his fault for being short.

"What, genius professor, you think somebody swam out there with her and held her down? In the middle of a college campus? Gimme a break."

I bristled.

"Look. We just told you she had bruises. What makes you think who-ever made those bruises wasn't willing to do a little more? Why don't you at least pretend to wait for the autopsy before you declare the case closed?"

I was no longer speaking calmly.

Kaiser's piggy face mottled with rage and he clenched his fists at his side. I was glad Margaret was there as a witness. One-armed I wouldn't be able to defend myself all that well. I took a step back.

Karl smiled at that. He genuinely enjoyed intimidating women.

"We'll need your statement. Don't leave."

Without another word to me or to Margaret, he turned on his heel and marched away toward his partner.

Margaret slowly blew out a breath while she looked at me.

"I take it you know each other."

I had to hand it to her. Dry humor in the pouring rain with a dead student to explain to the parents, to the administration, to the campus, and to the media. They're a tough breed these university deans.

"Yes, yes. I do know him. Look, Margaret, I want to take another look around. Kaiser will stomp around for twenty or thirty minutes before he even thinks to look for evidence. There's probably not much to see with the rain and all these people around, but I'd like to be sure."

Margaret frowned but didn't say anything. She turned and went back toward where the university police cars were parked.

I went forward as far as the police tape would allow. I looked at the ground by the low surround wall, trying to see where she might have gone in. That's when I saw the shoes. They were lying nearly hidden in the taller grass by the side of the pond on the far side away from the parked cars and the buildings. I walked on a pathway to avoid stepping on the grass so I could get a closer look.

Yes, they were definitely the shoes she'd had on yesterday. They were not together. One was on its side, about a foot from the wall around the pond. The little bow on the front was now dangling by a thread. The other was about two feet away, also nestled in the grass, but upside down and almost touching the wall. I moved closer to get a better look and squatted. I could clearly see the sole was split across the ball of the foot. If she'd jumped in on her own, would she have kicked off her shoes first? But if she had, how had they gotten so beaten up in less than a day? When she'd worn them to my office they were practically new. I took out my cell phone and snapped more photos.

"Ma'am, could you please move along?"

The voice from behind me sounded sharp and impatient.

I stood up and turned and there was Alice Matthews. She still looked irritated, but now because she was looking at my arm in the sling.

"Are you completely crazy? You're out here in the rain after you were mugged last night? What the hell is the matter with you?"

I was not being treated to Matthews's kindly manner this morning.

I explained my relationship to the student and Dean Lester's call, asking me to come. I decided to tell her about the shoes.

"Look, Matthews, see over there?" I gestured with my hand that was still holding the coffee mug.

"Those were the Kim student's shoes, I'm sure of it. She had them on when she came to my office and they looked like new. Now they're a wreck."

Matthews looked carefully at the shoes.

"Think she was running?"

She was quick.

"Well, that's what I was thinking. They're not exactly running shoes. But who or what was she running from? Or towards?"

We stood side by side on the path, looking at the shoes in silence.

"Shouldn't you be off duty by now?" I asked.

"Well, technically, yeah. I was about to go off shift when the call came. It was all hands on deck for something like this. Everybody came."

She looked at me.

"Listen, you really should go home, get into bed for God's sake. You look awful. I'll make sure the city cops bag and tag the shoes."

I really couldn't have agreed more. My energy level was flagging badly.

"Thanks for following up on the shoes. And I'd love to leave, but the detectives want my statement first."

"Go sit in the cafeteria. I'll tell them where to find you."

"Oh, thanks. Really. Thanks so much."

And that's how I ended up giving my statement to Ichabod Crane in a private dining room off the main cafeteria. I was totally fading, but I tried to get it all in. The bruises, the boyfriend, the Christian student group, my suspicions about the scholarship angle, the shoes.

Ichabod, his real name was Al Brown, wrote it all down without moving his facial muscles in any way. Must be a real advantage to be able to have that kind of a poker face when partnered with Kaiser.

Finally we were finished, and I staggered home to an empty house. Blessed be, the kids were in school, Carol and Giles were in class and I was alone. I set my alarm for 1 in the afternoon. I had a class at 3. I couldn't remember what the subject was.

6

When, however, men are prevented, by being alarmed, from doing wrong, it may be said that a real service is done to themselves. The precept, "Resist not evil," was given to prevent us from taking pleasure in revenge, in which the mind is gratified by the sufferings of others, but not to make us neglect the duty of restraining men from sin."

AUGUSTINE, *EPISTULA* XLVII, 5

I felt I was being watched.

I was.

When I opened my eyes, three pairs of brown eyes were staring at me. Sam, Mike and Molly were all sitting on the foot of the bed. Even Molly seemed to be looking at my bandaged arm and sling.

I looked at the clock. 12:45. Tuesdays and Thursdays were "early days" at kindergarten. That meant the teachers got to get off early and working parents had to scramble to make child care arrangements. Carol, Giles and I rotated pick-up on those days. One of them must have retrieved the boys at 12:30.

I tried to assume a happy tone.

"Hi, everybody."

"How'd you hurt your arm, Mom?"

The accusatory question was from Mike, always serious, always going straight to the point. He might have been the elder son by only twenty-three minutes, but it often seemed like he was the elder by twenty-three years.

Mr. Rogers sings, "I want you to tell me, I want to know" and as a toddler, Mike had loved Mr. Rogers and sung that song along with him with the same serious air. I'd found Mr. Rogers a little insipid, but the whole 'Dad coming home from work and putting on play clothes' had seemed to fill a void for Mike as he had no Dad. Sam had liked Sesame Street. Thank God nobody liked Sponge Bob.

Mike still wanted to know everything, straight up, right away. Sam, on the other hand, would much rather pretend everything was a joke.

But it was no joke. I was the only parent they had left and they knew it. Any time I got sick it scared them. I was rarely sick, so that was good, and I thought this might have been the first serious injury I'd had since they'd been born.

Truth then.

"Well, guys, last night while I was taking out the trash somebody made this cut on my arm with a knife. I kicked him and he ran away. The police came really fast and I had to get my arm bandaged up. I'm fine. A little tired, but I'm fine."

"Kick him bad, Mom? Did you punch him? Like this?"

Sam jumped off the bed and threw kicks and punches at an imaginary mugger, letting off steam. Molly thought this was a fine game and jumped off the bed to run around with Sam. They should have martial arts for dogs, they love it so much.

"Did they catch him?"

Mike had stayed on the bed, and on point.

"No, not yet. But I think they will."

I put my good arm around Mike and we watched Sam and Molly jump around some more.

When I didn't yell at him and tell him to stop making a racket, Sam turned around and looked at me. Molly stopped too.

"It's okay, guys. Really. The cut's not very deep and I have medicine to take that will help it heal right up. There are some very good people in the world, like the cops who came to help me, and the doctors and nurses (well, perhaps not one particular nurse) who fixed me up. There are some bad people, it's true, like the guy who gave me this cut. But hey, I stopped the bad man with an awesome kick."

I smiled, trying to look like 'Mom in charge.'

Sam bought it and started a tug game with Molly. Mike gave a big sigh and kept sitting next to me.

I squeezed him around the shoulders and then stood up.

"I'm going to be fine. Let's do big, big hug and then I need to get cleaned up and go teach a class. But let's be gentle, okay, so my arm can keep getting better?"

Two serious nods and a goofy dog smile.

We hugged very carefully.

* * * *

As I walked tiredly up to the front of Myerson, I could see four or five university police cars parked around the main quadrangle. I guess they were there to reassure students, faculty and staff that the university was being well guarded.

But from what?

I wondered if the crime scene techs had finished or even if they were still in the cul-de-sac, photographing, measuring, bagging, labeling.

I turned my back on the campus and went through the door.

"Kristin, hi. Hey, what happened to your arm?"

Henry, my office-mate, was coming down the stairs two at a time as I paused in the main foyer. I'd already been asked 'What happened to your arm' about seven times on the three-block walk to campus. I was considering having a tee shirt printed up with the slogan, "I was mugged in Hyde Park" and just wearing it. I might even do a brisk business selling them to residents (or tourists for that matter).

"Henry. Hi yourself. Just your typical evening taking out the trash in Hyde Park."

"What? You fell?"

Henry stopped on the last stair so our eyes were level. His eyes were tired, even strained behind his glasses and he was practically vibrating with tension.

"No, actually somebody tried to stick a knife in me. Luckily I was wearing my running shoes."

Henry sucked in a breath.

"Geeze, Kristin. No kidding? That's awful."

Henry came down the last stair and stepped around me and took two steps toward the door. Then he stopped and turned back.

"What do you know about the Kim student? Drowning in Mendel?" He sighed deeply. "I knew her, you know. That day of remembrance thing."

Last year the Korean students had held a service to commemorate the anniversary of the division of their country. I recalled that Henry had helped them plan it. Typical for Henry, descendant of the hated Japanese, to help the Korean students. The students and their concerns came first for Henry. It was one of the many things I liked about him.

I looked at him more closely standing under the one hanging light that illuminated the foyer of Myerson. I knew I looked horrible, but Henry did too. His dark eyes were rimmed with purple, contrasting with his pale skin. He looked totally beat, though we both usually looked beat from trying to manage family, teaching, and getting some writing done. But today, instead of acting tired, he was wired. He was shifting from foot to foot while we talked.

Maybe since he'd known Ah-seong, it was her death that had him so jumpy.

"Yeah," I said slowly, recollecting the service. I'd been there, but I'd forgotten Ah-seong had been in it. Seven Korean women in traditional dress had done a dance drama mourning all the Korean "Comfort women," the young Korean girls kidnapped and forced to serve in Japan's "prostitution army." Henry had read a small piece, denouncing that atrocity. It jolted me to remember now that Ah-seong had been one of those dancers.

"Henry, we need to talk. I spoke to Ah-seong yesterday and she was very troubled. I'm certain she'd been beaten more than once, and I don't know if that had anything to do with her death. Can you come back up to our office and talk for a while? My class doesn't start until 3."

"Nope. Can't. I've got a University Resources Planning meeting to go to. You won't believe how stupid those meetings are, but they take attendance and write it up in the minutes. I've got to go. I'll be back later."

Henry turned on his heel and rushed out the door.

Well. What was that? I didn't have the energy to ponder it and I just wearily trudged up the stairs toward the second floor. I'd almost made it when Dorothy Grimes, my esteemed boss's wife, plunged down the stairs right above me. She had her head down and her arms and legs were not exactly moving in sync. I was alarmed for a second she might stumble into me, and I had no good arm to try to catch her.

She stumbled past me, seeming not even to see me. She had on a raincoat over a nurse's uniform. That's right, I'd heard she worked part-time as a nurse at the university hospital.

On the next step below me she swayed and I put my briefcase down on the stair with an idea to turn and steady her. But as I was fumbling around, she picked up speed and went lumbering down the rest of the staircase like she couldn't wait to escape the building. I watched her until she reached the bottom, her soft-soled hospital shoes making a horrible squeaking on the rubber tread of the stairs.

I turned and picked up my briefcase. The faint smell of sweat combined with alcohol lingered where she'd passed. I hoped she wasn't returning to work because she seemed to be plastered. For the first time I felt a little sorry for Grimes if his wife was a heavy drinker.

I turned into Frost's office to get my share of snail mail and received my dose of being Frosted. She glared at me so hard I still felt it when I turned my back and reached into my mailbox. Even for Frost this was a little much, since I hadn't done anything lately to make her that mad at me. At least, I didn't think I had.

Well, who knows, I thought as I rooted around for my office key and then eventually got myself, my mail and my briefcase through the door. Could be Frost was mourning the Kim student in her own weird way. Like Henry who was normally a little wired got a lot more wired, Frost could draw on her seemingly endless reserves of anger to get her through. Why couldn't these people try denial?

I ditched my mail on my already overflowing desk and shrugged out of my coat. That I dropped into my chair. My office coffee mug was sitting in the middle of my desk, beckoning to me. I grabbed it.

Luckily I had time. Before I'd left the house I'd not only remembered the name of the course I was teaching (Christian Thought) but also the subject of today's lecture, Augustine of Hippo. Augustine had been a randy saint who prayed for chastity, but just "not yet." I had done one of my doctoral exams on him so I was set. I had grabbed the written exam out of my files before I'd left home. So I had plenty of time for coffee.

The faculty coffee station was located in the same conference room where we'd had our meeting. When we weren't using it for meetings or as overflow classroom space, it was the faculty lounge. Of course, we didn't have servants like they had at Oxford in their faculty lounges, asking you whether you'd like a coffee or a sherry when you wandered in. I thought fondly of the month I'd spent at Oxford this past summer. The Ginellis had taken the boys for a month in their motor home and I'd gotten to do some actual research for my dissertation.

The British pretty much invented academic privilege and they did it very well. You could actually "live in college" and have servants to cook your food, clean your room and yes, bring you coffee or sherry. It had been fun for a while, but sort of cloying. Occasionally you need to clean your own toilet or you start thinking fondly about colonialism.

Well, here at the Department of Philosophy and Religion we had an ancient Mr. Coffee machine and it was strictly do it yourself. Well, good. American philosophical pragmatism ruled. That's the only philosophy invented by Americans and it certainly had fit that other former U. of C. professor, Barack Obama, when he'd been president of the United States.

I pushed open the conference room door with my shoulder and looked in. Grimes and Abraham were the only ones there. Grimes had pulled out a chair from the conference table and Hercules was seated on the one couch we had at the back of the room. Rats. Neither of them had coffee. I glanced at the coffee pot and saw it was depressingly empty.

I quietly made my way toward the coffee bar set up. I could see that Hercules had been crying. His hands were hanging down between his knees and his shoulders were slumped. He was the picture of dejection. Grimes looked over at me with a 'How do I get out of this?' look on his face. I deliberately looked at the coffee machine. No way was I helping Grimes out. He was Department Chair, let him deal with Hercules.

It was going to take some doing to make coffee one handed, but I picked up the carafe of water that stood beside the machine. Well, good. There was some water in it.

"You are hurt?"

Hercules had raised his head and noticed my arm in the sling.

I turned and exchanged a glance with Grimes and we made an unspoken agreement not to upset Hercules any more than he already was.

"It's nothing, really. A little scratch. I'm just resting it. Shall we make some coffee?"

Hercules looked blank and Grimes didn't move from his chair.

Well, what did I expect? Help?

As I poured the water into the top of the machine and sprinkled some coffee into a filter above the pot, I thought it was odd to see Grimes sitting. I tried to remember if I'd ever seen him sit. He stood in meetings in his captain of the ship stance, he had one of those standing desks in his office, and in glancing into a classroom when he lectured, I had seen he taught standing.

As the coffee started to gurgle, I remembered Ah-seong was taking one of his classes, "Marriage and Family Ethics." So, he was sitting down. Another way of showing grief, I guessed.

Hercules got up and pottered toward the door, muttering "La pauvre." Hmm. As far as I knew he hadn't even known Ah-seong.

Adelaide was entering as Hercules was exiting. He paused to hold the door for her and then he shut it feebly behind him. Adelaide saw Grimes first and made to turn to exit again. Then she saw me and came over.

I was still standing by the Mr. Coffee, avidly watching each drop drip into the pot. Since Grimes had made no move to help me, he wasn't getting my precious coffee first. Adelaide either, for that matter. I protected the pot with my body.

Adelaide moved up next to me, took my big coffee cup from my hand, removed the pot and set a paper cup under the drip to catch it. She poured me a full cup and wordlessly handed it to me. Then she switched the coffee pot and the paper cup and took that partially filled one for herself.

"So, what's with the sling?" she asked as we moved toward two chairs at the conference table.

I waited until we were sitting and then I quietly described the mugging one more time. I didn't particularly want Grimes thinking he was included in the conversation.

Adelaide's serious grey eyes looked intently at me while I was speaking. She looked increasingly angry and what looked a little like remembered fear.

"I hope they catch the bastard fast!" She slapped a hand on the conference table. "What a time for our department—a death and a mugging."

"I do not see that the student's unfortunate death and Ms. Ginelli's injury involve this department in any way, Dr. Winters."

Grimes had horned in on our conversation anyway.

"You're incredible, Harold. Just incredible in your capacity to not see what is right in front of your nose. Kristin works here and Ms. Kim was taking a class. From you! Why she might have majored! Kristin even talked to her just yesterday afternoon."

Adelaide glanced at me.

"I saw her waiting for you at 2:30. Did she? I mean, did she talk to you? I'm sure the police will want to know what she told you."

"I know, Adelaide. I was at Mendel Pond this morning at 7. Dean Lester called me when she saw who the victim was. I gave my statement to the police then, though I imagine they'll be back in touch with me."

Actually, I imagined no such thing, that is, if Kaiser had anything to do with it. Not unless he thought he could prove I'd murdered her, anyway.

"Oh, my God. You were there? You saw her? Was she, had she been assaulted, could you tell?"

Adelaide leaned toward me, her shoulders hunched forward with tension.

"I doubt it," I said, thinking of what I had seen of the neatly buttoned blouse. There were those shoes though. Still, no point in alarming Adelaide further just on my speculations.

"It could have been a lot of things. It didn't look much like suicide to me, but hard to tell. She could have been chased and fallen in, or been pushed. It's much too soon to tell without even a medical examiner's report."

I put my hand on her shoulder and she immediately stood up, shaking me off.

"I've got some work. I just wondered, that's all. It's so common."

Yes, she was right about that. All too common.

I decided we were ready for a change of topic.

"Do either of you know where Dr. Willie is today?"

I glanced at Grimes, who was still seated, looking especially grim. Well, it was a grim day. Still, this was a question tailor-made for him. He was the kind of boss who would want to know where all his flunkies were all the time. He didn't fail me.

"He has a class today from 2 until 3."

I turned my chair toward Grimes.

"Doesn't he spend a lot of time with the football team?"

Curiously, it was Adelaide who answered from behind me.

"Yes. He was a physical therapist before he did his Ph.D."

I kept forgetting how long these people had known each other. And the second career thing was so common. So Willie had been a physical thera-pist. I thought Adelaide had been a high school English teacher. I wondered if Grimes had done something else before getting his doctorate in religion and philosophy.

What was it about religion? Did you kind of back into it, or did you just have to be older to appreciate it? No sensible person seemed to pick religion and philosophy as a career first time out of the chute. And with jobs disappearing faster and faster, perhaps few would choose it even as a second or third career.

I realized Adelaide was still talking.

"He helps out with the team, even travels with them sometimes but mostly it's, you know, group psychology coaching on teamwork, leadership, guys bonding together. Whatever."

Adelaide's voice was distinctly derisive as she described Willie's work with the team. She was not a fan of male bonding, apparently.

I turned my chair back the other way to look at her. Good thing they were swivel chairs as I couldn't have managed this back and forth with one arm.

"Why do you want to know?" she continued, tilting her head and look-ing uncomfortably directly at me.

Might as well tell her.

"Yesterday Ah-seong told me she was dating someone with an athletic scholarship. I figured it had to be football as they have about the only ath-letic scholarships . . . "

"No, Ms. Ginelli, you are not to become involved in this in any way," Grimes interrupted me. "Leave this to the trained professionals."

"You forget, Harold. She is a trained professional," Adelaide corrected him in a positively gleeful tone of voice.

"I'd thought she'd changed professions," Grimes countered in a clipped voice. "Perhaps I was wrong."

I now swiveled my chair again so I could keep both combatants in partial view. I hate to be spoken of in the third person when I'm sitting right there, the ways some adults do to children. These people might outrank me in an academic department, but I'd be damned if they'd treat me like a kid.

I got up and strode toward the door. As I opened it, I turned back and looked directly at both of them.

"She will do exactly as she sees fit," I added through clenched teeth.

"Dr. Grimes, Dr. Winters," I said and left.

I fumed as I walked back to my office. Sure, Grimes was warning me off. He was probably worried looking into Ah-seong Kim's death would take my attention away from something really important, like that stupid self-study research.

If it had been anybody but Kaiser assigned to the case, I'd have been giving myself the same speech. 'Stay out of it.' I hadn't worked on my dissertation in two weeks and it didn't look like I'd be getting to it any time soon.

But in addition to being a brute, Kaiser was genuinely stupid as well as lazy. He would never figure out what had happened to Ah-seong Kim if he was the one conducting the investigation. Ichabod had not inspired a lot of confidence either.

I'd been considering looking into her death while I was walking over to Myerson, maybe feeding information, if I got any, through Alice Matthews. Grimes trying to get me to back off was pretty much the last nudge I'd needed. I really hated the way he'd obviously assumed he could tell me what to do about this. I'd investigate even if it cost me my job. Maybe Matthews would help. But even if she didn't, I had to do it.

I owed Ah-seong that much. I'd failed her in life. Perhaps I wouldn't fail her in death.

I stopped by Frost's office. She was fortunately elsewhere. I stole some paper and a pen from her desk and left Willie a note asking if we could meet at 4:30 in his office and stuck it to his door. Then I crossed to mine and got my lecture notes.

I told the students, clearly subdued from the death of one of their classmates, about Augustine's theory of a Just War. He'd wanted the Christian pacifists of his time to take up arms against the barbarians invading Rome. Augustine had believed sometimes violence was justified, and it was especially justified in defense of the innocent, what he called "the vulnerable other." It was a good thought, protecting the vulnerable from barbarians. We certainly had an endless supply of barbarians.

7

The latest enemy of the vitality of classic texts is feminism.

HAROLD BLOOM, *THE CLOSING OF THE AMERICAN MIND*

I made sure the lights were out in the seminar room and started back toward my office. Even in the dim light cast by the new, energy-saving LED lights, I could see someone leaning against the door of my office. As I got closer, I saw it was a young Korean man, his hands in the pockets of his worn black leather jacket. His hair was cut short, the kind of haircut they give you in the military, and he was wearing clean, pressed jeans with a white-collar shirt. He straightened as he saw me and moved to stand blocking the hallway. Call me paranoid, but after just having been mugged I was a little nervous at his stance. It seemed somehow threatening. I was conscious that Frost had left for the day, and probably the other colleagues had too. We were alone in this corridor, perhaps even on this floor. I stopped about five feet away from him.

"Are you waiting to see me?"

"Are you the Professor Gin-elly?" he countered tersely.

"Yes, I am."

"Then I am waiting to speak to you. I am Myung Ha Kim, the brother of Ah-seong Kim."

Well, no wonder he seemed tense. I moved closer to get to my office door, intending to ask him to come in. My keys were in my pocket, and with one arm holding the books and papers I'd used in class, and the other arm in a sling, I fumbled a little. Myung Ha Kim made no move to help me. I just put the books on the floor and spoke.

"Why don't you come in, Mr. Kim? I can't tell you how sorry I am about your sister's death. How can I help you?"

He didn't abandon his stance in the center of the hall. That was a good thing since he raised a fist and shook it at me. If he'd been closer, he'd have hit me.

"You had no right to talk to my sister. You had no business talking to her. You are no Christian. You do not even know what it is to be Christian!"

I decided not to unlock my door. I grabbed my keys in my pocket, however, putting my fingers between several of the keys to make a weapon. If you grip your keys like that, it can make a fairly effective set of brass knuckles. But I kept my hand hidden. Perhaps this young man's anger was a mask for grief, though he was clearly blaming me. He was panting with rage.

I tried for a calm voice.

"I spoke to your sister because the Dean of Students asked me to. Someone was hurting her. Had you seen her lately? She had bruises on her neck and on her wrists. She needed help."

Myung Ha took a step toward me until we were about a foot apart. I gripped my keys more tightly. The top of his head only came up to my chin, but from what I could see where his leather jacket strained along his shoulders and biceps, he seemed to be in great shape. His pressed shirt did not do a lot to hide impressive pectoral muscles. He kept his fists by his side now, but he was clenching and unclenching them.

I took a step away from my door toward the middle of the hallway. He did too, keeping in my face.

He struck himself on the chest.

"I am the one she must talk to. Who are you to say anything? You are a woman and an American—how can you know what Korean woman must do? If she had listened to me and not you she would not be dead."

Okay. That was enough. I was sorry he'd lost his sister, though their relationship sounded like he expected to call the shots, but I needed to put some physical distance between us. I took two quick steps back down the hallway and turned toward him. When he started to follow me again, I spoke sharply.

"Stop there, Mr. Kim. I'm going to overlook your attitude here because you've just lost a family member in tragic circumstances, but you need to leave right now and not bother me again. If you don't leave right now, I will see that the Dean of Students has a talk with you and you could find yourself in big trouble. Am I making myself clear?"

For a minute he stood stock still, glaring at me. I thought I might need those keys as a weapon after all. But then he reached down and grabbed his backpack where he'd left it at the side of the hallway. He straightened and looked derisively at me, and then he retreated rapidly down the staircase.

My hands holding my keys were sweaty. It took me three tries to open my office door.

I slumped down in my office chair fairly stunned by the encounter with Ah-seong's brother. I could see why she might not have turned to him if she was having boyfriend trouble.

Suddenly my office phone rang, making me practically jump out of my chair from the excess adrenaline. I grabbed for it, knocking over what was left of the coffee in my big mug all over my books and notes on the desk.

I grabbed some tissues and patted them down on the mess. Then I stabbed the speakerphone button and continued to wipe.

"What?" I said loudly.

"Professor Ginelli, please."

"Speaking."

"Hello, it's Tom Grayson. I was calling to ask how the arm is."

Now I wished I'd answered a little more graciously.

"Doctor. This must be the modern equivalent of a house call. I'm flattered."

Oh. God. Stupid. Apparently flirting is not like riding a bicycle. You do forget.

"How is it? The arm I mean." Tom soldiered on. He seemed nervous too.

"Actually, I've hardly had time to think about it. One of my students was found drowned in the pond behind our building. It's been chaos."

"Yes. I'd heard about that. How tragic. I'm sorry to hear that you had to come to campus and face that. In fact, I called your home first. Someone who identified himself as Batman answered and said Mom was at work."

Had to be Sam. He had a lot of Batman outfits, primarily so he wouldn't sulk if his Batman garb happened to be in the wash. Grayson must be a dedicated physician if he'd still called me after learning I had a kid. I wondered what he'd think of twins. Well, I doubted the occasion would ever arise.

"I had a class, but I'd already been here at 7 am at the Dean's request. She was in one of my classes and someone I'd been counseling. I was one of the last people to speak to her, I think."

I heard myself say "counseling" and it brought back the vivid picture of Ah-seong recoiling from my use of that word. Well, and a one-sided lecture from me about Jesus scarcely counted as counseling anyway.

Grayson was still talking, and revealing himself as a pompous physician-type.

"In the rain? I don't think that was wise."

Well, hell. I certainly didn't need a lecture right now. I sighed, a little regretfully. But part of me was relieved, too. The last thing I needed was to start caring about this guy, and wondering if he cared for me. Too much baggage there.

I sharpened my voice.

"The wisdom or lack of wisdom of my actions is not really your concern, Doctor. You did me a favor and I appreciate it. I will say 'thank you,' again but I believe that should just about cover it."

I don't take orders at all well and I'd had just about enough of them today from Lester, to Kaiser, to Grimes and now this interfering doc. Combine that with the scare I'd gotten from Ah-seong's brother and I was ready to slam into somebody and Grayson was giving me a target.

Astonishingly, I heard a chuckle on the other end of the line.

"You're right. You're right. I've tried to shake that Hippocratic manner, but it's tough. They teach it in medical school, you know. Can you let me back into your good graces if I quit acting like a know-it-all doctor?"

I felt the anger drain out of me like water through a sieve.

"Yeah. Well. Okay," I said, being my usual sophisticated self.

Even though I was letting go of the anger, though, I wasn't exactly relaxed. This guy had far too much charm and I couldn't seem to detect a false note in what he'd just said. Danger ahead, said my nerve endings.

"I really called to see if we could have coffee this week. I'd like to get to know you better."

So Grayson had a purpose and it wasn't to make a house call over the phone. I waited some, testing how I felt about this.

"Kristin? Are you still on the line?" Tom asked.

I'd waited a little too long.

"Okay," I said.

I could feel my heart racing. Whew. When did this get so hard?

"Great. How about after the IRB meeting tomorrow?"

This guy had thought things through. I wish I could say the same for me.

"Okay," I said again. I was pretty sure it was not my snappy conversation that was attracting him.

"Good," Tom said. "See you then." And he hung up.

I ended the call but kept my hand on the phone. I looked at my hand, the blue veins starkly visible under my eternally pale Scandinavian skin, more pale now from loss of blood. That hand connected me to the receiver and the receiver connected me to another human being. An attractive male human being.

Emotion is a terrible thing. It seemed to me that my emotions had only two settings. Off and on. I realized I had turned the switch from off to on and was no longer living in the self-imposed cocoon where I had dwelt for the last five years, insulated from any emotional connection to other adults. The boys were all I needed, I had convinced myself. All my emotion, all my capacity for love, had gone to them and only them. But now I could actually feel the cocoon starting to tear, to open up. I didn't want it, did I? I slowly tightened my hand on the receiver.

No need to panic here, I told myself. There were good reasons I was feeling too much. My grief for Marco had never gone away. Never would. That wound was compounded by the real wound in my arm, a wound that was an all too visible reminder that I too could be taken from our boys. Add to that the shock and remorse over the needless death of a lovely young woman, my on-going resentment, even hatred for Kaiser and to top it off, the jolt to my nerves of the encounter with Ah-seong's brother.

Right. I wasn't attracted to the charming doctor. I was just nervy. And I knew I was lying to myself even as I grasped at the edges of the cocoon and tried to pull them back around me.

The phone rang literally under my hand and I jumped, jolting my other arm.

I stifled a groan and answered the phone.

"Yes?"

It was Donald Willie. He'd gotten my note and he was free now if I wanted to talk.

"Yes, thanks," I said, not really meaning it.

But first I picked up the phone and called the student scholarship office. I got an actual human being on the line and an actual answer to my question. Amazing.

* * * *

Donald's office was two doors down from Henry's and mine—two doors closer to Grimes and the seat of power. Not that we had any power in Philosophy and Religion any more.

It is odd though, I pondered, as I tiredly walked the short way to Donald's door, that in a world where religion and ideology are so much at the root of vicious, bloody violence from war, to terrorism, to attacks on Planned Parenthood to the police shootings of often unarmed or surrendering African Americans, to the rising again of Islamophobia and Anti-Semitism, to name just a few, nobody wants to study religion and philosophy any more. Maybe that's why. Understanding someone else's religion or ideology or history of being discriminated against makes it harder to hate and to kill. Hating and killing are now ends in themselves, I was coming to believe. At least they seemed to win elections.

Donald had left his door partly open for me, but still I knocked briefly on the door jam before I entered. I didn't much like his office. It always reminded me of a dentist's waiting room. He'd pushed his desk up against the far wall, and had placed a couch, two chairs and a coffee table in the middle. He even had magazines spread out on the coffee table. I'd bet he intended this set-up to look inviting and feel non-threatening to students. Too bad, though. It looked just like a dental assistant would direct me to take a seat and the doctor would see me shortly. I hated going to the dentist.

Donald was seated at his desk, his back to me. He was dictating into a microphone attached to his computer. I wondered if those kinds of voice-typing programs actually worked or if you had to spend a bunch of time correcting typos. Who knows? I was unlikely to try it. But I paused and kept silent, not willing to add my voice to his recording. He must have heard me because he quickly shut it off.

"Kristin. How's the arm?"

Willie's voice was all warm concern. He gestured for me to take a seat on the couch. Not being a fool, I chose a chair. Donald continued to stand, looking down at me.

"Adelaide told me of your adventure last night, and this morning too! Talk about one of those days."

Donald's voice came rapidly from under his brown, luxurious mustache. He seemed a little nervous under all that warmth.

"Can I go get you some coffee? Water? Anything?"

Okay. Definitely nervous. Usually Willie was, or affected to be, carefully calm.

Well, maybe he was just unsure why I'd come and wanted to talk with him. I'd certainly never dropped by for a chat before.

Not that I'd ever had anything particularly against him. He had always seemed an amiable enough guy. Yes, his large mustache and beard always seemed to overwhelm his thin, long face, but I didn't hold that against him. In fact, I thought as I sat there looking at him standing on the other side of the coffee table, I'd never given him much thought at all.

Besides, he was often absent, accompanying the football team. When he had spoken of that work in pre-faculty meeting gatherings, it had been with the most energy he ever displayed.

"No, thanks, Donald. Really. I came by to ask you some questions about student athletes."

Willie took the other chair and looked up at me, frowning slightly.

"Oh. Okay. Shoot."

"I don't now if Adelaide mentioned it when you spoke with her, but the student who was drowned, Ah-seong Kim, came to see me yesterday at

Dean Lester's request. Ah-seong had been referred by her dorm counselor to the Dean because she had come in on Saturday night with some bruises on her."

Donald's pale brown eyes widened, but he didn't say anything beyond a psychologist's stock-in-trade "hmmm."

I pressed on.

"Ah-seong was not very forthcoming with me, but I gathered from some things she said that she was dating a guy whose temper flared at her when he was under stress from trying to keep his grades up and also stay on a team. That made me think of student athletes. Especially football."

Donald leaned forward in his chair, his face tightening and he lost his neutral psychologist's tone.

"You think she was dating a football player? Why them?"

"I called the scholarship office before I came in here, Donald. Football is the only team that still has any specifically dedicated athletic scholarships. And they have pretty high grade requirements. With as much time as I've heard you say you spend with the football team, I'm pretty sure you know that, don't you?"

Willie sat back in his chair and tented his fingers like a TV show shrink. I sighed inwardly.

"Yeah. Well, I guess so." He paused. "But I just don't see why it has to be a student athlete who bruised her. She could have gotten bruises any number of ways. Perhaps in a fall?"

Ah. The ever-popular idea that battered women actually manage to bruise themselves.

I was not getting a lot of cooperation from Donald. I wondered if he was just being naturally protective of his precious football players or if he actually knew something.

It was my turn to lean forward and I did, pulling myself up straight so I could appear to loom over him. I looked directly into his eyes, willing him to get the picture.

"The bruises were around her neck and around her wrist, Donald. These are not skinned knees we're talking about. She might have had bruises elsewhere as well, but those were the ones I saw with my own eyes."

Silence.

I pressed on.

"She told me a guy who was stressed out because he 'needed to stay on the team' and keep his scholarship made those bruises. That adds up to football player to me. The only dedicated, endowed athletic scholarships are for football. You know that. Now, are you going to help me figure out who was putting those bruises on her or not?"

Donald's eyes narrowed at my tone and he looked distinctly less amiable.

"That's just such a common stereotype, Kristin. The macho athlete who knocks women around. In my experience, athletes are no more capable of that kind of behavior than anyone else. Less, actually, in my opinion, since sports themselves discharge a lot of negative emotion and team camaraderie provides emotional support."

I had pretty much had it between the events of the last twenty-four hours up to and including the encounter in the hall with Ah-seong's brother. I was not feeling diplomatic.

I abruptly stood up, startling Donald. He pulled back in his chair as now I really loomed over him.

"The names Ray Rice, Jason Kidd, Mike Tyson or Floyd Mayweather ring a bell, Donald?"

I bent over to tap on one of the magazines on his table and Donald flinched and tried to lean even further back in his chair.

"See this article in one of your sports magazines? See the headline here? And the tag line? 'Half of male college athletes admit to history of "sexually coercive behavior such as sexual assault."' Half. Get it? It's a study from a medical journal. We have an epidemic on college campuses of sexual assault, a lot of it by athletes, and you want to just brush me off with claptrap about it being a stereotype?"

Donald abruptly scrambled out of his chair and stood behind it, gripping the back.

"I'm surprised at you, Kristin. All of this is open to debate. The media blow all these kinds of reports way out of proportion, especially when it comes to professional athletes. And student data is very unreliable."

I stood facing him. I didn't need to grip a chair. I was going to be out of here in a second anyway.

"Donald, I don't think it's 'open to debate' when you see a video of someone being punched unconscious by her fiancé. Look, even the NFL has admitted there's a problem and colleges and universities all over the country are being investigated for failure to protect students from assault, especially sexual assault. We have not been investigated here. Is that what you want? Ignore the problems and then be forced to deal with the damage because an outside group forces you to do so?"

Willie's hand came down flat on the back of his chair, making a whoosh sound as the plastic-covered foam made a breathy protest.

"I had no idea you were such an aggressive feminist, Kristin. I thought as a former cop you'd have a more balanced view."

Yeah. I'd learned a lot as a cop about having a 'balanced view' of domestic violence.

I just stood there and looked at his hand that had hit the back of the chair. Willie got the point and his face colored slightly. Well, the little bit of his face I could see with all that facial hair colored slightly. He crossed his arms over his chest and stepped back toward his desk.

I keep looking at him, letting the silence do its work, but I was also thinking. This was not a philosophical discussion of whether feminist analysis was helpful or not helpful in illuminating the relationship of aggression and sports. I was becoming more and more convinced Willie knew something and his own anxiety and now aggression were attempts to hide that.

"Look, Donald. I came in here because I thought you'd want to help. A student has died, and she died with bruises on her neck and her wrists. She died. Get it? That is the most important thing. We could debate feminism for hours and nothing would change that fact.

"Another fact is that she told me she was dating a student athlete. You know these students. Are you going to help me narrow down whom she might have been dating, or not? Willie hunched his shoulders and tightened his arms around his chest.

"I am certainly not going to give you names of student athletes so you can harass them and accuse them without any evidence of God knows what."

I turned as if to go, and then, just when he would think this was over, I turned abruptly back.

"I'm going to talk to these guys with or without your help, Donald. I just thought it would be easier with your help. I thought you might have some insights. But apparently you don't."

This time I did turn to the door for real and I started walking out.

Willie spoke to my back.

"You know you have absolutely no authority to conduct an investigation into anything. You do know that, right? Why don't you back off and see if the authorities that are responsible for investigating do their jobs? Or are you working out your guilt here because she killed herself after talking to you?"

Ah, psychobabble. Willie was turning out to be about an inch deep, protecting himself with his arms and his arsenal of psychological one-liners instead of trying to think with me about a dead woman student. I had hoped Donald would be, what was his word? Oh, yes, balanced. I grimly chuckled to myself, glad I was facing the other way. Donald was trying to defend male privilege with a very thin shield.

I turned and looked at him across the room. He now had crossed his legs as well as his arms and he was leaning back on his desk. He actually appeared to have shrunk in size.

"I ordinarily would let the authorities handle it, Donald. Unfortunately, in this particular instance I've met the authority. Besides. Don't you think the truth is the business of everyone? Where's your Socratic method?"

Willie looked stumped.

Good ole Socrates. Gets 'em every time.

I was tempted to make a grand exit on that line, but Ah-seong came first. I came back toward him and fumbled in my shoulder bag one handed for a card. I felt for a pen and wrote on the back of my card.

"Here's my cell number. You could help here and it would not be to falsely accuse anyone of anything. It would be to find out what actually happened. Which I will do, with you or without you. Just think about it."

I held out the card but he did not take it. I placed it on the magazine with the story about athletes and campus assault. Maybe he'd take the hint and read the article.

I let myself out of his office.

8

Everyone must admit that if a law is to have moral force, i.e. to be the basis of an obligation, it must carry with it absolute necessity; that, for example, the precept, "Thou shalt not lie," is not valid for men alone, as if other rational beings had no need to observe it; and so with all the other moral laws properly so called.

IMMANUEL KANT, *FUNDAMENTAL PRINCIPLES OF THE METAPHYSICS OF MORALS*

After the kids had gone to bed, complaining about no Tae Kwon Do, I went online to my university account and looked up the student directory. Maybe Ah-seong's roommate didn't know whom she was dating, but I'd only heard that third hand. Many times people know more than they realize. And I had many more questions for the roommate anyway.

I searched for Ah-seong's name and got her dormitory and room number. She'd lived in one of the elaborate new dorms to the north of the campus named for a Russian immigrant alumnus and designed by a Mexican architect. Go figure. The announcement of the design of these brightly hued, multi-colored stacked boxes had enthused that the architect was going for a "tropical feel" for the buildings. When I'd read that I'd thought, 'Sure, that's what a largely gothic university campus located in a climate where there were weeks when the temperature did not get out of single digits really needed.' I'd only walked by this collection of low-rise, pink, purple, tangerine and lime colored rectangles and even then I'd thought it might be hard to find a specific building and room number.

Well, maybe I could get directions from the roommate.

I called the number in the directory. A female voice said a cautious hello.

"This is Professor Ginelli. Is this Ah-seong Kim's roommate?"

"Who did you say you were again?"

The voice was very soft and hesitant.

"Professor Ginelli. I knew Ah-seong as a student. Is this her roommate?"

"No, I changed roomed with Karen; she's the roommate. She didn't want to stay here and reporters have called and everything. It's been a zoo. I was just about to take the phone off the hook."

"It's important that I speak with Karen. Could you go find her and tell her who's calling and ask her to come to the phone to speak with me?"

The voice was a little stronger, though still hesitant.

"I guess. Yeah. Okay. Wait a minute."

Quite a few minutes passed, in fact, before a very subdued voice came on the line.

"Hello? I'm Karen Cartwright. You wanted to speak with me?"

I tried for my reassuring professor voice.

"Karen? Hello, thanks for coming to the phone. I'm Professor Kristin Ginelli. I knew Ah-seong Kim and I wanted to talk to you about her."

"About what?"

"Lots of things. This isn't a conversation we can have over the phone. Could you meet me for breakfast tomorrow? I'll stop by your dorm around 8 in the morning."

As reluctant as she sounded, odds were she wouldn't show up if I asked her to meet me in a restaurant. I'd collect her.

"I guess. I don't know what you want to talk to me for."

"I'll explain when I see you. And Karen?"

"Yes?"

"You're probably going to have trouble sleeping tonight. You've had a terrible shock. Student Health is open for walk-ins until 10 tonight. Go on over and tell them what happened. They may be able to give you something to help you sleep. You'll still feel crummy tomorrow, but not as crummy as you would if you'd been awake all night."

I knew what I was talking about. I was an expert in not sleeping from grief and feeling crummy. That's why I'd not hesitated to take the pain medicine after I was mugged. It can feel like giving in, but sinking into even a drug-induced sleep can be a way of fighting back. Or at least, giving yourself a break so you can fight again. Grief and shock had to be fought. Or the fog sucked you in and held you.

"I guess."

Karen was still passive, but that was normal. She was numb from what had happened to her roommate. I asked Karen to put her friend back on the line, the one who had been kind enough to switch rooms with her. When the friend came on, I told her to take Karen to Student Health so she could get some help.

I wanted to sleep myself, but before I did, I tried Henry at home. His wife answered. She was from Japan and her English was difficult for me to understand. Of course, her English was far better than my Japanese, which is non-existent. I gathered from what she said that Henry was not home. I didn't know which suburb contained his convenience store and I thought it politic not to ask. I wondered if he'd pick up his cell at work and decided he'd probably not be able to talk anyway. I just left a message on his work voicemail asking him to meet with me tomorrow.

Just as I was trying to get to sleep, Margaret Lester called and she did not sound happy.

"Kristin! Dean Wooster has just this minute finished chewing my head off. Both Drs. Grimes and Willie have reported to him that you are stirring up trouble about this student's death and I am to tell you in no uncertain terms to stop."

Margaret was plainly angry, but was it at me, or at Wooster for making use of the chain of command to get her to lean on me instead of calling me himself? Probably the latter, though of course I couldn't know for sure. Grimes and Willie had wasted no time in getting to the Dean. I found that quite interesting.

I tried for a reasonable tone.

"Margaret, you've met Kaiser. You know he won't look into Ah-seong Km's death very carefully."

"That's merely your opinion. And there may not be that much to 'look into' as you put it. This is most likely a tragic accident."

Ah, the administrative party line. 'Just so sad. A sad, sad accident.' I stopped being so reasonable.

"That's administrative baloney and you know it and so do I."

Margaret was silent for a moment and then she sighed.

"Yes, I do know it."

I felt bad for the position Margaret was in, but it was nothing compared to how bad I felt for Ah-seong.

"Look, Margaret. Here's what I plan. It's not all that complex. I'm going to have breakfast with the roommate and try to figure out the boyfriend's name. Then I was going to talk to him. I also want to drop in on the Korean Students Christian Association."

Suddenly I remembered something else.

"Margaret, you must know Ah-seong had a brother here who's also a student. Have you talked to him?"

Margaret completely stopped being the cautious bureaucrat.

"Did I? What a piece of work that kid is. I had him in my office for nearly an hour, alternately accusing me, the university, and various of her professors, especially you, by the way, of leading her from the true path of Korean womanhood."

"He paid me a visit this afternoon at my office. I thought he was going to deck me. I had to threaten him with an involuntary visit to you. He is certainly firm in his views of what's Christian and how his sister should have behaved. I assume he's a mover and shaker in the Korean Students Christian Association?"

Margaret sighed again.

"As a matter of fact, he's the president."

Figured.

"Well, I imagine I'll talk to him again then."

"He did get along fine with Detective Kaiser."

Why was I not surprised? Despite Kaiser's racism, he probably recognized a kindred authoritarian soul.

"When did he see Kaiser?"

"Kaiser was in my office for part of the time I talked with Kim. He wanted to ask him some questions about who his sister was dating, whether she'd told him of any problems and so forth."

Odd. Kaiser seemed to actually be investigating.

"Did he know whom she was dating and that the guy might have been putting bruises all over her?"

"He claimed she wasn't dating anyone, wasn't having any problems and that he was the only one she talked to."

"I don't buy it. I wouldn't talk to him if he were my brother."

"No. Me neither. But Kaiser bought it, or seemed to."

"Well, I still think the roommate is the most likely for Ah-seong to have confided in. Do you know if Kaiser has talked to her?"

"The police are supposed to let our office know if they will be questioning a student. They haven't mentioned the need to talk to the roommate."

Amazing. So Kaiser really wasn't investigating all that much.

"Typical of Kaiser, Margaret. Really. It's typical. He'll overlook the obvious every time."

I heard another sigh, or maybe this time is was a snort. I needed to reassure Margaret a little more that I was not her biggest liability in this.

"I won't stir up trouble, Margaret. I swear. And I plan to feed everything I get to the campus police and it can be passed right through channels to Kaiser and his partner."

I hoped I was right in thinking Alice Matthews would do that. I thought I was.

"Great. And precisely what do I tell Dean Wooster?"

"Tell him you spoke to me and it's your read that if I'm allowed to poke around a little without being sat on, or words to that effect, that I'll give up of my own accord. You can also tell him you'd hate to have me get mad about being reprimanded for asking questions and be provoked enough to take my concerns about the investigation, or lack of it, to the press."

Margaret's voice became very tense.

"You'd do that?"

Actually, I'd already been mulling over the press as an option this evening while I should have been working on my next lectures. I'd rejected it. At least for now. Involving reporters in an investigation was a little like using nuclear weapons. As the American Catholic Bishops had concluded a couple of decades ago, no use of nuclear weapons can be justified because there's no way to avoid having innocent civilians be killed by the thousands. The Bishops had used Augustine too. If a lot of innocents get harmed, you can't call it a Just War. Things you did not intend to target got decimated anyway.

The press was a little like a tactical nuclear warhead. You couldn't point them in any one direction and have any confidence they'd hit only the target. Or even hit the target at all. They were so interested in their online hits to sell whatever product was advertised on the same page as the news story that they'd sling as much mud as they could to increase traffic to their news sites. Especially in this age of electronic media it was far, far too likely that many innocents would get hurt. No. No press.

But Margaret didn't need to know that. She'd be more convincing to the Dean if she thought I might involve the press.

Well, so much for Kant's theories about the immorality of lying. I was going to lie in the interest of truth, something Kant had thought was impossible. Part of me was realizing these last couple of days were undermining my confidence in those philosophical principles I had thought I could hang my hat on when police work had gone to hell in a hand basket.

Too bad. The Bishops were right and Kant was wrong and I was going to lie to Margaret. So be it.

"Yes, Margaret. I would. If I thought there was no other way to get this investigated properly, I would do precisely that."

"I don't think Dean Wooster is going to take kindly to being threatened like that."

"Well, don't post it as a threat. Act like you see me as harmless, a kind of Barbie-cop, poking around incompetently with very little staying power. You just don't want to make Barbie mad enough to do something stupid like go to the press."

Margaret definitely snorted this time.

"We'll see. Though anyone who'd associate you with Barbie needs their head examined. Spider-Woman, maybe."

Margaret hung up the phone, a little too forcefully perhaps.

* * * *

The next morning found me entering the flamingo pink door of the dorm where Ah-seong had lived while she was a student. It was 8 in the morning, but no sign of Karen in the entryway. I knew the room number, so I went up the stairs and woke the friend who had changed rooms with Karen to let her sleep. She was groggy, but polite, and said she'd go wake Karen. She returned briefly and said Karen would shower and meet me downstairs 'in a few'. Minutes, I assumed. Then she grabbed a bag of toiletries and disappeared in the direction of the bathroom, leaving me standing in the open door of the dorm room.

I thought since I had to wait this was a good time to look around Ah-seong's side of the room. I went all the way in, shut the door, and took stock.

The inside of the rooms in this new dorm block were not fanciful tropical architecture. It was basically a cinder block rectangle with a single window opposite the door and twin beds pushed against the walls on either side of it. The shade was pulled down against the chance of morning sunlight. There was no sunlight as this was another grey Chicago morning, like so many were. With the shade down, the room was almost completely dark. I flipped on the single overhead light fixture and the harsh unshaded glare revealed one side of the room as obviously Ah-seong's.

The bed was neatly made with a faded coverlet, the desk was clear of all papers and the books were lined up in the small bookcase, all the spines facing correctly outward and evenly spaced on the shelves. There were two framed photos on the side of the desk.

I stepped closer to look at the pictures. One was obviously a family portrait. I recognized Ah-seong and Myung Ha. She was shyly smiling and he was poker-faced. They stood on either side of an older Korean woman, plainly dressed in a skirt and blouse. Three younger children, two girls about eight and ten, and a boy of no more than four, were grouped in front of the mother. They were standing in front of a very small cottage. There was no father in the picture. Perhaps he was the one taking the picture, but I somehow doubted it. This looked to me like a family without a father and without much money. It made me see Myung Ha in a different light, the oldest male child on whom the responsibility for the family fell heavily.

I glanced at the other photo. It was a snapshot of the memorial service. Ah-seong and the other young women who had danced were grouped in a circle, dressed in traditional Korean flowing robes. Their faces were raised to the sky, their arms reaching up, beseeching the heavens. I remembered the moment. It was the expression of outraged innocence turned upward, asking why, perhaps even asking God why. I suspected Ah-seong's brother had been livid if he had seen this performance and the young women's grief and anger directed heavenward.

I picked up a few letters stacked in front of the pictures. All but one were in handwritten characters I obviously could not read. I set those aside. The letter on the bottom was from the Financial Aid office of the University. It was neatly slit along the top. I took out the letter and read the happy news that Ah-seong's full tuition scholarship had been renewed for this academic year. It identified her scholarship as need-based. So much for my prejudiced assumption that she was the daughter of wealthy Korean parents.

I went over to the bookshelf and looked at the titles. Several I recognized as required texts used by our department. Others were obviously science texts. On the bottom shelf was a surprise. There was a copy of a controversial book by a Korean feminist. Twenty-five years ago when it first came out, it was so provocative that it had had to be published in the United States. It was now considered a classic in Asian feminist theology and still widely read.

I'd read it and really admired the spirit of the woman who'd written it. It was a critique of the combination of conservative Christianity and Confucianism that dominated South Korea at the time. Still dominated it, in fact, though with a hefty dose of free-market capitalism making the conservative ideologies even more rigid and hierarchical.

I pulled it off the shelf. I opened the flyleaf and Ah-seong's name was neatly printed in English. I flipped through it. She'd underlined with a thin red pen on nearly every page, sometimes writing in the margins. But not in English. Rats. I'd loved to know what she'd thought.

I decided to take the book with me and ask someone to translate the marginal notes. I doubted very much if her brother would want this book as a keepsake. I stuffed the book in my backpack.

I let myself out, shut the door and quickly retreated downstairs, feeling I had made a lot of unwarranted assumptions about Ah-seong Kim.

I had time to check my email on my phone but eventually Karen appeared, showered and dressed in jeans, work shirt, vest, anorak and hat over her wet hair. She was small but athletic looking, with a thin face that had a worried frown.

We walked out of the building and I steered her across the street to a row of the kind of little restaurants and shops that surround every college campus. I didn't want us to be seen eating in the cafeteria together. Besides, to get to the cafeteria we'd have to walk past Mendel Pond and that was something I thought neither of us would want to do.

I let her walk in silence. She'd be better after getting some coffee. I knew I would.

We went to the Agora, nicknamed "the Agony" by the students. Originally it had been Greek, but it had been through so many reincarnations and owners it was difficult to discern any vestige of Greece, apart from the name. The scared tables and the graffiti covered walls had endured from owner to owner. It was a typical college student hangout and it survived, I assumed, because the coffee was good. And they left the pot.

After we'd ordered coffee and drunk quite a lot of it, I started us talking about inconsequential things. I found out Karen was from Iowa and she was planning on going to medical school. Who at this University was not, at least when they were just at the beginning of sophomore year and before biochemistry cut its wide swath into the pre-meds?

Eventually I steered her toward Ah-seong and what she was like as a roommate. Karen had been a little shy of me at first, but her natural warmth coupled with her real need to talk to somebody about the death of her roommate soon took over.

"She hardly talked, you know? I mean I'm not always chattering, like some people. But I like to talk. She was so silent, it was weird. She'd come and go and I'd hardly even know she was there. She didn't even dress in the room. She'd take her clothes to the shower and get dressed there. She studied in the library. I guess she did. She never studied in the room. She was like, I don't know."

She fiddled with a strand of blond hair that had escaped from under her hat.

"Like a nun or something. She read the Bible before she went to bed. I mean, I was raised a Christian too, but golly. Read the Bible every night? Like for an hour? What's up with that?"

I sat quietly not wanting to interrupt the flow of Karen's words.

"You know, like the first week we were roommates she did try to talk to me about this book she was reading and stuff, but I didn't much get it. She talked about Korean women and the 'three obediences.' I mean really. I tried to listen, but after a while I just told her to forget all that. She didn't need to worry about that. She was in the United States now, for Pete's sake. She didn't much talk to me much after that. I hadn't meant to shut her down, not really.

I just thought she'd be happier if she quit worrying about whether she was being obedient enough, or good enough, or something."

Karen took a sip of her coffee, staring past my shoulder, perhaps realizing she'd failed this vulnerable woman in some way and regretting it. I knew how she felt.

"When did you first notice she was coming in upset?"

"Oh, geeze, I guess it was a few weeks ago. Just about two weeks into the semester. One night I was up late and she came in. You know, I'd kind of gotten used to not seeing her. She'd leave before I was awake and come back after I was asleep. But this time she came in and she was crying. She was trying not to show it, but she was. She sat on her bed and hung her head down."

Karen looked down at the donut she'd ordered but not eaten, unconsciously mimicking Ah-seong. I was suddenly, horribly aware I'd seen Ah-seong in that posture too.

"Did she say anything?" I asked.

"She said she was sorry."

"Sorry?"

I'm sure my eyebrows were up around my hairline.

"Yeah. Sorry. Go figure. What, sorry for bothering me by coming in crying? I said, 'forget it,' and kind of like, asked if everything was okay, could I do anything, was she sick or in trouble? She just shook her head no and went to bed in her clothes."

"And did she ever talk with you again about something bothering her?"

"One night. I don't know exactly, a couple of weeks ago maybe, but I remember it was a Sunday night and I was totally going to have to vamp on the studying because of this big bio test the next day and I was way behind."

I thought vamp, in undergraduate speak, meant stay up all night like a vampire.

"So what happened?"

"Well, wouldn't you know it, Ah-seong comes in again in tears. So I ask again, 'What's wrong? Come on, it's something. And she says, 'I do not understand men, what they want.' I said, 'Like who does?'"

Karen's cornflower blue eyes narrowed and looked like lasers, ready to zap some guy.

"So I went over and sat on the bed next to her and that's when I noticed she had these red marks on her arm. All around the wrist, like somebody had grabbed her wrist too hard. So I pointed to the marks and said, 'What gives? Is some guy pushing you around?'"

"And she said, can you believe it, 'It's my fault. I am too unloving. I'm not a good Christian.'"

"So I let her know what was what. No guy can hurt you and have it be your fault. It's his fault, pure and simple. After all, I said to her, 'you're the one with the bruises, right?' I mean Jesus said turn the other cheek and all that, but that's okay only up to a point."

Karen leaned back against the high back of the chair, straightening her spine along its length. As I gazed at her Iowa-fed, blond countenance I wondered how her middle-class white confidence had played with Ah-seong. Probably not well. Then I realized I hadn't done any better. Perhaps I'd done worse in how I had come across to Ah-seong. Also, I mused while I took another sip of coffee, there must be some pretty liberal churches out there in Iowa if Karen thought there was a point where Jesus stopped applying. And she'd pretty much dismissed Kant's ideas of absolute ethical norms, too, though as a pre-med I doubted she'd read Kant. Well, to Karen, women shouldn't get bruised by guys and that was that. I totally agreed with her.

"Did you say anything else?" I asked.

"Well, I told her she needed to talk to somebody better than me, somebody who knew more about what she was going through than me."

Karen leaned forward, her hands, with their little square-cut polished nails, clenched in front of her. She was remembering, unconsciously repeating with her hands her struggle to get Ah-seong to get help.

"I told her she could go to Student Health, or maybe there was a professor she could talk to who would understand. Set her straight."

"And what did she say?"

"She actually looked up and smiled. She told me she would talk to one of her teachers."

Karen gazed at me with a distinctly accusing look.

And here I'd thought Margaret had forced her to talk to me. And this was what, probably three weeks ago? Had she talked to somebody else before she talked to me? I needed to tell Matthews. It was important that the police know that Ah-seong might have talked to a faculty member before she talked to me.

Who was it?

"Do you know if she did talk to any faculty member, or to anybody else for that matter?"

"No, I don't." Karen sighed.

"Right after that she was gone almost all the time. And it wasn't accidental. I thought she was avoiding me, trying not to talk. Until this past Saturday night."

"What happened Saturday?"

Though I'd heard some from Margaret about that evening, it was important to hear it from Karen.

Her small face flushed and she looked past me again, into a place that it was clear was very hard for her to think about.

"She came in late and she was really losing it. Her blouse was torn around the neck and I could see some red marks. The blouse was all pulled to the side and it was hanging out of her skirt. There was a spot of blood at the corner of her mouth."

Karen hunched forward and wrapped her arms around her torso. She wasn't cold. She was hugging herself for reassurance. I bet she was thinking, had already thought, could that happen to me?

She looked up at me.

"Well, I thought she'd been raped or something. She was shaking so much I got a blanket and wrapped it around her shoulders and sat next to her. I talked to her for about an hour and she wouldn't say anything. She just kept shaking and crying. Finally I went and got the dorm resident. I let her handle it and slept out that night. Anne, you met Anne? She's got a futon in her room."

"What about Sunday?"

"I never saw Ah-seong to talk to again. When I got back to the room the next morning she was gone and she didn't come in the next night."

Karen's clear blue eyes clouded with tears. I handed over an unused napkin.

"Just a few more questions. Do you have any idea whom she was dating?"

She wiped her eyes on the napkin, but then answered clearly enough.

"A couple of weeks ago I saw her from a distance across campus with a guy. He was really huge. Of course, she's so short. I mean, I mean, she was so short."

She used the napkin again to wipe away tears.

Oh, a huge football player. That will narrow it down.

"Was he white or black?" I asked. Of the four football scholarships, two were held by black guys, two by white guys.

"Ah, he was black I think."

Karen's face had paled during our talk, but now it turned red. She looked like she thought she'd told me something shameful about Ah-seong. Multiculturalism must not yet have reached Iowa, apparently.

"Did you ever meet him?" I asked more abruptly than I'd intended.

"No, no."

"What about her brother? Did you ever meet him?"

"I met him once."

Karen practically spit the words out.

"He came to the dorm to get Ah-seong one time and I was down the hall. She introduced us and he looked right through me, like I didn't even exist. I asked him what year he was and he didn't even answer. He just took Ah-seong's arm and practically dragged her out the door."

She paused, thinking.

"And I talked to him on the phone a couple of times when he called the room. Same thing. Couldn't even be bothered to be civil to me. And sometimes if I came up to the door, I could hear him in the room yelling at her. It got so I'd just turn and leave. And she was always embarrassed by the way he treated me. He's wonky and he creeps me out really."

Myung Ha creeped me out too, and I'd probably think he's wonky if I knew exactly what it meant. But was he a murderer? Or had he pressured his already stressed out sister so much that she'd killed herself? It was clear I was going to have to talk to the wonky creep again. I'd try to catch him out in the open somewhere, preferably in the middle of the quadrangle. And the quadrangle made me think of Mendel Pond.

Karen was starting to gather up her things.

"Wait, Karen, just one more question. Do you know if Ah-seong could swim?"

"Swim?"

She looked briefly puzzled and then the reason for my question dawned on her and her pale face became paler.

"Well, everybody has to, right? Be able to swim, I mean? There's a test. Freshman year. Everybody has to pass it or take a required credit of swimming. We didn't room last year, but she'd had to pass the test or have taken the required swim class and passed it. You can't not do it. They make a big deal about it."

Of course. I'd forgotten. The swim requirement. Though I made a mental note that I'd have to talk to somebody in athletics, I bet Ah-seong wouldn't have been the first student to fake a swimming requirement by getting somebody to take the test for her.

I doubted it, though. She didn't seem like a person who'd fake her way through something. Odds were she'd passed outright or learned to swim at the University of Chicago. For all the good it did her.

I paid the bill and we left.

9

There is nothing in nature so despicable or insignificant that it cannot immediately be blown up like a bag by a slight breath of this power of knowledge.

FREDERICK NIETZSCHE, *ON TRUTH AND LIES IN AN EXTRA-MORAL SENSE*

I parted from Karen when we reached the main campus and hurried to my office. Henry wasn't in our shared cubicle. He'd left me no note and there was nothing from him on my voicemail. Why had he suddenly turned in to such a ghost? I scribbled a note to him to be sure to get in touch with me today, I added my cell phone number though I knew he already had it, and I stuck the note dead center on his computer screen where I was sure he would see it. I sped down the hall to my class.

Today I had to leap forward a millennium and teach "Modern Philosophy." Modern Philosophy could mean anything after the eighteenth century, modern therefore being a very loose term, but I was teaching it as a kind of 'how did we get into the mess of the twenty-first century' kind of excursion, hoping to hold their interest by relating these 'old, dead white men,' as so many thought of them, to their present.

We were working our way through a book on Freud, Nietzsche and Marx, called, very imaginatively, *The Modern Magi*, named after the three "wise men," that is, ancient philosophers, whom biblical tradition said had brought gifts to the baby Jesus. These three modern thinkers had certainly brought "gifts" to more recent centuries, but very often these gifts had turned out to be exploding cigars. Or had humanity just not understood the gifts, or used them stupidly and violently? The Star over Bethlehem became the horrible yellow star the Nazis had forced Jews to wear. Freud, Nietzsche and

Marx had been used to serve Stalin, and Hitler too. As I stood up in front of the class, I had thought to use the exploding cigar metaphor, but now it seemed too tame. Bomb or IED might be a better way to begin.

Even using an Improvised Explosive Device as the opening of my lecture, I mostly failed to get through their complacency as we got started on discussion. There were no more Communists now, we were even friends with Cuba, so Marx was irrelevant, Freud was for helping crazy people, and Nietzsche was somebody who thought what didn't kill you made you stronger. In other words, Nietzsche had become an Internet meme. I wasn't going to get into politics, but I wondered what they thought of their current president in light of Freud, Nietzsche and Marx.

But then I finally got a little opening on socialism and student debt. Thank you, Senator Bernie Sanders. Student debt is clearly today's college student's link to the Great Depression, and they are not wrong about that. So I got a chance to bring Marx back in and there was a decent discussion for a while about what exactly is socialism and is it a good or a bad thing? But as the class moved on toward the end of the hour, their energy waned. Sanders had touted the need for an ongoing revolution in our politics and in our economics, but I didn't see any signs of an impending revolution among these students. They merely gathered their books at the end of the hour and departed.

Maybe Nietzsche was right and ideas are just the fictions we tell ourselves to keep from screaming at the cold and uncaring stars.

Who was I to criticize these students for retreating into complacency, even in the face of the fact that our world was lurching toward totalitarianism? Wasn't I the one who had chosen to treat ancient philosophies like Valium, retreating into their smug assumptions of universal truths? Except Nietzsche didn't work like that for me. When I read Nietzsche it was like having three cups of espresso in a row. No fuzzy fictions to wrap around myself to keep reality from intruding.

I dragged myself out of these fairly useless musings and went back to my office. No sign of Henry. I dropped the books and lecture notes and picked up my coat.

Ah-seong's death was no fiction. I needed to talk with someone about how the "official" investigation was proceeding. If it was proceeding. Before I left the office, I called over to the campus police station and found out that Alice Matthews came on duty at noon. It was 11:50 now. I headed out.

* * * *

The building that houses the campus police force is ivy-covered, brick and graceful. It sits nestled in tall trees, next to some tennis courts. The yellow and red leaves are starting to float down and cover the still green grass. It is an older, charming addition to the academic landscape.

That is, until you get inside. No Chicago police station is crummier, more poorly painted, inadequately lit or odiferous. The first time I'd been there last year to pick up my faculty-parking permit, I'd been amazed how familiar it felt.

This building could not be so schizophrenic by accident. The outside reassured students, administrators, and local residents that these university police folks fit right into the academy community; the inside was designed to intimidate suspects and remind the police who worked the campus that serious police business was conducted here.

Sometimes I wished Myerson, where my office was located, could be this gritty inside instead of being fake medieval through and through. As I walked up to the door of the campus police building, I idly wondered if I could skew this curriculum study that Grimes had foisted off on Henry and me and convince the department that we should darken our walls, knock out half the lights and teach only Nietzsche. Well, maybe also the French post-modernists and maybe an existentialist novelist or two.

Probably not.

I walked up to the front desk. The uniformed officer there looked carefully at my bandaged arm in the sling, I assumed awaiting a complaint. I didn't react and just asked for Alice Matthews. After looking at my faculty I.D., he directed me two flights up, and 'to the right.' I asked for an office number as 'to the right' seemed a little vague, and then started climbing the stairs.

As I walked up the stairs not daring to touch the filthy handrail, I was suddenly back to my own precinct. For all its bad memories, there had been times when I had felt I was doing some good, as well. At least at first.

The staircase gave on to a corridor with crackled linoleum on the floor and peeling walls that had once been green. Had they imported these authentic details from a downtown police station that had closed? It was so dimly lit, I was temped to take out my cell phone and use the flashlight app. Turning right as directed, I saw a door open down the hall and from the back light I could dimly discern Matthews. She waved and motioned me down. They must have called up from downstairs.

I followed Matthews into a small office that fortunately had a window. I sat in a rusted folding chair. Ivy made graceful swirls on the outside of the windowsill. I looked from the ivy to the peeling walls, to the battered desk and cracked floor and shook my head.

Matthew's brown eyes laughed at me, barely visible wrinkles making wings at their sides. She was very good at reading people.

"The building's incredible inside, isn't it?" she chuckled.

"Yes, it puts me in mind of Dante, a new circle of hell. The linoleum floored circle of hell."

"This was a small school before the university bought it. Apart from dividing up classrooms into these little cubicles and adding a holding cell in the basement, at least I hope we were the ones who added that, we've not changed anything in thirty years."

"Reminds me of Branch 26, out California Ave."

"Yes, I know it. You were a cop before, I take it?" Alice asked.

"I was. Yes. Up until five years ago."

She waited for me to elaborate, but I didn't. I never did. Matthews got the message and got down to business.

"So, how can I help you?" she asked. She eased an arm over the back of her chair and waited.

"Officer Matthews, I'll be blunt. I know Detective Kaiser very well. I don't have a very high opinion of his investigative ability. I've been asking around about the death of the student, Ah-seong Kim, and I'd like to tell you what I've learned, and I'd like to go on doing that until we're sure what happened to her."

Matthews leaned down and opened a drawer of her desk. She took out a metal box, opened it and extracted a pack of cigarettes. She silently offered me one. When I shook my head no, she hesitated. I motioned her to go ahead and she opened the window, pulled another rusted folding chair over, sat by the open window and lit a cigarette with a practiced motion. It looked peculiar to me to see her kindergarten teacher's face with what looked like an unfiltered cigarette in the middle of it.

She was obviously, even tritely, waiting me out. Finally, after another deep drag, she seemed to make up her mind.

"Call me Alice. Mind if I call you Kristin?"

I said, no, of course not.

"I can't do a lot. We just fetch and carry for the city cops in an investigation like this." She took another long drag on her cigarette and blew the smoke adroitly out the window. I wondered if any passerby might think this office was on fire.

"But they will keep you informed, right?" I asked.

"Yeah, in a way. Detective Kaiser and Officer Brown have already been here. Kaiser ruffled a lot of feathers. He treated us like we were school crossing guards. Both the full-time and the part-time police here are experienced professionals. It didn't go over large, I can tell you. I imagine almost anyone here who's met Kaiser will help you, at least quietly."

She smiled quietly and looked out the window.

Ah, Karl's ineffable charm.

"Do you know when the autopsy is likely to be completed?"

"Kaiser told the Watch Commander forty-eight hours. That should be today. But I doubt they'll be in a hurry to inform us. I'd say tomorrow at the earliest and probably later than that."

Alice flicked her ash out the window. It floated out and was caught on the Chicago winds that blew so mercilessly from the west. The ash would probably be in Michigan by dinnertime. As I watched the ash disappear, I thought of Ah-seong. I thought of cremation and scattered ashes. And I made up my mind to tell Alice exactly what I intended to do.

"So, Alice, I have been pursuing some leads, frankly. I am looking for the guy she was likely dating, the one I thought she told me made the bruises on her. I've narrowed it down to one of two scholarship students on the football team. The roommate, her name's Karen by the way, said the boy-friend's African American. I'll try to clinch who it is and talk to him today or tomorrow."

I pulled a small notebook out of my purse with my good arm and flipped it open. Alice looked at the pad and then at me, but only nodded her head slightly. Didn't hazard a comment.

I took that as a sign to just motor on.

"Karen, the roommate, thought Ah-seong could swim because of the P.E. requirement, but somebody needs to check on that. If the autopsy indi-cates she did drown, that is."

Alice shook her head and managed to wave smoke through her hair.

"Kristin, drowning's such a dicey call on autopsy, I'd say we need to know either way if she could swim. The best an autopsy does on drowning is tell you if there is debris in the lungs, or that there's no debris in the lungs. You know, maybe she was alive when she went into the water and inhaled some stuff or no. But she still could have been pushed, hit over the head, held under, lots of possibilities on drowning."

I nodded. She was right.

"Alice, do you know how deep that pond is?"

"Yeah, Kaiser wanted to know that too. We checked."

Alice flicked more ash out the window, took the remains of her ciga-rette over to her desk, opened up her drawer and took out another metal box. In the box was sand. She stubbed out her cigarette in the sand, closed the box and put both boxes back into the drawer. Then, without missing a beat, she opened a file that was right on top of her desk. Clearly Alice was not pushing Ah-seong's death aside either.

She looked up at me.

"The pond, you know it, right?"

I nodded.

"The narrow end is only four feet deep all the way across, but the wider end is six feet deep at the center. She was what, five feet tall, tops? The bottom slants down, like a bowl. And the bottom is mud and debris over concrete. For all those plants. You wouldn't want to try to find a footing in that gunk, even if you were tall enough, and the plants could catch you, drag you down anyway."

Alice tapped the paper in the file with a long, bright red fingernail and then looked at me.

"Yeah," I conceded. "You're right. But she wasn't dragged down, trapped by the plant matter. She was found floating. I didn't see it myself. She was on the ground by the time I got there, but several witnesses said she was found floating. What's up with an hours old body that floats?"

I leaned forward and rested my little notebook on a corner of Alice's desk so I could make a note one-handed.

Alice looked back down at the file again.

"I think we've got that one. A bubbler goes on from two in the morning until five. It's supposed to aerate the pond. You know, for the plants. If the body was directly over the bubbler, and that bubbler mechanism is located right in the center of that bowl-like depression, her clothes, may be her lungs, could have had air pushed into them. She'd have floated with that air and could still have been when the trash guys found her."

Her nail moved slowly down the page, I assumed looking for any additional information.

"If she was murdered, she was put in that pond before two," I said without looking up from my pad when I was still making shorthand notes.

"Why do you say that?"

Alice reached for a pad of her own.

"The murderer knows the pond will likely be deserted after 1 in the morning. That's when the gates are locked on that side of the quad and that area becomes a cul-de-sac. Nobody can walk through so they go around. Little danger of being seen."

I drew a feeble sketch on my pad and pushed it to where should could see it.

"But," I continued slowly, thinking it through. "The murderer would want time to get away without somebody, maybe in a building nearby, like Myerson, seeing a body slipped into the pond and someone walking away.

The murderer would want the body to sink. If the bubbler was churning up the pond, it would be clear the body would get churned up too. No, if it's murder, it was before 2."

"No, before 1," Alice said, tapping my pad with its sketch.

"Come again?" I looked up.

"How do you get a body to Mendel Pond after the gates are locked? Carry it all the way across the main quadrangle? Or drive across the main quadrangle? Too obvious. The safest way would be to come directly through the gates and slip her in."

Alice took a pencil and added the driveway to my sketch, the traced the route with the tip.

I looked at the sketch again.

"Or come out of one of the nearby buildings."

I added a square to the sketch to indicate the back of Myerson. Suddenly the proximity of my department to the pond was more than a cause for mourning each time I went to my office. Myerson's back door gave directly on to the widest part of the pond.

I drew a door in my square. Then pointed.

"The least visible way to bring a body to the pond is to walk her there while she's still alive and kill her either at the pond or just inside Myerson's back door and then put her in. And doing that after 1 means it is more likely that area will be deserted. So she's killed before 2 but after 1."

Alice pointed at pond in the sketch.

"But we're jumping to the conclusion that she was murdered. Why couldn't she have been frightened by someone and been running and fallen in? That explains the condition of the shoes."

Alice sat back and looked at her top drawer. She was likely longing for another cigarette. But then she looked back at me.

"Though it doesn't explain why the shoes were in the grass in different places instead of in the pond or still on her feet."

"Yeah. The shoes are weird," I said. "I'll give you that. Besides, this pond is not Lake Michigan. It's relatively small, and the part of the pond closest to the road and the paths is narrow. She could have just run around it. Or through it. That's only four feet deep at most there. You said so. Even if she fell in there, she would get wet, but she wouldn't drown. Not without help."

Alice frowned, narrowed her eyes.

"So somebody chases her and holds her down? After what? Removing her shoes?"

"Well," I said slowly. "She could have kicked the shoes off and jumped in. Tried to get across the pond if he, and we're only assuming it is a 'he,' if he cut her off from the gate if the gate was still open. Then he went in after her and held her down. If so, the autopsy will show new bruises on her shoulders. The ones around her neck seem to have been made on Saturday night."

That brought back more from the conversation with Karen.

"The roommate told me that it seems like somebody tried to rape, or succeeded in raping, Ah-seong on Saturday night. The cops really need to talk to the roommate, Alice. That was two days before she died and when the roommate first saw the neck bruises. I saw the wrist bruises, that were fading a little, on Friday. The poor kid was getting pounded on regularly, and rape could have been part of it."

Oh, God. Why hadn't she told me who was hurting her? The abuser's best friend is his victim, too cowed, too ashamed, too full of self-blame and loathing to even ask for help. My stomach started to hurt but it wasn't from hunger. But this wasn't about me.

"That reminds me. The roommate told me that a few weeks ago Ah-seong told her that she was going to talk her problems over with one of the teachers. And I doubt she meant me. I saw her for the first time the day before she died. Maybe even the day she died, depending on when it happened. Do you know if the people she was taking courses with have been contacted, asked whether she had talked to them recently about any problems? Has anybody asked faculty or staff to come forward who might know something?"

Alice made another note on her pad.

"I don't know, Kristin. I'll check with the Watch Commander. He looked like a storm cloud after Kaiser left. The WC here is a decorated, twenty-five year man from Minneapolis. From what I saw at the general meeting when Kaiser spoke to us, he treated the WC like he was a rookie. A dumb rookie."

And here I had thought Karl would obstruct my investigating this. He was positively helping.

I summarized Henry Haruchi's working with the student group on the memorial, and that she was taking a class with Grimes. I said I didn't know her other classes.

"But she's also in the sciences, though I can hardly see her talking to her biology teacher about such things. But you never know. And then there's her advisor. That's a possible. I actually don't know who her advisor is. Easy to find out, though. And teachers from previous semesters are another idea. She could have had a better rapport with one of them."

Alice was writing quickly.

"According to Dean Lester, her brother told Detective Kaiser that she only talked to him and that she didn't have a boyfriend, didn't have any problems, and so forth. It's what Kaiser would want to hear, but I've met the brother and I'm beginning to think he was one of her problems."

Alice paused in her note taking.

"How so?"

"Well, when I met him he yelled at me for talking to her and corrupting her ideas of Korean womanhood and Christianity."

I went on to fill Alice in on Ah-seong's participation in the dance at the memorial service. More notes were added.

"The whole service upset the conservative Korean students. Some of them actually protested outside. And I found out that Ah-seong was reading a classic book by a Korean feminist. If her brother had found out she was reading that book, he'd have been livid."

Despite my desire to be frank with Alice, I decided to leave out just how I knew Ah-seong had been reading that particular book and that the was now in my possession. Removing items belonging to a possible murder victim is frowned upon in law enforcement. It can be considered 'impeding an investigation.' Even a cruddy investigation.

"Just how livid?" Alice snapped, her copper skin flushing. She was angry but kept it under control.

"I don't really know. The roommate said her brother was yelling at her all the time and he dragged her from the front hall of her dorm."

Alice leaned forward, her expression sharpening.

"Could the brother be the one who was making the bruises?"

* * * *

It wasn't that far from the campus police station to the hospital building where the Human Experimentation Committee met. I grabbed a sandwich from the hospital lobby cart and ate it on my way to the meeting. I took care to stop in the restroom, however, and made sure I had no crumbs on my mouth and I even brushed my hair. I was a little nervous about seeing Tom again.

Being nervous was totally unnecessarily, as it turned out. Tom never made the meeting. I checked my phone a few times under the table, but no texts.

As I was leaving the meeting room, I heard someone say, "Professor Ginelli?" from somewhere around my waist.

I looked down to see a blue helmet of hair and a tiny woman in a pink smock under the hair that marked her as a hospital volunteer. Her powdered face with a network of wrinkles looked up and positively beamed at me.

"Yes?" I replied a little cautiously.

"I have a message for you from Dr. Grayson. He's still in surgery but expects to be finished between 6 and 7 this evening. He wanted to know if you could still meet him."

That's right, I thought. Tom would have had to tell someone to tell me his message. No texting while doing surgery. Good safety precaution.

The faded blue eyes under the blue hair were twinkling with enjoyment at what she supposed was her role in a romance.

I thought for a minute. I rarely have coffee for dinner, and I wanted to go home and see the boys.

What the heck. I asked her if she'd take a message back to Dr. Grayson and she bobbed her blue helmet up and down. I told her what to tell Tom. She looked a little puzzled, so I had her repeat it and even spelled out one word. She nodded and bustled off.

I hoped she had understood. The failure of messages to be received was the basis of much Shakespearian tragedy.

10

Among the states that are generally regarded as paying attention to the training of youth, there are some which seek to create an athletic habit of body, but do so at the cost of serious injury both to the figure and the growth of the body.

ARISTOTLE, *POLITICS*

After dinner, I conned Giles into taking the boys to Tae Kwon Do class. I wanted to go watch the football team practice, and it was the only way to keep from having to take them with me. What I planned to do tonight could not be done with two six-year-olds in tow. And I am not alluding to meeting Grayson. And yes, that had been my message to Tom, to meet me where the football team practiced at 7.

It was not as easy as it might sound to get Giles to take them to the class. Giles is a pacifist and disapproves of the martial arts on principle. His natural reserve and his caution about talking about his childhood and youth in some conflicts in his native Senegal meant I had only a sketchy picture of his past, but I had gradually pieced together that he had seen enough violence to last him a lifetime.

I had had only small success in pointing out to him that peasants or even slaves forbidden to have any weapons to protect themselves had invented many martial arts. I kind of like that element of the underdog in many of the martial arts. Capuera, a Brazilian martial art, is done to music and can look, to the untrained eye, like dancing. The slave inventors of Capuera danced their moves to fool their Portuguese masters in Brazil into thinking that the natives were frolicking in their spare time. At least that's what the masters thought until one of them was brought down with a flying sidekick.

92

Using an enemy's superior weight or other advantage against him—
what Bruce Lee called 'the art of fighting without fighting'—has always
seemed to me to be a justified way of equalizing power. I was darned glad I
knew Tae Kwon Do when I had been facing a knife-wielding attacker in the
alley. I could have been injured much worse than a deep cut on my arm. I
could very well have been killed. So, I agreed with Augustine that violence
could be justified under certain conditions. Giles thought I, and Augustine,
were wrong.

So I just told Giles the truth about why I wanted to find a particular
football player. It worked.

Can telling the truth be manipulative? I wondered briefly about what
Kant would have said. Nietzsche would have told me I'd only told *a* truth,
anyway.

* * * *

The night had turned sharply colder. Only a week more and it would be Hal-
loween. The full moon over Parker Field House looked like a communion
wafer, brittle at the edges. I walked towards the gym in its grudging blue
light. My arm in its sling throbbed from the cold.

The "Cage" is directly behind the gym and the only way to enter it
is from inside the gym itself. I dug out my faculty I.D. and ran it through
the scanner at the front door. I'd worked out in the gym, and only seen the
"Cage" through the clear glass doors that shut it off from the rest of the
facility.

I pushed open the door and entered. It was astonishingly large. It
looked like a kind of enormous shed, complete with dirt floor, and about
four stories high. The smell was what hit me. It was like compost mixed with
sweat. I saw some bleachers over to the right and a few people sitting there.
I made my way over and took a seat close to the door.

I was one of a handful of people there. I had to admire these dedicated souls who would actually want to watch an indoor scrimmage. I had
thought I'd be the only one there. Well, me and Grayson. That is what I had
told the hospital volunteer to tell him, 'Meet me at the Cage at 7.' It wasn't
hard to see he wasn't there. Maybe he hadn't gotten out of surgery when he'd
thought. Maybe blue helmet hair had missed him and the message had not
been delivered.

I huddled into my coat (the Cage is unheated) and turned my attention
to what was happening on the floor. I had gotten the names of the four students on athletic scholarship from the scholarship office and a call earlier to

the athletic office had given me their numbers: 4, 11, 22, and 30. I scanned for those numbers on the jerseys on the floor.

I found 4 and 11 easily. And then I saw 22. Numbers 4 and 11 were white. I dug out the little list I'd made from my coat pocket. Kent Samuelson and Tim Conroy. Number 22 was Howard Brown.

I wondered if a kid this age was going to be able to commit a murder at the beginning of the week, and practice football like nothing was wrong on Wednesday. There would most likely be tells, if he even showed at all. Simplistic? Yes. But most investigation is simplistic. Watch for the reaction that should be there and isn't, register whether there's extra emotion that shouldn't be there, and is.

I watched Brown. He was lanky and a little ham-handed, but he moved okay. I watch him catch a pass and return it. From this distance, it was hard to see facial expressions, but he had no body language that spoke of anything other than a stiffness in his right knee. He wore a ace bandage there. I could see it sticking out from the below the knee length tight pants they all wear. I wondered if somebody had kicked him in the knee. Somebody wearing little black pumps with bows on them.

I couldn't seem to spot number 30. I checked my list again. Edwin Porterman. Not showing up for practice might be a tip-off.

I was so intent on watching Brown and looking for Porterman that I started when Tom Grayson sat down beside me.

"Hey, you made it," I said, standing to let him get past me to sit on the bleacher bench. I wanted to be on the outside in case I wanted to get up quickly and intercept someone.

"Yeah. Thanks for suggesting it. You must be quite the football fan to come out to watch a scrimmage."

Tom unbuttoned his topcoat and looked for a minute like he was going to take it off. Then he seemed to realize it was colder in here than outside and he kept it on.

"Well, I'm not here exactly as a fan. I'll explain later."

I turned back to scanning the floor of the Cage.

"I want to apologize for standing you up for coffee."

Tom sounded tentative.

"It's okay. You're a doctor and you were doctoring. It's fine. I'm just glad they sprung you so we could get together."

I took my eyes off the floor for a minute to turn and smile at him. He didn't smile back.

What was this about?

"Are you sure you're not upset?"

He looked intently at me as he asked.

"No, I expect it happens all the time. What's to get upset about?"

I pulled off my itchy wool hat, hoping I would not get hypothermia, and I smiled again, hoping it would work this time. No smile in return. At sea as to what was wrong, I turned back to watch the practice again. This was more uphill than I had expected. Plus I was trying to detect and date at the same time. Probably too much multi-tasking.

Grayson sighed and I tore my eyes away from trying to see the numbers on some kids pushing tackling dummies around at the far end of the Cage. What? This was no big deal and he was acting like it was.

"Tom, what's the matter? Did you think I'd act like a spoiled child for your missing our coffee?"

I patted his arm with my mittened hand.

"Really. It's no big deal. Who'd make an issue of something so simple as rescheduling a coffee?"

"You'd be surprised, Kristin. I'm no longer married because my former wife wanted our lives not to be interrupted or our plans canceled by surgeries."

He looked down at his own leather-gloved hands.

"Why'd she marry a surgeon then?" I asked, looking up again from scanning the floor.

Now it was Grayson who was intently examining the kids running around on the floor. But from what I could see of his face, he wasn't seeing the players but a past that was very painful.

"Money, status. I don't know. And it's not just been her. Other relationships haven't been able to stand up to all the changed or cancelled plans, missed meals and calls in the middle of the night. I'd hoped to get off on the right foot with you, though."

I turned on the bench to really face him.

"You know, Tom, surgery isn't the only field where there are more schedule changes than schedules. I was a cop, remember? I was married to a cop. He was never home, or when he was, it was just so he could get called out again. It can be disruptive, I grant you, but you just roll with it. Marco had to roll with it when I got called out. A lot of cop marriages don't survive it, it's true, but actually I found out that I'm okay with abrupt schedule changes. Really."

I turned back toward the floor, but it wasn't a bunch of football players I was watching. I was watching as I replayed my words to Grayson and seeing myself break a rule. I never discussed Marco with anybody. Just saying his name to someone outside the family was something I hadn't done in all these years. I forced myself to focus what was happening on the floor. The game was about to start.

Suddenly I spotted number 30. He was sitting at the end of the play-ers' bench, hands hanging down between his knees. Donald Willie, my colleague who claimed he didn't know anything about Ah-seong having a football-playing boyfriend, was sitting next to him with an arm around his big shoulders, talking intently into his ear. I think we had our boyfriend.

" . . . thought that you would see things that way."

Grayson was talking and I'd missed about half of it, I guessed.

"Tom, I'm sorry. I missed part of what you were saying."

I hoped he'd just attribute my red face to the cold. Boy had it ever been a dumb idea to think I could watch for Ah-seong's boyfriend and make conversation with Grayson at the same time.

Tom stiffened a little.

"You seem kind of distracted here, Kristin."

Oh, great. Now we go from 'I don't want a clinging vine' to 'why aren't you hanging on every word.' Amazing.

Tom wanted to get us off on the right foot. Well, me too. And nothing works for that like being frank.

"Tom, I'm interested in what you have to say, but I'm also here trying to figure out whom that student who died in the pond was dating. She never told me his name, but she did say he had an athletic scholarship."

To my amazement, Grayson started to laugh. He sort of rumbled and chortled, gazing at me with what actually appeared to be enjoyment.

I forgot all about the guys running around on the floor below and stared at him. So did a few people sitting near us. He was laughing so hard now tears appeared in his eyes.

"I'm so worried you're mad at me and you can barely fit me into your detection schedule here. I believe I've just been told to chill, so to speak." He chortled again.

I looked at his tearing eyes. He'd actually managed to fog up the lenses of his glasses. Anybody this self-aware was probably too good to be true, but I liked him at lot at that moment.

I smiled at him and used my mittened hand to pat his arm.

"Doctor, just take a seat and wait until your name is called."

I turned back to watching Willie and Porterman, but I was aware of the continuing rumbling chuckles next to me for a few minutes more.

* * * *

Porterman did not get off the bench and join the scrimmage. After a while, Willie left him and went to speak to one of the coaches. About twenty min-utes into the scrimmage, Porterman abruptly stood up and headed for the door that connected the Cage to the gym. I bet he was headed for the locker room.

I leaned over to Tom and told him we needed to go. But not why. As I was climbing down, I contemplated how to send him on his way so I could talk to Porterman when he came out of the locker room, if that's where he had gone.

On the other hand . . . I glanced back at Grayson. He was a guy and therefore could go into the locker room and check.

Tom looked at me quizzically as I stopped.

"Tom, the tall black kid that just left the floor, I think he's gone into the locker room. I'm pretty sure he was the one dating the student who drowned in the pond. I'd like to ask him a few questions. Would you go in and see if he's in there?"

Tom raised his eyebrows at me, but turned to go into the locker room. Then he turned back.

"What's his name?"

"Edwin. Edwin Porterman."

Tom nodded and disappeared into the door for the men's locker room. After a short while, an enormous guy with a frown on his face emerged. Tom was right behind him.

"You wanted to see me?" His deep voice had the timber of a major cord played on an organ.

"Are you Edwin Porterman?" I asked, more tentatively than I had intended.

"Yes," he said, not looking pleased.

"I'm Professor Ginelli. I knew Ah-seong Kim. I talked to her shortly before she died. I'm trying to find out more about her. Were you and she dating?"

"Yes."

Well, that was informative.

I had better get right to the point before Edwin decided to walk away from me, as there was nothing I could do, or Tom and I combined, to stop him if he decided he didn't want to talk. Standing in front of him, I realized just how tall he was. I'm six feet tall and my eyes were at the level of the middle button of his pressed, button-down Oxford shirt.

Wait a minute. Pressed Oxford shirt. Sharp crease in his trousers. Leather shoes.

Yeah. Yeah. Probably my own stereotype of how football players dressed on campus, but still . . . serious brown eyes behind horn rimmed glasses looked down at me. Edwin was waiting for me to speak.

But now I couldn't figure out what line to take.

"Could we sit down a minute and discuss Ah-seong?" I gestured to a group of chairs and couches in a kind of lounge area down the hall.

Edwin turned silently and walked toward the chairs. Tom and I followed. Tom sat on the plastic sofa; Edwin and I took tubular armchairs.

I turned my chair a little to where I could look directly at him. He looked gravely back.

"Edwin, I'm trying to figure out how Ah-seong died. How did you know each other?"

He sighed deeply, looking down at his hands.

"We met right at the beginning of this fall quarter. We were standing in the checkout line at the bookstore together for about forty-five minutes. She was so tiny and she had this huge pile of books. Heavy books, mostly in the sciences. I offered to hold some for her and we started to talk. She was so . . . "

Edwin's eyes became liquid and he turned his head away. He didn't raise his hands to his face. They remained hanging down while the tears glistened on his face. I sat there quietly, waiting and wondering if this was an act. It certainly didn't seem to be. This was grief in its purest form. He started to talk again, very quietly.

"Anyway, we dated some. We both had heavy schedules, so it was mostly a quick coffee and studying. I helped her some on the math. She'd tell me about Korea."

He trailed off.

I decided to be more direct.

"I saw Ah-seong in my office less than twenty-four hours before she died. She had bruises on her wrist and on her neck. Do you know how she got those bruises?"

I noticed Tom, who was sitting quietly on the couch, tense at my question.

Edwin abruptly stood up and clenched his hands. I sat back and contemplated this large young man towering over me. Grayson appeared to be about to stand too. I made a small gesture for him to remain seated. His standing would just escalate things.

"I wish I knew who'd hurt her," Edwin said, anger and grief both audible in his voice, and his chest heaving with emotion.

"I asked her and asked her the first time I saw a bruise on her wrist. She told me not to be concerned. Yeah, right. Not concerned. Her wrist was the size of a chicken wing. A small chicken wing. If I could have known for sure."

Edwin turned away and then grabbed the hapless coke machine in the lounge. He held the machine for a moment like he was thinking about lifting it, but then he just put his head on the cool glass front.

I went over and stood next to him, putting one hand on his back. I could hear a muffled sob.

"I feel the same way, Edwin. I'd like to know who was hurting her. I think that's crucial to finding out how and why she died. She told me somebody with a scholarship who was stressed out over grades made those bruises."

Edwin turned his head and looked at me. He stood up and almost smiled.

"So you thought it was me, right?"

I nodded.

He turned away from me and addressed the empty hallway. Though his back was to me, I had no trouble hearing him.

"I have a straight four point average. I'm an economics major. Playing on this football team stresses me about as much as having to play cribbage with my Aunt Melda. I've played against Junior High School teams tougher than the guys we face. It's just a way to foot the bill and not have to turn to Uncle Sam for the money."

He turned and looked directly at me.

"I have a Rhodes Scholarship. I delayed it for a year to do more work here and then I'll be studying at Oxford next year. I didn't hurt Ah-seong, believe me. I would have protected her if she'd have let me."

He sat back down heavily.

I could check on his grade point and the Rhodes Scholarship thing, but I was pretty sure he was telling me the truth. If he had straight A's in economics here, the kid was a genius. The Economics Department at this university had won so many Nobel Prizes, they tended to regard it as an in-house prize.

"So who was hurting her, Edwin?"

I looked down at him. I wanted to comfort him like I would have one of the boys if they were hurting, but Ah-seong came first. I was pretty sure Edwin agreed with me.

He sat up and looked at me.

"You know her brother's also a student here?"

"Yes, I've met him," I said and sat back down next to him.

"Well, if you've met him, you know what a piece of work he is. He came by my room about three or four weeks ago, told me to stop seeing Ah-seong. That I wasn't suitable. I laughed in his face. He got all puffed up look a rooster, told me he'd cripple me, break my knees if I didn't go right off her. I told him to take a hike. You want my opinion? Check the brother. He's a first-class bastard."

His hands were gripping the metal arms of his chair so hard I thought I'd see finger marks in the cheap metal when he got up.

Well, well. Another insight into Myung Ha. Everybody's favorite guy.

"Do you know if the brother is on a team of some kind?"

"Yeah. Ah-seong was worried when I told her about her brother's visit. He's a black belt and he's on the University's Tae Kwon Do team. Well, it's not actually a team, it's a club. But they travel and compete against other schools. I think they're supposed to be good."

I sat and thought for a minute. If Ah-seong had a need-based scholarship, odds were her brother did too. There was a high grade-point requirement for getting and keeping those scholarships. Maybe Myung Ha was finding it hard to keep his grades up and spend so much time on his Tae Kwon Do.

"Did she ever admit to you that her brother hurt her?"

Edwin's reddened eyes looked directly at me.

"Nah. She would never. Family's everything to Koreans. You never tell an outsider anything. Not anything."

Edwin Porterman sank back in his chair and looked down at his hands again. I looked at Tom. He gestured that we should go. I couldn't have agreed more. I stood and looked down at Edwin.

I felt both inadequate and like an idiot. I'd assumed so many things about this kid before I'd even met him. Here he was, Aristotle's ideal of the educated athlete. Maybe this university hadn't been wrong about trying to give athletics a back seat to academics. I shuddered to think what Edwin's life might have been like at one of the powerhouse football schools. But maybe I was underestimating him again. Maybe he would have been exactly the same, using athletics instead of letting it use him.

I put my hand on his shoulder. As big as he was, he was still a young man, a hurting young man. A young man too young for the death of a young woman he'd plainly come to care for very much.

"If somebody killed her, Edwin, I'm going to find out."

He looked up at me out of his grief.

"You do that."

* * * *

Tom had been remarkably patient. I'd give him that. When we got out into the cold fall air, he expelled a pent-up breath that made a long plume of frosted air.

"This evening has not gone exactly as I'd planned," was the first thing out of his mouth.

He jammed his hands in his pockets and started to walk rapidly down the sidewalk.

I have a pretty long stride myself, and I caught up to him easily.

"Me neither. But this is what I'm like. Well, not all the time, but sometimes."

Especially recently.

"It takes some re-evaluating," Tom said, not pausing in his rapid walking.

Oh, so now what? I was going to be weighed in the balance, thumbs up or thumbs down?

I was hustling along beside him, working myself up into a fine snit when he abruptly paused in his hiking. He didn't say anything more. He just pulled his hands out of his pockets, pulled me to him and kissed me. Kissed me very thoroughly.

Then he resumed walking.

I didn't.

I just looked at his retreating back. I wondered why I couldn't have just eased out of my self-imposed emotional cocoon instead of bursting it to blue blazes.

Oh well.

It was a great kiss.

11

From birth to death Asian women have to fight against "death wishes" from male-dominated society.

CHUNG HYUN KYUNG, *STRUGGLE TO BE THE SUN AGAIN: INTRODUCING ASIAN WOMEN'S THEOLOGY*

I was awake half the night, first because of the about-face I'd been forced to make about Edwin Porterman, and then because of Tom. Since I couldn't sleep, I got up and looked through the Korean feminist book that Ah-seong had underlined so heavily. Big mistake. It didn't exactly help me sleep either. Even though I couldn't read the marginal notes, I could look at what she'd underlined. And what she'd underlined had really kept me awake.

Finally it was morning. I drank a cup of coffee while the boys ate their cereal and then glanced at the clock. I wanted to get over to the Korean Students Christian Association breakfast meeting. When Carol took them upstairs to begin the laborious process of getting them dressed, I headed to the cafeteria where the group met.

I grabbed another coffee and a donut there and with my arm still in the sling had to elbow my way into the private dining room where they met. I spilled about a third of my coffee on the floor. Not the most impressive entrance.

I put the remaining coffee and the donut down at an empty place at the conference table centered in the room and shrugged off the backpack I'd taken to wearing instead of carrying a briefcase. I put the backpack on the floor and took my napkins over to wipe up the spill I'd made on the floor. The room had fallen completely silent at my entrance and nobody offered to help me clean up the spill. They just watched.

I stood up from my cleaning and looked back at them. Dr. Andrew Lee, at the head of the table, had risen when I'd entered and he had a deep frown on his face. Four young women kept their eyes down, and seven men, including Myung Ha, looked directly at me. Some of the eyes (the ones I could see) looked hostile. The others were perhaps fearful or cautious. Open bibles lay in front of each person.

I tossed the wet napkins into the trashcan by the door and headed to the place where I'd left what remained of my coffee. But Andrew Lee didn't seem to want me to sit down and just join the group.

"What do you want, Professor Ginelli?" His voice was cold.

"I read in the student newspaper that 'all are invited' to your breakfast bible studies. Did I misunderstand?"

I struggled for an even tone of voice and I don't believe I succeeded.

Lee made a curt gesture with his right hand, symbolically cutting through my words. Louder than any shout could have been, it said 'cut the sarcasm.'

When I'd met Lee before, he had been friendly in a reserved sort of way, and he had always been very polite. His compact body, dressed immaculately in coat and tie as always, was now literally shaking with tension. Behind his glasses, his eyes were narrowed. He barely moved his lips as he spoke, hissing the words out at me.

"You have demonstrated no interest in bible study before this. I do not believe you respect what we do here, how we study the scriptures. To be invited to join us, you need to show some respect for our ways."

I remained standing, but I grasped the back of the chair in front of me with my good hand and jerked it back toward me. The screech of the chair legs on the stone floor was the angry scream I was in danger of making. One of the young women closest to Lee looked up at me, startled by the sound, and I suppose at my temerity in standing up to him.

"Well, respect cuts two ways, Dr. Lee. It seems to me that you want others to respect your views, but I haven't seen a lot of evidence so far that you're willing to respect the views of others, especially those who disagree with you, like the student Ah-seong Kim. She raised some questions here, didn't she? And I'm beginning to believe at least some in this group didn't like that one bit. She wanted to bring in some other views, right?"

Lee stiffened.

"No one is forced to attend these breakfasts, Professor Ginelli. Everyone here has come purely because they wish to study the scriptures and pray together."

Despite his obvious tension, he made a graceful sweep of his arm to encompass the room. Well, not me, but everybody else in the room.

"I don't think so. Not everyone. Did you know that it was more than prayers forcing Ah-seong Kim to come to these breakfasts and quit asking questions? Right, Myung Ha?"

I looked directly at him, sitting in what I supposed was a place of honor on the right side of Dr. Lee.

He sneered at me and shrugged.

"You know nothing of my sister, her life, her Christian faith. Do not pretend she would talk to you."

The arrogance in his voice grated on me. I reached down into my backpack and pulled out Ah-seong's copy of the feminist theological book I'd retrieved from her room. I held it up, cover open, so the whole room, including Myung Ha and Dr. Lee, could see her name written on the flyleaf.

"Maybe she didn't tell me much, but this book and her underlinings and notes tell me quite a bit. Ah-seong had begun to think for herself, hadn't she, Myung Ha, and you certainly didn't like it."

I slapped the book down on the table. Several of the young women jumped at the sound.

I fixed my gaze on Myung Ha. The sneer was gone and he was clearly furious, but trying to control himself in front of Lee. He glared at me and I glared right back.

"Myung Ha, why don't you tell Dr. Lee and your friends about the bruises you left on Ah-seong when you beat her up? Was it for asking questions or her not wanting to come to these breakfasts any more or was it even for more than that?"

As I'd hoped, Myung Ha was pushed beyond caring what his professor or his friends thought. He jumped to his feet, knocking over his chair and with three lightening quick steps he was around the table to where I was standing. I pulled the chair in front of me out even further and shoved it between us. While I had no background in lion taming, it seemed an easy enough maneuver.

"Mr. Kim!"

Dr. Lee's sharp voice rang out and halted Myung Ha in his tracks. He turned toward Lee, breathing hard.

"You will resume your seat immediately!"

Myung Ha hesitated.

Lee was having none of it.

"You are dismissed. Come to my office this afternoon and we will discuss your behavior."

Now I was very glad of Lee's icepick voice.

Myung Ha abruptly turned on his heel and left the room, not taking all the tension with him, but certainly a good chunk of it.

Lee's face had turned ashen and he looked at me almost in a daze.

"I apologize for Mr. Kim, Professor Ginelli."

I pushed the chair I'd used to fend off Myung Ha back under the table and leaned forward, holding the back of the chair.

"I have good reason to believe that Ah-seong was raising questions neither her brother nor some in your group liked. I think her brother was physically intimidating her into shutting up and continuing to come to these breakfasts. And that's what I'm going to tell the police. Then you can explain to them how respectfully you treat one another."

Angrily I shoved at my hair with my good hand. Then I picked up Ah-seong's book from the table, and made quite a show of tucking the book well down into my backpack. I zipped it shut. I looked slowly around the room and saw tears in the eyes of the young woman who had been so startled by my yanking a chair around. I smiled at her and left, abandoning my uneaten breakfast on the table.

I didn't bother to get another donut or coffee on the way out of the cafeteria. I was sick to my stomach at all the forces that had trapped and ultimately conspired in the death of Ah-seong Kim. Whether someone had held her under the water in that pond, or she'd jumped in herself in despair, it was ultimately all these barriers to just being the human being she aspired to be that had killed her. There had little help available for her to deal with all these forces, and I indicted myself as one of those inadequacies.

As I crossed from the cafeteria to Myerson, I looked at the pond. Even under another slate grey Chicago sky, it still looked lovely and innocent, reflecting the sky and adding just another charming addition to the pictur-esque college campus. There were probably tours going on right now for parents with their daughters, showing them this entrancing vista, a window on college life. Too bad the window was really painted trompe l'oeil. Good expression, trompe l'oeil. Fool the eye. Yep. That's what all this expanse of trees, brick, ivy, grass and sparkling water did. Fool the eye.

I was fairly worked up by the time I stomped up the steps of Myerson to head to my office. And once again here came Henry, rushing down the stairs.

"Henry," I said loudly, "I really need to talk to you."

"I can't, Kristin. I'm late."

Since I'd taken to wearing a backpack to carry my books and papers, I had a hand available to reach out and grab Henry's sleeve as he tried to brush by me.

He stopped and blinked at me with a startled expression on his face.

"What? I said I've got to go."

"You've been ducking me, my friend. We need to talk. I've left you countless messages. I can't help but feel it's deliberate."

I had kept holding his sleeve as I said this, and I could feel him actually squirming to try to get away.

"I'm incredibly busy these days, Kristin. I just haven't had the time. And now I've got to go, really." He gently lifted my hand from his sleeve and turned to leave.

"I'll walk with you then, wherever you're going."

I turned back toward the door.

"No!"

Henry's 'no' was so sharp and so unlike him that it startled us both. I looked him in the eye and he looked away and spoke in a calmer tone.

"Okay, but only five minutes, okay?"

I gestured toward a bench on the lawn outside Myerson. With only five minutes, I figured it would be better not wasting time going any further.

Henry sat on the edge of the bench, his hands on his knees like he was poised for flight. He looked at his watch again.

I tried to capture his attention.

"Look, Henry. This is serious. Ah-seong is dead. The police who are supposed to be investigating her death are largely incompetent. I'm trying to help by getting a clearer picture of what was going on in her life. Did she ever talk to you, tell you about herself?"

Henry paused so long I thought he was trying to use up the five minutes in silence. Finally he cleared his throat.

"She was in tremendous turmoil. She was beginning to question her traditional culture, and ask herself what obedience she owed her family. She was even becoming politically more liberal, questioning the way conservative Christianity in Korea is so entangled with their right-wing politics and out-of-control capitalism. That dance, it was a turning point. She kind of went public with her feminism and her politics. She took a lot of heat from some in the Korean student community after that, though of many are supportive."

Oh, great. Now I had to consider whether this was a politically motivated killing?

"How do you know that?"

I tried to look him in the eye, but he averted his head and addressed the open campus beyond us.

"Oh, we talked some. Planning the service and all that push back she was getting."

Well that was probably a lie, or at least a distortion.

"No, Henry. If she took heat for having participated in the service, then she would have had to tell you that after the service, not before," I said firmly.

Henry moved even farther on the bench, like he was merely squatting over it. He looked over the campus again.

"Right, right. Of course."

He was distracted and so out of focus to me. Where was the Henry I knew? I could not get a handle on this.

He glanced at his watch again.

"So? I asked.

"So what?" he replied.

"So when did you talk to her after the service and what did she say?" This was like pulling teeth.

"I really don't remember. Around sometime. I've got to go, really."

He stood up and slapped his hands together for warmth. It really wasn't that cold a day.

I didn't stand. I raised my eyes to look at him and I caught his eye for a brief second. He looked away.

"What gives, Henry?"

"Nothing. I'll see you."

And he was gone, literally jogging away from me across the lawn.

I got up and walked slowly back toward Myerson and up the stairs to my office.

Henry was the one person I knew at this university whom I'd expected to be able to talk to, mull over ideas, and try to figure out what happened. Instead I was starting to wonder what his relationship with Ah-seong had really been like. How many evenings a week was he really working at that convenience store?

As I walked down the hall toward our shared office, I decided I needed to search his cubicle. It certainly wasn't breaking and entering. Probably trespass, though.

Too bad.

12

The man is best who sees the truth himself; Good too is he who harkens to wise counsel. But who is neither wise himself nor willing to ponder wisdom, is not worth a straw.

ARISTOTLE, *ETHICS*

I unlocked the office and for the first time regarded Henry's cubicle not as a pathway to mine, but as an end in itself. But what end? What could I possibly find? Well, I couldn't know until I'd looked, though Plato would tell me it was impossible to search for something if you didn't know what you were looking for. For if you didn't know what it was, how could you possibly recognize it when you see it? Nice problem. He devoted the dialogue *Meno* to it.

What was Plato's solution to the problem of finding something new? Oh, he said we didn't really find it, we remembered it from before we were born. In that case, I hoped I had been a better detective before I was born than I was proving to be in this life.

I was just stalling, not wanting to rifle a colleague's desk.

And as I looked at Henry's space, I realized he'd know if I moved anything. It was so neat. Everything was aligned, and most things were in hanging files. It took me about four minutes to conclude I wasn't going to find anything useful, like a note to a clandestine assignation with Ah-seong Kim.

The bookshelf was equally unrevealing. Mostly books on Buddhist philosophy. Two shelves above the computer were books borrowed from the library. Probably books he was using to work on his dissertation. I felt a momentary pang of guilt about my neglected dissertation.

The rest of the shelves were occupied with computer manuals. To the left of the computer was a stack of printed material. I looked at the first few pages, but it meant nothing to me. Just patterns of numbers. Numbers? What was Henry doing in his spare time, trying to beat the lottery?

I turned on his computer and it asked me for a password. I'd kept the original password the IT department had given me with the computer, "Welcome!" Nobody would guess that, right? I tried "Welcome!" on Henry's machine, but he had changed it. I tried his name, his birthday, his kid's name, his wife's name, nothing.

This wasn't getting me anywhere. I retreated over to my cubicle and made a call to the Economics departmental secretary. Amazingly enough, she picked up the phone and when I identified myself as a faculty member, answered my questions.

I sat at my desk to try to make sense of all I'd learned so far when the phone rang and jolted me nearly out of my seat. Just a little too much left over adrenaline from the prayer group, I suspected. Ringing phones were starting to give me heart attacks.

It was Alice Matthews. We exchanged hellos and she got right down to business.

"I called to let you know we got the autopsy report this morning. It was completed yesterday, but we just got it. The WC told me he was surprised we'd even been sent a copy."

"What's the conclusion?"

"Well, the report determines the cause of death as drowning. But there are plenty of findings that the medical examiner notes before that conclusion."

"Like what?"

"Wait a minute."

I could hear rustling of paper.

"First, the drowning finding is based on the fact that she had a ton of debris in her lungs—plant matter, soil, even some sticks. She wasn't dead when she went into that pond. She sucked in a lot of stuff trying to get some air."

Alice paused and I was sure she, like me, was picturing that agonizing death, struggling up, gasping for air, getting water in, sinking, struggling up again. A vicious cycle that could go on for as much as ten minutes, depending on the victim's physical condition, the depth of the water, lots of things. Did she scream? At least at first? How could this monumental a struggle happen in the middle of a college campus and nobody sees anything, nobody hears anything? Drowning is a slow, agonizing death following a desperate struggle. In a little pond?

I realized Alice was talking again.

"That's about as conclusive as these findings of drowning ever get, you know. Junk in lungs, probably drowning; junk not in lungs, some other cause. In this case, thumbs up on the drowning part."

"What about bruising?"

"Let me get to that."

More pages rustling.

"Here. There are bruises on her chest and neck, but they had started to heal, so not made at the time of death, which . . . ." Alice paused.

"Which they determine was between 10:00 p.m. and 3:00 a.m. Certainly no later than 3:00 because of rigor, etcetera. But here's something. The wrist bruises are older, not made at the same time as the neck and chest bruises. But there is some bruising and tearing around the vaginal area. They're saying about the same time as the neck bruises. I think the roommate was right. She was either raped that Saturday night or had some very rough sex."

Alice's voice was strained.

"So they're not even treating it as a suicide, just an accident?" I asked.

"Well, the WC said Kaiser'd said no note, no statements to anybody about being depressed. He even mentioned the statement you'd given Brown. She didn't tell you she was depressed, did she?"

I thought back. The bowed head, the slumped shoulders, the turning in on herself. That certainly said rape victim to me, especially in light of what the ME's report said. But I couldn't say without a doubt she had indicated depression.

"No, no, she was down, but I thought the main emotion coming from her was fear. Of course, fear and depression can be related."

"What do you think? Who was beating on her, forcing her like this?" Alice's compassion for Ah-seong could be heard in every word.

"I think the brother probably made the wrist bruises, yanking her around, but the others? I don't see it. It seemed to me that he was into controlling her, but not incest. No."

"What about the boyfriend?"

"Edwin Porterman? What a surprise he was. He's an econ major with straight A's. He told me that and I just checked with the economics department. They love the guy there. Ups their diversity quota, I assume, but the he's brilliant, no doubt. I had him as a possible for the Saturday night episode, maybe date rape, but the football team was gone from Saturday morning until Sunday noon. There was an away game. But it needs to be checked. The game was only in Wisconsin so he could have come back on his own, I suppose."

There was a pause. I assumed Alice was making some notes.

"So where does that leave us?" she asked abruptly. "Her brother is yanking her around so she'll be a dutiful Korean woman, and somebody she's not even dating rapes her and then she falls into a pond and accidentally drowns? It doesn't add up to me. Not at all."

Alice was right. It didn't add up at all and all the Nobel Prize winning economists in the world couldn't make it add up.

"Well, then, the ME's drowning conclusion leaves room to question how she got into that pond. Remember the shoes? My bet is whoever forced her Saturday night chased her and then pushed her into that pond by Monday night."

Suddenly Alice got a call and said she had to ring off.

I sat there, thinking. I wished I felt as sure of my assessment as I sounded. It is one thing to speculate with Alice and another to try to prove accidental drowning was actually murder.

I turned to my computer to look up a number for the Asian Studies department. In a surprisingly few minutes, I had an appointment for tomorrow morning to meet with their Korean Language professor. I had mentioned to the department secretary that I needed a few phrases of Korean translated, and he was most gracious. My appointment was quickly fixed for 10:00 a.m.

I got Ah-seong's book out of my backpack again and flipped through it. I wondered if any of her marginal notes would actual reveal who had killed her. Yes, I still thought she had been killed, murdered by someone quite clever. I put the book in my top desk drawer.

I looked at my watch. It was only 2 in the afternoon. I needed to stop thinking about Ah-seong's death for a while, step away and get some distance. I knew exactly what I needed. Coffee and a dose of my doctoral dissertation research. Nothing else had proved as effective for me in recent years in shutting off emotion as a dip into ancient philosophers. Perhaps there should be warning labels, "Caution: Do not operate heavy machinery while reading these thinkers."

* * * *

I had hoped to get to the coffee pot in the faculty lounge, grab a mugful and head to the library. No such luck. When I entered the room, Grimes, Winters, Willie and even Abraham were there. Even at faculty capacity, the huge room dwarfed our diminished department.

I had brought my mug and I went to fill it at the coffee machine. Grimes and Willie seemed to be going over some papers on the conference table; Abraham and Winters were looking at some photos on his phone.

I wondered if they were pictures of his grandchildren. He loved showing them around. Just the family at home here.

Adelaide looked up and gave me a smile.

"You're usually not here today, what gives?"

"It's been kind of an unusual week," I said, trying to keep the sarcasm out of my voice. "Actually, I'm on my way to the main library to put in some work on the dissertation."

Grimes looked up from the papers and frowned at me. It looked for a minute like he was going to get up and come over to me, but he stopped in the act of rising and merely turned his chair toward me.

"Now that Ms. Ginelli is here, I think it is appropriate to tell everyone that I had a call earlier from Dean Wooster. That student's death, the Kim woman, has been ruled an accidental drowning by the Medical Examiner. The case is closed and will remain closed."

Grimes's voice turned unpleasantly unctuous.

"I expect, Ms. Ginelli, that your playing detective was out of a sense of guilt that you should have done more for the young woman when she came to see you. But it was an accident. There was nothing you could have done."

Grimes looked at me with what I think he thought was a paternal gaze, his carefully groomed white hair and his tanned skin glowing in the refracted light from the windows. He was posing. It was nauseating.

I looked at Donald and he had the grace to look a little sheepish. It was clear his interpretation of my investigation as a guilt trip had been passed on to Grimes at some point.

"Thanks so much, Dr. Grimes, but your information is not quite accurate. Medical Examiners give findings, such as that Ms. Kim drowned. The police draw their conclusions from the report, so the 'accidental' part is a conclusion. It's a conclusion, I might add, that I find highly dubious. Did Dean Wooster tell you the rest of what was in the autopsy report?"

I took my coffee and walked closer to Grimes and Willie, wanting to see especially Willie's reaction to what either Grimes or the Dean had left out.

"No," Grimes said sternly. "There was nothing else. She died accidentally and that's all there is to it."

He looked a lot less paternal now, and more like the shark he was reputed to be.

"No, not quite," I said.

I was sorry to have to do this with Adelaide and Hercules present, but they deserved to know, and reality is often upsetting.

I knew the others were listening, but I moved even closer to the table and spoke over it, directly to Grimes.

"The autopsy report also indicated there were signs of sexual assault no more than a couple of days old."

I thought it was fair to call the injuries to her vaginal area evidence of sexual assault.

Behind me, I heard Adelaide make a small sound, like a stifled groan. I turned to look at her. Her face was set and pale. Then she looked down again at Hercules' phone, but I was sure it was not the pictures she was seeing.

I turned back to Grimes.

"Maybe it was just an accident that she drowned," I continued. "But when a woman just happens to drown right after she has been violently assaulted, it raises my suspicions just a tad."

Willie glared at me, his beard positively quivering with indignation.

"So, you continue to have suspicions of Edwin, despite all he told you?"

His narrow face seemed ever more feral to me.

I looked at him for a moment, assessing his anger. Was it for Edwin, or was it really for himself?

"There are a number of people whose movements on Saturday night I'd like to know."

Willie snorted.

"Don't you sound ridiculous even to yourself? You are a failed police-woman and so you try to compensate in this ridiculous fashion. The real police have ruled this an accident. An accident. As in not murder, not suicide."

He finished this statement by hitting the flat of his hand on the table. A favorite gesture of his, smacking things.

Willie scraped his chair back so hard the rollers almost carried it into the wall. I leaned over the table and spoke slowly and deliberately.

"Willie, your touching faith in 'real police work' shows you know next to nothing about it. It's the shortest distance between two points, and damn the evidence. Or create the evidence if you don't have it. Not all the time, but a lot of the time.

"I continue to believe Ah-seong Kim was murdered precisely because there is too much evidence contradicting the accident theory. And it's just that. A theory.

"I have a book of hers that she underlined extensively and took notes in, a book on feminism and religion in Korea. The pattern of the underlin-ings alone show that what she was concerned about in the text were all the statements on the extent of male violence against women. When I get the marginal notes translated tomorrow, I'm going to give them to the police. I will try to make them take another look at their accidental death ruling and if that doesn't work, I'll look for more evidence and I'll look and I'll look until I find the truth. Truth, Donald. Not theories."

I stood up. I would have crossed my arms over my chest if it hadn't been for the damned sling.

Willie jerked around and addressed Grimes.

"Harold, I'll be in my office if you want to go over any more of these figures with me."

Willie huffed out, leaving me looking at Grimes and Grimes, unfortunately, looking back.

"I think, Ms. Ginelli, that you and I had better go to my office so we can continue this, I can't very well say 'discussion,' can I? This exchange, in private."

Grimes rose ponderously and walked slowly out. He seemed older, somehow, and sort of stiff. As he walked by me, he grimaced. I wondered what was wrong with him besides my unacceptable behavior.

After he'd left, I looked over at Adelaide and Hercules. Hercules, contrary to my expectation, hadn't burst into tears. He merely looked thoughtful, like he was mulling over what he had heard. Mulling very hard. His black eyes met mine with what I read as approval.

Adelaide had recovered somewhat. She rolled her shoulders under her loose fitting dress and looked up at me.

"Be careful, honey. He's looking for ways to terminate your contract. You want a witness in there with you?"

I was touched.

"No, but thanks. I'll brave this one on my own."

I was sorry, however, that I was no longer entitled to wear a firearm. Oh well, if the NRA has its way, soon we'll all be toting guns on college campuses, not just in Texas.

I knocked on Grimes's door and he said to come in. Frost was in there with him, dispensing what looked like Advil and a glass of water. Oh dear, I'd given the boss a headache.

Frost gave me the worst glare I'd ever seen in my life. Even the emergency room nurse could take lessons from her. The temperature in the room lowered by several degrees as she froze me in her icy stare. Then Grimes finished his water, handed the glass to Frost, and she departed, closing the door with glacial politeness.

"Please sit down."

I shook my head no and continued to stand. Grimes was sitting again and he didn't seem to appreciate having to look up at me across his desk. What a shame.

"Ms. Ginelli, the next few minutes are going to determine your future in academics."

I almost laughed aloud. Such a misperception of one's own power and authority. I just kept looking at him.

"I tried to give the most tolerant interpretation of your recent behavior that I could to the Dean. He was not so charitably inclined."

I believed him. I'd met the Dean.

"I'm going to give you a clear and simple ultimatum. Either you immediately stop this embarrassing and distasteful business of running around questioning people and stirring up trouble, or we will terminate your contract at the end of the semester."

Grimes leaned back in his big chair and folded his arms.

So that was that.

I nodded so that he'd know I'd heard and then I turned to walk out. I knew that if I had any chance of keeping my job I'd best just keep my mouth shut and solve the case. Then we could sort out whether I still had a job. That was the intelligent, diplomatic thing to do. Right. I turned back to Grimes, sitting so pompously and importantly behind is desk, caring not one whit about a dead young woman and a murderer loose on our campus. Caring only about his little, narrow, and in the grand scheme of things, wholly unimportant fiefdom.

So I told him what I thought.

"You now, Dr. Grimes, you are exactly what is wrong with American humanities. You have gotten the impression that what you do is actually real, that it counts for something, when in fact it is so wholly irrelevant to the way the world works, it's a joke. Around the world, in Africa, in Latin America, in Asia, there are places where ideas are dangerous. They're real. They're about the world and how it works. They're about people's lives and what actually makes those lives nasty, brutal, and short. You rail that the university is cutting your budget and you don't see it. You're already extinct. You only need to realize it and you'll fall down."

Grimes, to my immense satisfaction, looked stunned.

I turned on my heel and walked to the door. Before I left, however, I glanced back.

Good. His mouth was still open.

And there was some more good news here. It looked like I wouldn't have to do that curriculum analysis for the self-study after all.

When I reached my office, I was breathing hard. I decided to put off the library for a while and grade some papers that were overdue. If they chose to try to fire me and I chose to make an issue of it, I didn't want there to be any evidence of incompetence in my work. I kind of lost myself in the students' convoluted prose. When the phone rang, it startled me. I glanced at my watch. An hour had passed. I grabbed for the phone.

It was Margaret Lester and she was furious.

"Kristin! Get yourself over to my office immediately!"

Her voice brooked no questions, but I asked one anyway.

"Why? What's happened?"

"Your buddy Detective Kaiser is here with his minions."

Buddy?

"They're ready to charge Edwin Porterman with assault and possibly with murder. I take it you identified him as Ah-seong Kim's boyfriend?"

Oh. Damn. But how did Kaiser know that? I certainly hadn't told him. Had Matthews? That seemed as unlikely as Karl having investigated on his own.

I answered Margaret in what I hoped was a calm and rational tone of voice.

"I found him and gave his name to the campus police to check his movements. I certainly didn't call Kaiser."

"Well, they got the information from somewhere and they're in my office now yelling at him. I'm at the phone at my secretary's desk. Please get over here."

The desperate appeal in her voice moved me, but not as much as the danger of Edwin in the hands of Kaiser.

I swore I'd run all the way over and hung up. Then I dialed Alice Matthew's cell phone. It went to voicemail, and I left a brief and desperate message. Then I texted her the same information with an urgent, 'Come to Dean Lester's office right away.'

I grabbed my coat and ran.

When I reached Margaret's outer office I could hear Kaiser yelling through the solid wood door of the inner office. If Kaiser was this abusive with the Dean of Students as a witness, God help Edwin if they were able to get him downtown.

I jerked open the door to Margaret's office and slammed it behind me, hoping to draw Kaiser's fire. I succeeded.

He snapped his head in my direction without moving his brown, polyester clad body in any way. It looked like the way a turtle keeps the shell still and moves its head. Only turtle shells are a more attractive color than the mud colored, food stained suit Kaiser wore. He snapped at me.

"Ginelli! What the hell are you doing here?"

I nodded pleasantly in a way that I knew aggravated Kaiser no end and took my time taking off my coat. I gazed around seemingly calm, looking for a place to hang it. It gave me a minute to glance at Edwin.

He was sitting perfectly still in a wooden armchair. His sweater clad arms lay along the armrests of the chair. His face looked quiet. Only his hands clenched at the ends of the armrests betrayed his agitation. His self-control was impressive, as was his sweater. It was a soft grey interspersed with a few blue threads. It buttoned up the front, so it was fairly formal. It went perfectly with his charcoal slacks, black socks and dark leather shoes. He could have been posing for a Ralph Lauren ad, if Ralph Lauren ads weren't so racist.

Edwin looked contemptuously at me. I bet he thought I'd fingered him to Kaiser. What a mess.

I turned slowly to face Kaiser. I took in Icabod, cowering in the far right corner, sitting notebook in hand and as far away from the dangerous black suspect as he could get.

"So, Karl," I said conversationally. "Who gave you Edwin's name here as Ah-seong's friend?"

Karl rasped out what I took to be a chuckle.

"Friend? Yeah, I've heard it called that. And that information is none of your damned business."

"Dr. Donald Willie," Margaret said coolly, cutting in.

Both Edwin and I looked at her, surprised for different reasons. I felt bad for Edwin if he'd thought Willie had cared about him. Donald's mentoring athletes only went so far, apparently.

"Dr. Willie called me a little while ago to tell me he felt in all good conscience he had had to call Detective Kaiser here and tell him that he had seen Mr. Porterman many times this fall with Ms. Kim. The detectives here called soon after to tell me they were coming over to campus. I suggested we all meet in my office."

Conscience? That's one word for it. Self-protection was a better word. I remembered Ah-seong's panicked response to the word "counseling." Who was more likely to have been approached for counseling by a troubled student than the professor who taught psychology? I was also remembering that couch in Donald's office, where counseling sessions might have gone a lot further than Ah-seong wanted. And Willie'd only learned that there was actual evidence of vaginal bruising a little over an hour ago. Seemed like too much of a coincidence to me.

I was surprised myself because Margaret had already known I had not been the one to tip Kaiser about Edwin. Yet she'd punched my guilt button pretty effectively to get me to run over here. Why?

Margaret continued in a tone so dry I suddenly wanted a drink of water.

"I have secured counsel for Mr. Porterman. He should be here shortly. Meanwhile, I suggest you direct your questions to Ms. Ginelli here."

Margaret's cap of brown hair with its grey streaking in the front nodded rather regally in my direction. Then she raised her arm and made a kind of ushering motion with her hand to effectively direct Karl's attention to me. She was standing quite close to him by now and she did this almost literally under his nose.

So that's what Margaret had needed me for. I was to be a tasty morsel, or rather, more like chum to throw out in front of the shark to distract it from a struggling diver while the rescue team got there. I've said it before. They're tricky, these administrators.

I looked at Edwin and he was looking far less angrily at me, though I could tell he'd been hurt by Margaret's revelation of who had revealed his relationship to Ah-seong. I decided to play along and bait Kaiser until the cavalry arrived.

"So, Karl," I said, in the most grating tone I could manage. "Found yourself a nice black suspect and decided Ms. Kim's death wasn't an accident after all, hmmm?"

I was glad I wasn't alone with Kaiser after I said that. He turned those dead, flat eyes, and really they were kind of like a shark's, on to me and actually took two steps in my direction before he recollected we weren't alone. His perpetually greasy face was shimmering with rage. Especially because what I'd said was probably true. But whatever miserable thing he was going to say got interrupted. The door behind us was jerked open again. At this rate, Margaret was going to need a new door.

A uniformed Alice Matthews marched into the room, her normally pleasant face rigid with anger.

She addressed Margaret.

"Dean Lester, Ms. Ginelli texted me you needed me here. Said it was an emergency."

Margaret stared at her.

Kaiser barked a laugh and started to say something that would at best have been unprofessional, and probably racist and sexist to boot. I interrupted him for his own good.

"Officer Matthews, did you check on Edwin Porterman's movements on Saturday night, October 15th?

I hoped Matthews was as good a cop as I thought she was and had done the checking. She hadn't had much time, though. With a stifled sigh of relief I saw her reach into her jacket for a notebook. She flipped it open and began to read in a murderous monotone. Kaiser's attitude had not escaped Alice.

"Edwin Porterman did not travel with the team to Wisconsin. He had sustained a slight injury to his lower back in practice and the coach decided he should not play. After being checked out at the medical center, he returned to his dorm at 8:30 on Saturday night, October 15th. His resident advisor identified him."

Uh-oh.

Kaiser started to look more kindly at Alice Matthews.

Alice flipped a page in her notebook.

"At 9:00 p.m. he went to Ah-seong Kim's dorm. He was seen by at least two students knocking on her door."

Now Kaiser was positively beaming at Alice.

Alice plowed right on.

I glanced at Edwin. He looked mildly interested and not at all alarmed.

"Mr. Porterman apparently did not find Ms. Kim in her room. He scanned his I.D. in at the economics library at 9:15 p.m. and he has also been identified by the student on duty at the door. He sat in plain sight of library personnel until 2:00 a.m. when the library closed. He then returned to his dorm at 2:15 p.m. according to his roommate, who was still up studying."

Didn't these kids ever sleep?

Alice snapped the notebook shut with a click. It matched her clipped voice.

"The economics library has only one door open after 9:00 p.m. and all other doors are alarmed. That library does not connect to the tunnel system."

She snapped the notebook open again.

"On Monday night, Edwin Porterman was at his aunt's house. Emelda Porterman lives in Hammond, Indiana. He took the train, arrived at 6:30 p.m., was picked up by his aunt and had dinner with her. He spent the night and returned by train to campus the following morning. The aunt confirms he was at her house all night."

Wow. I was amazed at how much information Alice had been able to get in such a short period of time.

Alice raised her wide brown eyes up to those of Kaiser and said, with no inflection, "I'll have a report emailed to you by 6:00 p.m. today."

Kaiser said "Bah" and turned away to look out the window.

I'd never actually heard anyone say "Bah" before.

Alice then looked over at Edwin and gave him her kindergarten teacher smile, complete with dimples. She then looked at me, but I didn't rate the same wattage smile he did. Then she turned on her heel and left.

There being nothing at all left to say, I offered to walk with Edwin to his next class. I was taking a chance, getting him out of there, but Margaret's brown head nodded fractionally when I said it. No need to wait for the attorney then. Good. Though I'd bet the attorney still billed for his time if he was already on his way.

Kaiser stayed where he was, looking out the window. It wasn't the view that was holding him there, I was pretty sure.

Edwin got up and I followed him out the door. I didn't shut it immediately, however. I managed to hear the first part of Dean Margaret Lester's lecture to Karl Kaiser on the elementary need to do one's homework.

Then I shut the door quietly and we left.

13

One hardly dares speak any more of the will to power: it was different in Athens.

FRIEDRICH NIETZSCHE, *NOTES (1880-1881)*

Were I a drinking person, I would have headed straight for a local bar after Edwin and I parted ways halfway across the campus. As it was, I needed a fix of my drug of choice so badly my hands shook. The heck with the student papers. I was going to read ancient philosophy until I was so calm I could pass for a Zen Buddhist.

I headed for the main library, an astonishing pile of large concrete blocks that seemed to have been precariously stacked and then abandoned by a giant child. I intended to lose myself in the bowels of the stacks. I still had more than an hour before the kids would be ready for dinner. The cool, musty smell of books upon books in sequestered library shelves always had a calming effect on me.

And it really was a good idea to work on my dissertation since it didn't seem like I was going to have a contract after this academic year. Maybe even after this calendar year was over, depending on how much I had pissed off Grimes.

I had my small, portable computer in my backpack with my dissertation proposal and my advisor's comments. His critique began with the line, 'You're trying to ride two horses. Pick one.'

Didn't I know it? I had been vacillating over this dilemma for a year. Did I go with the ancient philosophers, the ones who comforted me with their conviction that there was such a thing as absolute truth, or did I agree with the post-modernists that truth was a fiction created and maintained by shifting power relationships?

I liked the ancients. I could easily understand Plato and Aristotle. I could almost snooze while reading them. The post-modernists took a lot of concentration as layers and layers of conflicted meaning were probed. If you lost focus for even a few minutes, you'd have to go back to dig again into the dense analyses. As stressed as I was, I chuckled a little over an old joke I liked. 'What do you get when you cross a post-modernist with a member of the Mafia? An offer you can't understand.'

Still chortling a little, I scanned my I.D. into the reader at the main entrance of the library and then headed for the computers on the main floor for the locations of the books I wanted. With my indecision still firmly in place, I needed a lot of books.

The ones I most wanted were not in the regular stacks, I found. They were kept in the rare book room in the basement and I needed to get the key.

I glanced around the reading room as I headed to the huge main desk and there, in the otherwise empty room, were Professor Lee and Myung Ha Kim, tête-à-tête, so to speak. They were talking in hushed tones, but they were obviously not in agreement. I could see Myung Ha vigorously shake his head no several times. Lee had an arm leaning on the table, half lifting himself out of his chair as he pursued whatever point he was trying to make with Myung Ha.

As I approached the desk, I could see out of the corner of my eye that they had both looked up and fallen silent.

Conscious of their scrutiny, I asked the young woman at the desk if I could speak to the librarian, Mary Carpenter. You couldn't get a key to the rare book room from just anybody.

After a short time, Mary came bustling up, her arms cradling a short stack of books like a mother carrying her firstborn. She was already frowning at me. Why do so many librarians seem so suspicious of the people who want to use books in the library, or, gasp, take them out of the library? Perhaps all patrons are potential book abusers. Well, in a sense, probably they were.

Mary peered at me over her half glasses, apparently assessing my capacity for mayhem in the rare books section.

In my most mature voice, I asked for the key and was reminded that I could only remain in the rare book section until 6:00 p.m. Since that suited me fine, I agreed. The key was then grudgingly given, and only after solemn promises had been obtained from me that I would return the key in person no later than 6. I gave my oath and departed, not glancing over at Lee and Kim.

I descended to the basement and walked through the vending area that had been installed last year, tepid soda dispensed in plastic bottles or dried crackers and stale candy. Despite not having had much to eat today, I did not pause to sample these delicacies. I was running on caffeine and nerves. Besides, I thought there might be a squashed granola bar in the bottom of my backpack if I did get hungry. Though, if Mary caught me eating in the rare book room, or even on a table outside the rare book room with a rare book anywhere near me, I would probably be banned from the library altogether. Sobering thought.

I opened the door to the new basement section of the library. The outer door was unlocked during the day, since the stacks themselves were gated and locked. Hence the key I had gotten. The outer door was probably closed and locked by Mary herself promptly at 6.

I flipped on the light switch by the door and the hum of florescent lighting spread out in sound waves overhead. These were special lights, designed not to fade the paper of these books. They cast a vaguely bluish light. The stacks themselves ran along two opposing concrete walls of this large rectangular room.

It was cool in here. A complicated looking panel indicated temperature (60 degrees) and humidity (45 percent) as well as time and something called "rotation" blinked above the light switch. A stern warning was attached to the panel. "Do not adjust settings."

I heeded the warning and left the panel strictly alone. I turned my attention to finding the stacks where the books I needed were located. The labels for the Library of Congress numbers along with an additional "Stack Number" were displayed on electronic panels running across the top of these stacks, but independent of their current location. That was because the recent renovation of this area had included the installation of moveable stacks.

Moveable stacks are a series of regular set of library shelves, two shelves wide, but at the bottom on each end the whole unit is on wheels that ride on narrow metal tracks. All the stacks are pushed together with only one empty stack width left available.

How do you get to the books, then? You take your Library of Congress number over to a panel at the far end of the room. One screen instructs you to enter that number. When you type it in, it displays a stack number. Then you type in your desired stack number in the adjacent screen, rather like I could have typed in my choice for either Snickers or Vanilla Wafers in the vending machines outside, pressing F2 or G7, and a motor kicks on. The stacks are motored automatically along their little train tracks until the desired stack has a space about three feet wide for you to walk in and get your desired volumes. This system sounds complicated, but it saves a huge amount of storage space since the sometimes hundred of feet that would ordinarily have to be devoted to each aisle between immovable stacks have been eliminated.

Access to these moveable stacks is blocked, however, by a sliding grate attached to the floor and to the ceiling on another track. This just pulls along by hand, once you have unlocked it using Mary's well-guarded key, and then you just pull the grate along by hand to get at the aisle and stack you want. It sort of reminded me of the barriers they used at my high school to shut off certain corridors when we had school dances.

I went to the end where the grate lock was located and unlocked it. Then I went over to the keyboard that worked the motor and typed in my selection. There was a click and then a fairly loud clunk as the motor kicked on. As the stacks slid slowly by me, I wondered what each of them weighed. When the kids and I had moved from my graduate school apartment to our current house, each small book box I had packed was hard to pick up. I could only imagine what these ten-foot high and twenty-foot long double stacks would weigh. Tons, I guessed. No wonder it took a motor and a train track to move them.

I glanced again at the little piece of paper where I'd written the call number of the book I needed and I entered the stack space that had opened up. I was so intent on following the sequence of numbers to find my book that I was slow to react to the sound behind me.

The sound was the grate being pulled across, sealing off my exit from the stacks. For a moment I was only puzzled. I called out, thinking to let someone know I was still using this section when I heard another sound. Two sounds, actually. A click and then a thunk.

The motor to move the stacks had been turned on. The stacks were already starting to move, narrowing the space in which I was standing. I turned and tried to get to the grate, but I was too far back in the stacks. I screamed that I was still in the stacks, but there was no response.

I looked for something to brace the stacks open. Books. All I had before me was books. Hundreds of books. Thousands of books.

And shelf space.

The bottom two shelves were a folio section, where very tall books would be shelved flat to preserve them so the space was wider and higher than a normal shelf.

As the aisle narrowed slowly, inexorably together, I frantically pulled out all these large books from the doublewide space at the bottom. I hoped I could slide into it.

I crouched down as the closing shelves began to crush the volumes I'd thrown on the floor. The crunching of the bindings and the crackle of the paper was amazingly loud. I thought wildly how furious the librarian was going to be with me for letting all these rare books be smashed. But then maybe I was going to be crushed along with them and I wouldn't have to face her. I crouched down and tried to wiggle into the shelf.

My sling had come off in my panicked hurling of large books to the floor. Despite the pain, I forced myself all the way into the space I'd created as the snapping bindings and the crunching of old paper reached a crescendo. My injured arm ended up beneath me and I could feel the stiches pulling out. My legs were unnaturally angled, one knee pressing on the bottom of the shelf, the other literally being banged by the smashing folios.

Then the lights went off and there was silence.

The stacks had closed. Into the silence and the darkness I screamed for help. I screamed because my left arm was being pulled apart along the muscles so recently closed with stitches. I could feel the blood trickling down my arm and then wetting my chest.

I fought down the rising panic, but the dark and the pain were fighting me back. I screamed until I could scream no more. Then I must have fainted.

* * * *

I swam into consciousness briefly. I was hot. I hurt everywhere. And my mouth was so dry I could feel each separate crease in my tongue. I was too exhausted to scream any more. I could feel I was still bleeding. If it had remained cold in the rare book room, maybe I would have had a chance. But whoever had locked me in here and tried to crush me in the stacks had also turned up the heat to unbearable levels.

I mourned for my boys and I cursed my stupidity. Then I fainted again.

* * * *

My eyes hurt. There were lights and noise around me. I felt myself being lifted and the unclenching of my stiffened muscles was unlike any pain I'd every experienced. I couldn't scream any more, but I heard someone groaning. A stab in my right arm. And then there was nothing.

* * * *

I was swimming. I was in a pond and the leaves of the beautiful long-stemmed plants were closing over my head. I could see them from below, their undersides a cool and pleasant light green. Through the ceiling of water I could see the sky, a pale but vital curving dome. I gagged and choked as I tried to fight my way to the surface, up to the sky, past the plants, but they were clinging, holding me down. I struggled with all my might. But it was no use. They held me down and the water closed over my head.

* * * *

I could hear voices and I wanted to open my eyes. But my eyelids were so heavy it took all my concentration just to slit them. The stab of light in my eyes was so painful I gasped and the voices came nearer. I opened my eyes a little further and Tom Grayson was bending over me.

I tried to talk, but only a little croak came out. It wasn't even a respectable frog sound.

"Kristin? Kristin? It's me, Tom."

His tired eyes were narrowed, concerned.

I tried to smile but oddly my face wouldn't seem to move. I tried to nod. Nope.

Tom spoke quietly.

"You're going to be fine. You've lost a lot of blood and you were very dehydrated from the heat, but we're pumping plenty of fluids back into you. Your arm will have to be repaired, it's torn up pretty badly, and you're bruised in a number of places, but that's basically it. Here, let's try some ice in your mouth. You must be pretty dry."

That was an understatement. My mouth was as dry as the ancient paper that had crumbled into dust before the advancing library stack. Not a good image. A panic image. I breathed heavily.

Tom put his hand behind my head and angled it slightly. His touch made the panic recede some. His long fingers placed a piece of ice on my tongue. The cooling brush of the ice on my tongue was exquisite. I began to suck it slowly and the lovely drops trickled down my throat.

Tom lowered my head.

"How'd I get rescued?" At least I tried to say that, but the words wouldn't form correctly. I could only mumble.

Tom seemed to understand though.

"At 6 o'clock, when the key to the rare book room had not been returned, the librarian marched down there apparently to give you a dressing down about failing to abide by the rules. I can scarcely believe they would think you, of all people, would be willfully breaking rules."

Tom's attempt at humor was a little heavy handed, but his smile helped. I would have smiled back, but I still couldn't seem to move my face.

"Later she told the police when she found the door locked, she assumed you'd closed up and had just forgotten to take the key back upstairs. But she always checks the thermostat before leaving and makes sure the grate is closed and locked. Students, and faculty I might add, have been known to change the temperature despite the posted warning and they can be careless about closing and locking the grate. She was very specific about that."

Tom paused and slid another piece of ice onto my tongue. While I blissfully sucked it, he held my wrist to take my pulse. Whatever my pulse was, he seemed satisfied that he wasn't going to kill me with the next bit of information. Just the little bit of water in my mouth had made me feel so better, I felt I could listen to what my would-be book stack coffin must have looked like when they opened the door.

"Anyway, so the librarian opened the door and the heat was blasting away. Ms. Moorehouse was furious to find the heat had been turned up so high. She flipped on the overhead lights and saw the crushed books spilling out of one set of closed stacks. Then she heard you moan. She called security. She tried to open the grate, but it was locked.

"Security arrived pretty fast, apparently, and the guy shined his flashlight into the stack where the books were spilled out and they saw you trapped in a shelf and barely conscious. While the librarian called 911, he broke the lock with the butt of his gun and pulled it across so they could get to you."

Oh, I bet Moorehouse would never forgive me for all this damage in the rare book room.

Tom was talking matter-of-factly, but his face was grave. The locked grate proved I had not been the victim of some run-away modern library technology. Somebody had deliberately closed me in there and turned on the moveable stacks to crush me between them. The locking of the grate had been a mistake on the part of the would-be murderer. Because it showed it was attempted murder.

"What time is it?" I tried to say that but again I was just able to slowly mumble. What the heck was with this not being able to really move my face or talk right?

"It's about 10 in the evening. You were unconscious for a while when they brought you in. We got the bleeding stopped in your arm and pumped fluids."

I struggled to get a little more upright. Not only would my face not move, my whole body was flaccid and I couldn't seem to move very much. I started to panic a little. When Tom saw that I couldn't get my body to obey my mind, he put a hand on my shoulder.

"Don't be alarmed. We gave you a muscle relaxant to ease the strain after you'd been cramped for all those hours. The drug makes your muscles turn to jelly and you can't seem to move, but that will wear off gradually in the next hour or so."

That's why I was having so much trouble talking. It wasn't only the dry mouth. My facial muscles were all slack. I struggled to form some words.

"Kids . . . Giles and Carol . . . need to call."

Tom got a peculiar expression on his face. Even with his graying hair and his eyes that seem never to have slept, he looked like a high school guy bringing a girl home late for a date. Sheepish, I guess you'd say.

"They're right outside."

He paused.

"With their grandparents. I called your house when you were brought in. They're all here."

Tom's voice dropped an octave on the word "all."

I had not looked forward to the eventuality that Tom and Marco's parents might some day meet if Tom and I continued to see each other. But did they have to meet when I was drugged and barely conscious? On the other hand . . . maybe that was the best way. With any luck, I wouldn't even remember this evening tomorrow.

Tom stood and took a deep breath. He walked slowly to the door and opened it. In just a few seconds the Ginellis, Mike, Sam, Carol and Giles had all piled into the small hospital room. As the children carefully kissed my cheeks, cautioned by Mama Ginelli, I looked over their heads at Tom's tall form framed in the doorway. Our eyes met briefly and then he shut the door.

I tried to will my good arm to reach out for the boys, but even yet I couldn't quite get the muscle coordination right. A part of my mind registered that I now knew how Ah-seong Kim could have been put into that pond alive and slid obligingly to the bottom, breathing water into her lungs the whole way, but not being able to struggle back to the surface.

She'd been given some kind of muscle relaxant.

14

Q. So there is a certain "discontinuity in your theoretical trajectory . . ."

M.F. This business about discontinuity has always rather bewildered me.

MICHEL FOUCAULT, *POWER/KNOWLEDGE*

As Natalie started shooing everyone out of the hospital room, warning darkly that I would take a turn for the worse if they did not let me get my sleep, I whispered to Vince to stay. I was starting to be able to form words and he seemed to understand. He nodded his heavy head and went over to shut the door behind his wife. Then he pulled a chair up to the bedside and levered his bulk into it. Even his baggy golf sweater wasn't able to cover his stomach any more, and his white tee shirt was clearly visible between the straining buttons.

But while I wouldn't want to have to count on Vince to chase a suspect for more than two feet, I totally trusted his judgment as a cop.

I turned my head toward him as quickly as my still flaccid muscles would allow. I wanted to say this fast before Natalie came back to find out where he was.

"Vince, you've figured out I didn't just fall down in the library, right?"

Vince took out a cigar, fiddled with it, and gave me his level stare.

"Yeah, sure. Hell, you've pissed somebody off good and they're tryin' to make a permanent dent in you. Doesn't take genius to figure it out."

He looked at my heavily bandaged arm and sighed.

"Looks like they damn well gave it a good try."

"Yes, well, they didn't succeed and I don't want to sit around waiting for them to pick a time and a place to try again. I'm going to close up the house on Rosemont. I'd like you and Natalie to take the kids in your mo-torhome and get out of town."

Tears burned hot in my eyes.

"You've got to keep them safe for me, Vince. For Marco. What I can't stand about all of this is the threat to them."

I turned my face away.

I felt Vince's heavy, calloused hand patting my good arm.

"Ah, kid. If ya were my own, I couldn't love ya more. The boys, they'll go with Natalie and hang Beverly. They can all stay in Wisconsin. I'll stay here with you. We'll get this SOB."

Vince's large hand patting me felt like being massaged by a brick, but it was comforting all the same.

I was touched. But Natalie drove the motorhome about thirty miles an hour in the fast lane. She'd get herself and the boys killed by furious motor-ists before they reached the Wisconsin border.

"You can't, Vince. You know Natalie can't drive that battleship by her-self, and it takes the two of you to control the boys on a trip. And I trust you to see trouble coming. I'm not going home and set myself up to be attacked again. I'm going to ask Carol and Giles to go to Carol's sister in Lombard, and I'll go stay with a friend. I won't go to my office and I'll work with the cops to find out who's doing this."

Vince sat back as far as the metal armed chair would allow him and he narrowed his eyes. He stuck the unlit cigar between his lips and chewed meditatively for a few minutes. Vince was great at the silent treatment. Like I said, he'd been an excellent cop. And damn him, he got me. I felt a blush starting below the neck of the hospital gown and moving up to my hairline.

"Uh, huh. Who's the friend?"

"Ah, Vince. He really is just a friend."

I looked at his lined face, lines carved so deeply by the death of his son. Tears pooled in the corners of my eyes.

Vince grunted, embarrassed. I thought he might pat my arm again, but he just looked across the bed toward the other side of the room, looking internally at his son and feeling his own loss again. The cigar rotated in his mouth, but otherwise he didn't move. He looked like a sad Italian Buddha.

"Five years is a long time, Kristin. Maybe too long."

We sat in silence for a few minutes, each with our separate thoughts. Vince would never have another son, but maybe I could still have a life. Things were changing yet again. Vince didn't like it, but he could see it too. And like really good cops do, he didn't flinch from calling it the way he saw it. I regretted there were so few like him. And it seemed like they were get-ting fewer all the time.

The door whooshed open on its pneumatic hinge and Natalie stuck her iron-grey head in.

"Vince, what on earth? Let the child sleep and get that cigar out of this room."

She held the door open, certain after thirty-five years of experience that Vince would obey.

Vince, having been given his marching orders by two women, heaved to his feet and started for the door. Then he turned.

"I got yer cell. I'll call. We'll talk. Talk to the kiddos too."

I nodded and he lumbered out, shooing Natalie in front of him like a destroyer with a very round tug.

Staying with Tom was only a half formed plan in my mind. Tom hadn't even been consulted. I guess if he didn't like the idea I could stay in a hotel.

My day caught up with me and I slept.

* * * *

The whoosh of the door opening woke me. It seemed like I had only slept a few minutes, but morning light was framing the window shade. Then my vision cleared and I was appalled to find Karl Kaiser, not Tom Grayson, swimming into sight.

I struggled to sit upright and stay decent. That's never easy in a hospital grown. At least my muscles seemed to be obeying me. It's a terrifying feeling to want to move and be unable to. It had given me a whole new perspective on paralysis.

Icabod Crane was with Kaiser. The best part of that was that I would not have to be alone with Karl.

Icabod folded his long, thin body into a metal chair in the corner of the room and he took out a notebook.

Kaiser coughed to clear a wad of phlegm that had come up into his mouth. He scanned the room, I guess looking for a space to spit it out. Since it was a hospital, there were no spittoons. He swallowed it. I felt my stomach churn.

"So, Ginelli. Somebody tried to flatten you I hear."

Kaiser moved closer to the bed, but then actually paused to look at the computer screen propped on a cart near the bed. The display showed my vitals, breathing, pulse and so forth. Nurses and doctors used these instead of written charts these days to enter or get patient information. I started to be indignant at the invasion of privacy, but then I realized he clearly couldn't make much out of the differently colored lines. Astonishingly, he tapped a key, but the screen stayed the same. Hospital personnel had to scan their

I.D.'s on the side of the keyboard to get access. Karl clearly didn't know that, but he was already managing to piss me off.

"Seen enough?" I asked sarcastically.

He turned from the screen with no sign he had heard me and moved to the chair Vince had pulled up by the bed the night before.

"Suppose you go over your adventure in the library with us, eh Ginelli?"

I sat up a little straighter.

"I'm surprised you're here, Karl. I thought you'd be running around trying to find another convenient black guy to frame for Ms. Kim's death. That is, since you've revised your view that it was accidental. Or have you?"

"Kid just fell into that muck there. Accident. Forget that. This here is attempted murder, of you, in case I need to point that out for you. Somebody tried to off you. Go figure. A sweet gal like you."

Karl chucked at his own wit. I glanced at Icabod, but he didn't crack a smile. I was actually starting to like him a little.

I looked Karl directly in the eyes. Good thing my mouth was really working now.

"It's amazing to me that you have the gall to call yourself a detective. A student drowns, I ask questions about it, and somebody tries to murder me. Now, how does that add up? I annoyed someone by asking questions about an accidental drowning?"

Karl half rose in the chair and leaned over so that I could actually smell his horrible breath. I moved my good arm to cover my injured one. I wasn't sure Karl wouldn't 'accidentally' lean on my injury.

"Listen. I don't want your smart-mouth opinions. I don't want your so-called theories. I want you to tell me what the hell happened to you last night. I came to you because that campus cop broad said you were at death's door and couldn't come in to make a statement. So give. Now."

He sat back down, but the miasma of his stinking breath lingered between us.

Alice Matthews. She must have been the one to tell Kaiser he had to come to me. I appreciated the thought, but I would much rather have staggered downtown than have to talk to Kaiser while I was in a bed, even a hospital bed.

But it needed to be done. So I tried to breathe as little as possible and told him and Icabod everything that had happened from the time I got the key to the library to when I'd woken in the hospital. Then I backtracked, and threw in my visit to the Korean students breakfast, my talk with Henry, and even the reaction of my dear colleagues in Philosophy and Religion. I stopped from time to time to spell out names for Icabod. It seemed he was keeping up nicely. Then I even told them about Ah-seong's book, implying that she'd given it to me, which, in a post-mortem sort of way she had, and that all of the above, perhaps with the exception of Henry, unless he'd heard it from somebody else, knew I had that book and I planned to get the marginal notes translated the next day. Today. Looked like I was going to miss that appointment.

"So this book that you shot your mouth off about. Where is it now?"

Even Karl had been able to make one and one add up to two.

"In the top drawer of my desk in my office." I paused. "If it's still there."

I was silent while Karl glared at me. Yeah. It was evidence and it was probably gone. That had been the point of this whole exercise in the library. To get me out of the way and to get that book.

Karl interrupted my reverie.

"So you think it was lifted while you were being squeezed in the library?"

He chuckled. It was a ghastly sound. Karl could bring out dirty nuances in a nursery rhyme. I bet he had an anonymous Twitter account devoted to harassing women who stood up for themselves and other women.

"Why don't you investigate, Karl? Send somebody to check my desk drawer. That's what other cops do. They actually go places and check for evidence."

Kaiser wasn't the only one capable of being nasty.

He snorted and glanced over at Icabod who was scribbling furiously. We both waited until Icabod glanced up and gave a jerky nod.

Karl launched himself at me again, linguistically speaking.

"And you didn't see anything, any part of the perp who pulled the grate? A foot, a hand, anything?"

Back to basics. Who'd you see? What did they say? Well this case was a little more complicated than that.

"No. I was bending down with my back to the opening, looking for a book."

"So, issuing invitations again? I'm surprised he didn't take you up on it, come into the stacks for a little bump and grind and then take you out. Why fancy it all up with machinery?"

I took a deep breath and kept my gaze level. I recognized Karl's 'make'em furious' technique in its most heavy-handed fashion. He knew I'd hate the crudity and being made to feel like I had cooperated in my own attempted murder. Still, maybe the muscle relaxants were still working because I controlled my mouth. Sort of.

"I don't know. You're the detective, remember? I did your job enough when I was on the force. I won't do it now."

I leaned back against the pillows and enjoyed the flush of rage on Kaiser's face. Still I was glad there was a witness in the room.

Just then the door opened and Tom walked into the room, rubbing the hand sanitizer from the dispenser outside the room into his hands. He stopped when he saw there were others with me. I introduced Karl and Icabod. Karl grunted something resembling a greeting. Icabod said nothing. They both took themselves off.

Tom looked even more tired than usual and that was saying something. I felt I should move over and let him rest on the hospital bed for a few minutes. Or an hour. I wondered if he had spent the night in the hospital.

"Hi."

"Hi, yourself. You seem to be recovering. Who were those guys? Clearly not friends here to cheer you up."

No, that was certainly not true.

"Cops," I said shortly. "I needed to make a statement about what happened."

I think Tom could tell I didn't want to talk about it. He went to the computer, scanned his I.D. and busied himself tapping keys for a few minutes.

"Well, you seem to be doing fine overall. Let me just check a few things."

For the next few minutes, Tom busied himself doing doctor things to me, checking my blood pressure, my temperature and my reflexes. They still seemed a little slow to me, but Tom made no comment either way. He unwrapped my arm and I winced at the horrible gash that was there. He felt me recoil.

"Well, you're going to need plastic surgery. I never recommend pulling the stitches out by hand. But it will look better than this soon. How's it feel?"

He pushed at the edges of the wound and I jumped.

"Tender. Hmm. Let me see."

He fiddled around some more, but it didn't hurt quite as much even two inches away from the wound itself.

Then he sat down in the chair next to the bed Karl had just vacated. I thought I could feel a speech coming.

"Kristin, you've put yourself in tremendous danger to figure out what happened to that student. I think you need to ask yourself if you're doing the right thing."

Tom's narrow face was grim.

Well, as scoldings go it wasn't too bad. He hadn't outright yelled. Though I suspected Tom rarely yelled.

I put my good hand out toward him, but stopped short of actually touching him. I felt too unsure of myself for that.

"Tom, I do ask myself. I asked myself that a lot when I was trapped in that shelf and I cursed what an idiot I had been to let myself get trapped like that. I know I'm a civilian now, but I can't seem to help it. I wish I could, but it seems it's just the way I'm made. I just have to keep digging."

I paused and pondered for a second. Did I want to let this guy in or not? Yes, I thought. Yes, I do.

"That part of me, the relentless curiosity, it went away for a while in my grief, but it just went underground, apparently. Lately, I've been sort of coming to the surface, reaching out instead of hiding. This is part of that. I know it sounds crazy to say that making somebody so mad they want to kill you is a sign you're healing, but it's true for me. And Tom, you're part of it. You're part of my healing, of my waking up."

I hate it. I blushed again. Damned Scandinavian genes.

Tom looked at me and put his hand in my outstretched one.

"You're going to make me crazy, you know that, don't you? I wanted someone who was self-reliant, who wouldn't lean all over me and I got Wonder Woman."

"Have you? Have you, you know, got me?" I said very softly.

His hand tightened around mine.

"That's the way I read the vital signs, don't you?"

I nodded, too full of emotion and painkillers to risk a verbal answer. I did think though that this was a good time to land my idea on him.

"Tom. I'd like a favor. I'd like to stay at your apartment for a few days. I want to heal and to think about all of this. No one would think to look for me there. The children are going with their grandparents and Giles and Carol, you met them too?"

He nodded.

"They're going to a relative's house."

Tom looked a little poleaxed.

"You want to stay with me?"

"Yes, but let me be clear. I'm just asking to borrow a spare room if you have one, or the couch. Nothing else. Not yet. I'm not ready, but I'd like, I mean I need to . . . "

God this was hard. I wanted to say 'I need you' but maybe I just wanted to feel I needed him. Was this the worst kind of emotional deception?

"I need to know you more, and I guess know me more too." I paused. "Maybe it's unfair, what I'm asking and not asking for. And besides, I've got a murderer trying to kill me, so I do know that can be a drawback in any relationship."

Tom frowned. Clearly my attempt at humor had been a mistake.

I waited.

Then Tom leaned forward a little and spoke softly.

"I have a spare room. Two actually. I just hope separate bedrooms doesn't mean I can't comfort you from time to time?" Then it was Tom's turn to pause. "Though you realize I need to refer you to another doctor now, right?"

He smiled.

I really like his eyes, the way they crinkle up at the corners.

"Yes, I do know that. All of that."

Then we made plans for Tom to refer me to another doctor and get the discharge process underway so I could get out of the hospital and he left.

I took out my phone and using only one hand awkwardly texted Carol where I would be. Tom had written down his address for me on a pad and I copied it into the text. After I had sent the text, I pondered the scrawl of the address, wondering what would come of this step. Then I texted Elaine our neighbor to ask if she would take Molly for a while. She texted a 'yes' right back. Okay. Everybody dealt with. For a while, anyway.

Then I brought myself back to the problems at hand. I tried to adjust my throbbing arm so that it was a little more comfortable. My arm. Suddenly I saw, as vividly as if it was happening again, that knife swooping down on me in the alley. And the stocking mask. The unprovoked nature of the attack. I sat up so abruptly I grunted with the pain. Somebody hadn't just tried to kill me once. Somebody had tried to kill me twice. That was no random mugging the night Ah-seong had been killed. I should have realized it sooner. Whoever had killed Ah-seong had tried to kill me as well because of what they feared she'd told me that afternoon. Having failed, that person had lain low, realizing that I had nothing definite the way I was thrashing around, asking all kinds of questions. But yesterday, I'd shot my mouth off about having something of Ah-seong's that might actually reveal the murderer. And so they'd acted again. And failed again.

The door opened interrupting my thoughts. Dr. Ellen Burton introduced herself as my new primary care physician, referred by Dr. Grayson. She worked over my arm, closing up the wound and binding it more securely for discharge.

I barely noticed what she was doing. Over her head I looked at the blank white wall, reflecting. Yes, the murderer had failed twice, but I'd failed too. Spectacularly. I knew Karl Kaiser or one of his minions would not find Ah-seong's book in the center drawer of my desk. It had been removed while I had nearly died in the rare book room.

15

Richer savor lies
in a conquest by violence
than in soft consent.
Baron Scarpia, Act II

GIACOMO PUCCINI, *TOSCA*

"Ready?"

Tom was at the door of the hospital, ready to take me away.

"Ready? Am I ever."

I was dressed in clothes Carol had brought from home last night. The outfit in which I'd spent time bleeding and sweating in the rare book stacks had been trashed. Even if it could have been saved, I'd wanted no reminders of that horrid experience. I thought maybe I'd apply to get a work-study student to check books out of the library for me from now on. I didn't relish the thought of walking through any more library stacks, moveable or immovable, from now on.

And I certainly didn't need another minute in the hospital. I felt surprisingly okay. Well, maybe not so surprising. When your blood and other fluids drain out of you, I suppose it really perks you up to get a fill-up. It felt odd to feel almost normal.

Physically, anyway.

Alice Matthews had called while I was waiting to for the discharge to come through. She'd accompanied Kaiser to my office in Myerson and it had indeed been burglarized. Ah-seong Kim's book was no longer in my center drawer. It certainly tied the attack on me to her death, though Alice said that amazingly enough Kaiser was still resisting that conclusion. The office door had not been forced. It was a key entry, and the door had been re-locked behind the burglar. Nothing of Henry's had seemed to have been touched, so whoever had stolen Ah-seong's book from my desk had known which one was mine. The cops had dusted, but hadn't found anything but my prints and some smudges. Well, who doesn't know about wearing gloves when you commit burglary?

Though crooks can be remarkably stupid. I remembered the case we'd had here in Chicago where a bank robber had written the note demanding money on the back of his own deposit slip, pre-printed with name, address, zip code, everything. When he got home with the money he'd gotten from the teller, the cops were waiting for him. What a laugh we'd gotten at the station about that.

But this university related murderer wasn't stupid. Just vicious and clever.

Tom drove me to my house to pick up some additional clothes for the next few days. He insisted on going in with me and almost got knocked flat by Molly. Molly hates to be left alone, and without the kids or Giles and Carol she was desperate for attention. She's also no kind of watchdog, unless we were going to be robbed by squirrels.

"Down, Molly, down!" I realized my throat still hurt some from shouting in vain in the library stack. It didn't matter though. I could have shouted the house down and Molly still would keep jumping up to be petted.

I pulled her off Tom by her collar. That he didn't immediately start bushing the hair off of his suit jacket was kind of promising. I distrust people who don't like dogs, and in our house dog hair is kind of considered a condiment.

"Tom, I'm going to take her next door to the Jackson's house. They always take her when we're away. We bird-sit for them when they're out of town."

Tom was chuckling at the thought of someone bird-sitting as I towed Molly away.

I got her over to the Jackson's through the gate in the fence between our two yards. We leave the gate open almost all the time, so they hardly seem to notice when Molly is actually staying with them, she's over there so much. When Sam and Mike are with their grandparents, I find her at their house watching cartoons with their two kids. To Molly, a kid is a necessity of life.

As I came in the back door, Tom was coming up the basement stairs. I really should have told him no criminal would visit our basement. It's really a cellar, with a dirt floor and the detritus of a hundred years scattered about. And the smell is worse than the Cage where the football players practice.

"Nothing, and I mean nothing, down there."

Tom was deadpan about it.

"Yes, I know exactly what you mean. Let me just get a few things together upstairs and I'll be ready to go."

I went up to my bedroom and started to think about what I might need. Robe, pajamas, toiletries, those were simple. But what were Tom and I going to do for the next two days? Besides the obvious, which I'd said I didn't want. Well, correction. Didn't want right now.

I glanced at my dresser top and realized that sitting there were my two tickets to the opera for Saturday. Tonight. I'd forgotten all about it. I usually went with a friend whom I should have asked days ago, and of course that had completely gone out of my mind.

I am a Chicago Lyric Opera subscriber. The Lyric is wonderful. It is fully sold out every year. It produces an imaginative and wide list of operas. And I am really an opera junkie. I have two tickets to each opera every season, I subscribe to the libretto series (the complete English words of each opera in booklets), and I go to the free lectures they give any chance I can get. In short, I'm hooked. It just gets to me, somehow.

I've learned to be careful about which of my friends I invite to go with me to the opera, however. I'd invited a woman in the psychology department to go with me to *Madama Butterfly*. I routinely weep through the whole last act. Even the opening bars of the last aria can make me tear up. My colleague sat dry-eyed through the whole thing. As we were walking out, she looked at me with concern as I was blowing my nose and dabbing at my eyes, and she asked me if I'd 'been under a lot of stress lately.' Not an opera lover.

I stuck the two tickets in my pocket. If a man can go to the opera and not whine about it, there's not much wrong with him.

So in addition to grabbing a few pairs of pants and blouses, I stuck in a loose fitting calf-length black wool and silk blend dress that I know looks wonderful on me. It should. It's an Armani. Armani's clothes look sensational even without people inside them. It had a high neckline and long-sleeves. It would hide my bandage and make me look totally sophisticated at the same time. I threw in the matching shoes, hose, and bag and went downstairs. Now, all I needed was to convince the doctor that the patient would heal much more quickly if she could imbibe a little Puccini. For the opera was *Tosca*, one of my all time favorites.

I left my bag at the top of the stairs and called to Tom to ask him to carry it down for me.

As I followed him, I felt almost lighthearted. Apart from the really nasty fact that somebody wanted me dead, I felt more optimistic about the future than I had in years. Five years, to be exact. As I looked at Tom's retreating back, I enjoyed the feeling of looking forward to the next moment, rather than trying to trick myself into coping for just one more day.

While Tom put my bag in his car, I put on the alarm system for the house. I even activated the motion detectors. If somebody did break in looking for me, the alarm would summon the police immediately if a door or window breach is followed in ten seconds by the motion detector being tripped. It would be nice if the murderer could be caught breaking into my house, but I doubted it would be that simple.

Tom drove to his apartment. It was in a wonderful old art-deco building overlooking Lake Michigan. We rode up to his apartment in silence, shy with each other. The elevator had a stained glass panel framed at the back and a parquet floor. Each floor of this building only had two apartments. We rode to the top floor, got out and he opened the door to his place.

I stopped in the hallway just stunned. It was incredible. The whole front wall was two stories high with floor to ceiling windows, inset with more stained glass in the arched tops. The lower windows up to about ten feet were clear glass and gave onto a spectacular view of the lake. It was a clear, cold day and the lake was calm, a pearl-grey mirror reflecting the scudding clouds. In the distance, a lake tanker moved across the horizon.

I tore my gaze from the windows and looked around the room. I nearly laughed out loud. What a decorating scheme for this incredible place!

All along the left wall, Tom had installed what appeared to be state of the art audio-visual equipment. When I'd gone out to get us a new television for the Rosemont house, I'd browsed some in the higher-end area and been stunned at the cost of some of this stuff. I wandered over to look at the labels. The huge curved television was nearly six feet across, I guessed. I squinted. Samsung. Then there were flanking towers with speakers and amplifiers and a fitted system underneath with other gadgets, including what looked like a tablet to run it all. Not for six-year olds, that's for sure. Though the boys would love this whole thing.

And in front of all this high-tech gadgetry was one black leather recliner chair. More upscale than a La-Z-Boy recliner, but it was the same principle. The rest of the furniture, probably purchased by his ex-wife, was pushed along the far right wall, in as thoughtful a grouping as one finds in discount furniture stores.

Tom had disappeared down a hallway with my things. He was probably checking if the bed in the spare room had sheets. I looked back at the view and then at all the technology and the chair positioned in front, the rest of the furniture abandoned to the side. It was a lonely room, as I thought about it. I stepped further into the center of the room and I nearly slid to the floor. My foot had slipped on a CD case lying there. I bent to pick it up and saw it was an album by, good heavens, Justin Bieber. I stood back up, leaving the offending object on the floor.

I glared down at the CD. Did Tom have a kid (or kids?) from his former marriage? Now that was something I hadn't considered. New vistas of relational difficulties opened up before me. I looked down at the cute and vaguely smarmy face of Bieber, so beloved of young girls, like it was a live grenade. Besides, who listened to CD's anymore? I didn't want to know. So I kicked the CD case under the recliner.

Tom came back and I looked innocently at him. I wasn't going to bring up the subject of kid or kids from his former marriage right now.

"Right." Tom said. "So how about some lunch and then maybe a nap for you?"

He addressed this outrageous statement to the furniture grouping on the right.

"Well, lunch sounds okay. Where's the kitchen?"

"No, I'll get it. You sit."

I'm not that great with being taken care of. I struggled not to snap at him.

"Tom. It's okay. I'll sit in the kitchen while you make sandwiches or something. I'm feeling fine, really."

Tom looked at his recliner like he expected it to add to this conversation. Then he looked over at me with an embarrassed shrug.

"I wasn't going to fix anything. I never buy food. I was going to order it from the deli across the street. They'll bring it up."

So gourmet cooking was not one of his hobbies. Fine. I decided to treat this weirdness like there was nothing wrong.

"Great. Ham and swiss on rye with Dijon mustard. And a big pickle. And coleslaw. And a Dr. Pepper."

Like any working mother, I was an expert at ordering in food.

Tom nodded and took out his phone. While he ordered our food, I sat down in the big leather chair. Whoa. It was like being embraced by a big leather cloud. I didn't actually sit in it, it kind of absorbed me. I grasped the arms to swivel it around a little and touched some controls. I looked at them. Excuse me. This was so not a La-Z-Boy. It was a Hammacher Schlemmer heated massage chair. I was so tempted to turn it on and try it out, but I decided if Tom was embarrassed by his empty refrigerator, he would be mortified if I started vibrating in his chair. Too bad. I made myself a promise to try it before I left.

I did tilt the chair back a little and looked up at the raised plaster designs on the ceiling. They were so beautifully made, so intricate, that I tilted the chair a little more to get a better look. I lay there, alternately picturing the workers who had the skill to make something like this, and thinking how increasingly rare such handmade details were. My thoughts drifted to Tom. His voice was still rising and falling from across the room, probably ordering our food. I had thought I would be more nervous, here in his house, and now in his big, comfy chair, but I was feeling relaxed. More and more relaxed. And then I must have fallen asleep.

* * * *

I dragged my eyes open and was somewhat surprised to see that the sun was going down. Long blue shadows had replaced the silver on the lake. I struggled to sit up and I dislodged the blanket that Tom must have placed over me. Now I was the one who was embarrassed. Some guest I was, passing out in a chair before I'd been in his apartment for half an hour. And I was a little irked that Tom had been right about my needing a nap.

I wrestled the cloud chair into a more upright position and pushed my hair out of my eyes. I spotted Tom sitting across the room at the dining room table he now clearly used as a huge desk. The elegant mahogany table, what I could see of it, was piled high with paper, manila folders, a portable computer, and a printer. A desk lamp diffused yellow light on to the keyboard of the computer and Tom's arms. His face was in shadow as he gazed intently at the screen.

As I pushed the blanket onto the arm of the chair, Tom looked up.

"Hi," I said, more softly than I'd intended.

"Hi yourself. Feeling better?"

"Yes, and I'm starving. Did you actually get me my sandwich?"

"In the refrigerator. With your pickle and your drink."

I moved to get up and Tom crossed the room to extend a hand to help. But then he pushed my hair back from my shoulders and stroked down my back. I felt the tingling all the way down to my sneaker-covered toes. Then he stepped away and turned on a light by the far wall. He turned back to me.

"So, do you really want to eat your dried out ham, or shall we go out and get dinner some place?"

He continued around the room, lighting the lamps scattered at random through the furniture maze.

Now was the time to lay the opera tickets on him. If we got there early enough, we could have some fairly decent small plates type of food. I tensed. But suppose he hates the opera? Relationships have floundered on much less.

"How'd you like to go to the opera? I have tickets for tonight. They have food there."

I fished in my jean's pocket and held up the two tickets triumphantly.

"*Tosca*," I said, I hoped enticingly.

"That's not one of those interminable German ones, is it?" Tom asked, frowning at me.

Uh oh. Not a fan.

"No, no. It's by Puccini. Italian."

"How will we know what they're saying?"

Really not a fan.

"They project the English electronically right above the stage. You can read it perfectly clearly. But it's the music that carries you away. Maybe you'll like it."

Tom is no fool. He could hear the tentativeness creep into my voice.

"As long as it's not four hours long. I have to operate early tomorrow."

"No. I swear. Two and a half hours. Tops."

Well, I shouldn't lie.

"Plus intermission."

He looked at me and nodded.

"Let me show you your room so you can change."

As I followed him down the hallway, I thought that there are worse things than not loving the opera. And nobody's perfect. And I detest Wagner.

* * * *

The Lyric Opera House is everything an opera house should be. It has sparkling golden chandeliers, huge banners with spangles and floating streamers, and a crowd of over-dressed operagoers. In my Armani sheath, I fit right in. I'd washed my hair. No mean feat as I'd had to do that one-handed with the other arm stuck outside the shower curtain to keep the bandage dry. I'd left my hair just hanging down my back and the simplicity fit the dress and gave me a single fluid line. I hoped it did. The look in Tom's eyes when I'd come out of the guestroom dressed in this getup had been very appreciative. He'd even not nagged me about going without the sling as we'd consumed our food and wine standing at the tall tables sprinkled around the upper foyer. I'd taken a pain pill when I'd woken from my nap and I was feeling pretty good. I'd also realized with something of a jolt that my breeziness earlier with Tom had been due to the pain medication. Well, no wonder people did drugs. It really made you feel great. At least until you crashed or got addicted, or both.

I particularly love Italian opera. It's so completely over the top. I actually feel like I've gained weight after I've been to something by Puccini. Forget your spaghetti Westerns; the real pasta is in Italian operas.

My seats are great. They're in the first balcony, center. The sound at the Lyric is excellent, but in the center it is especially round and full. Box seats also give you more legroom, which I need and, as we seated ourselves, I saw Tom appreciated as well.

Tom stayed awake for almost the whole first act. Then he dozed off until intermission. I went and got him an espresso and he drank it while he went out in the hall to answer a page. But neither the caffeine nor the call about a patient kept him awake for long. By the third act, he was deeply asleep, snoring softly, his head on his chest. Well, I was glad he was getting the rest.

I turned my attention completely to the opera. It was the most dramatic moment, when Baron Scarpia advances on Floria Tosca. He has had her lover, Mario, tortured to extract information from her and to pressure her to submit to him. Now he has sent Mario to be hanged.

Tosca cuts a deal with Scarpia. Save Mario from the gallows and only pretend to shoot him. With a safe conduct from Scarpia, Tosca and Mario can then flee the country. If Scarpia will save Mario and give them the safe conduct, Tosca says she will submit to him. Scarpia has savored the idea of forcing Tosca to submit, loving abusing his power over her more than even if she had given herself to him willingly. It is a "richer savor" his corrupt heart contends, to conquer a woman by violence, than to get a "soft consent."

Scarpia pretends to save Mario and then he writes out the safe conduct. He turns and grabs Tosca, bending her down on his desk. She struggles and kicks at him, and then, freeing herself slightly, grabs the letter opener from the desk and stabs and kills him. She looks down contemptuously at the dead man, ridiculing those who love to abuse power.

"And before him all Rome trembled."

I'd always want the diva that plays Tosca to spit when she said that. But perhaps divas don't spit on stage.

And abruptly the stage changed from the velvet and gilt of Rome in 1800 to Chicago in the twenty-first century. And I knew, as surely as I was actually seeing the events of last Monday night played out on the sage, who had killed Ah-seong Kim and why. Sex harassers around the world and through time are all the same. It's all about power and control. The main motive isn't the sex, it's making a woman submit to you when she doesn't want to. Ah-seong had been killed because she'd been seduced, and then, when she had tried to put an end to that mockery of a relationship, she'd been grabbed and forced. That time, she had decided to fight back. Unlike Tosca, she hadn't managed to kill her attacker; she'd been killed instead. But she had fought. Her little broken shoes were testimony to that. She'd kicked and kicked, probably trying some self-defense move she'd learned. And her

Baron Scarpia had subdued her, drugged her and placed her limp, but still breathing body under the cool, indifferent water where her lungs had fought for air and her flaccid limbs had refused to obey her passionate desire to get to the surface, to breathe, to live. Now I knew who it was, I knew how it had been done and I knew why.

But how was I going to prove it?

After Tosca plunged to her death, I woke Tom and we went back to his apartment.

16

In the surging swell,
in the ringing sound,
in the vast wave
of the world's breath –
to drown,
to sink
unconscious –
supreme bliss!

RICHARD WAGNER, *TRISTAN UND ISOLDE*

Tom and I spent Sunday walking along the lakefront. I looked out over the vast expanse of water, thinking of Ah-seong Kim, seeing her sinking, struggling to breathe, drowning, and, then, frankly, thinking of the stupidity of Wagner. Tom was right to reject Wagner. Not only were Wagner's operas too long, they were also idiotic. Isolde really should have known the difference between love and death, as a feminist poet once said. In fact, Isolde might have thought dying for love was idiotic, if she'd actually ever existed, but Wagner clearly did not know that love and death were not the same. Ah-seong Kim did, of that I was now certain.

We didn't talk much. I don't know where Tom's mind was. I was recreating the events of the last week in my own mind, searching for evidence of the pattern of violence and deception and abuse of power that I now was sure was there. Once you can clearly see the pattern, the case is solved. The only problem is getting hard evidence, the kind of evidence that will stand up in court. I needed physical clues like bloodstains, or murder weapons with fingerprints on them, or eyewitnesses, and I had none of those. What

I had was pattern. And with pattern comes the possibility of prediction. I stopped walking, struck with an idea. Tom glanced back at me, but I stood rooted. Not just predicting new violence. I suspected that this murderer had killed before. It was too pat. There had been practice. Practice before. I started walking again. Perhaps I could find that trail. And then I would know even better how to predict his next move. Though predicting what violent people will do is an extremely inexact science. And it is dangerous.

When we returned to Tom's apartment after dinner at a local Thai place, I had made up my mind. Tom dragged a sofa over to the middle of the room from his collection of furniture so we could both sit in front of the entertainment system. Watching him shove the recliner over to make room for the sofa, I'd briefly let my imagination wander over the possibilities of that lovely, soft chair. But dwelling on those possible delights was all I planned to do this evening. I had other plans for the good doctor.

Tom picked up the pad device from the shelf below the television and we sat down on the sofa. He tapped into the cable channel list with a very practiced movement, skimming down the list of shows. All I saw was a blur. I don't like scanning the cable channels even with our much more primitive television remote. I had it programmed for "child safe," though heaven knows how long that would last before the boys figured out how to bypass the parental safety codes. They could get to their children's programming and they could recognize their favorite shows all too well on the screen. Pokémon was the current favorite. If I never saw that weird yellow rabbit-looking thing again, I'd be very happy. I had flatly refused to download the app on my cell phone so we could go capture Pokémon in virtual reality. I was already sick of the students walking around the campus looking at their phones on the trail of these creatures. I suspected Giles might cave soon and let them play with him.

Tom was still skimming through his list of cable channels. It seemed to be relaxing for him. Good. I needed him to be relaxed.

"Tom?" No response. "Tom?"

He glanced up at me, as from a great distance.

"Tom, before we watch something I have some questions for you."

Well that got him to focus. His eyes lost that slightly dazed look and narrowed with what I took to be anxiety. The terrifying word "question" from a woman could cover all sorts of relational minefields. I could see some of the possible meanings flash across his face.

"Ah, certainly, Kristin. What about?"

"I'd like to describe for you specifically how Ah-seong Kim died, what the autopsy report said, and then what I'm thinking about her murder."

If I'd thrown a bucket of ice water over him, Tom could not have looked more surprised, and then, in a moment, furiously angry. His blue eyes became dark behind his glasses as he registered my request and what it meant.

"Are you completely insane?"

The tablet slipped from his hands to the floor and he seemed not to notice.

"You're going to keep pursuing this? After all that's happened to you? Where's your sense of proportion?"

Tom stood and faced away from me. He must be really upset to not even notice he was about to step on his expensive device.

I leaned over and picked it up. I stayed quiet, letting him vent.

He swung back toward me, body rigid, arms folded across his chest.

"What do you want from me? Back up at the next murder attempt on you? Or do I just get to patch you up again after you get torn apart by this maniac?"

He deliberately turned away from me again and sat on the edge of the leather chair. He took a breath and then turned to face me. His normally warm eyes were still narrowed in anger, and, I realized, in fear. He cared enough about me to be frightened for me. Well, that was an intelligent response. I was frightened for me too.

But if we were going to continue this relationship, he had to understand that running away from problems was what I now feared most, feared more than I feared Ah-seong's murderer. Well, almost more. I just wouldn't, I couldn't, let myself slip back into that mind-numbing cocoon from which I was only now escaping.

All cops have to come to terms with how they'll handle violence. There was now mandatory psychological counseling for anyone who'd discharged their weapon in the line of duty if they'd hit or killed someone. Though given the current reactionary political climate, I wondered for a second if that would just be cancelled as 'too soft' or some such right-wing excuse for police violence. Anyway, the psychological cost would remain high, no matter what the politics.

Some cops dealt with it and went on, but a lot self-medicated with fattening food, alcohol and sometimes even drugs. After a violent episode, some cops were never really the same. Sometimes they quit the force like I did, some retired in place, phoning in their work and putting in the time to real retirement.

Having your husband shot and killed in the line of duty was a double whammy given the way it had gone down. Marco's death and my suspicions of what had really happened had undermined my ability to trust the police and threatened my sense of family, of the security of home that made it possible to go out into the streets of Chicago every day.

But I was getting it back. I could feel it. I was scared, but I wanted to get this murdering jerk, I wanted it for Ah-seong, but also, if truth be told, for myself. I wanted that sense of completion, of justice served. I do think there is a moral universe, as bent and broken as it may be. When you get the right perp, the rusty scales of justice creak just a little, right themselves and balance returns to the world.

My whole sense of self and of the possibility of justice was riding on nailing Ah-seong's murderer and I had to make Tom see that. And I had to make him see that the self that wanted that righting of wrong was me, really me. I'm not really the objectifying philosopher. I thought I could be, but I really am a down and dirty scrapper in the down and dirty twenty-first century.

So I leaned forward on the couch and looked directly into Tom's eyes. I told him, with as much passion and conviction as I could muster. I told him how I'd wanted to be a cop, what Marco's killing had done to me and how I'd grabbed my babies and crawled away to lick my wounds. I let myself touch the cold, numbing denial I'd used to keep on living, and I think he could see in my eyes the price I had paid for that refuge. And I let him hear my conviction that I could do this. I could get this done. I tried to let him really see me.

"No, I don't want backup from you Tom and I certainly don't want to use you as my concierge doctor. What I want, what I need from you is trust. Trust that I know what I'm doing and that everything that is really me can't walk away from what I think I know. Trust me enough to help me do this."

I waited. I'd given a pretty long speech.

Tom shifted back in his recliner, but he didn't speak. He sat still, looking at me. I was not breathing normally. It's truly terrible to let another person in, to let them see who you are. I was beginning to bitterly regret my outburst. I should just get my things and move to a hotel.

Just as I started to move to get up and do just that, Tom spoke.

"You know that cliché, be careful what you wish for, you just might get it? I swear to God I must have wished you up one night when I was alone and I couldn't stand the inch-deep relationships I was having. But if I don't have a cardiac episode from what you put me through, I think you can be my reason for living."

Tom leaned forward and opened his arms to me.

What do you know? We did end up together in that recliner of his.

* * * *

Some time later I moved back to the sofa. Alone. I tried to get back to my investigative self, but it was damned hard. I looked suspiciously over at Tom. If he was trying to deflect me, more subtly this time, he was doing a damned good job of it. I felt about as sharp as that marshmallow fluff stuff the kids liked so much on their peanut butter sandwiches. But Tom didn't look particularly devious. He looked like a large cat with twinkly blue eyes that'd just had an enormous dish of salmon.

I sat up straighter on the couch, pushed my hair back, buttoned and zipped up various parts of my clothes that were, shall we say, disheveled, and tried to get back on track.

"So, Tom," I began. "Here's what I think."

The relaxed look left his face.

"Wait a second, Kristin."

He angled the chair back up, reached around in its many leathered folds and came up with his glasses. He put them on and I had to stifle a smile. I hoped he had another pair, because these glasses were bent out of shape on one side. Tom realized it too, probably since the world would have looked a little tilted. He took them off, bent the temple piece back into shape, and put them back on. And then he sighed.

"Okay. I'm listening."

"Anyway, I think the murderer, and I'm sure it's a murder after the last attack on me, got a dose of muscle relaxant into Ah-seong and slipped her limp, but still breathing body, into the pond. She inhaled large amounts of debris, that's in the autopsy report, but her muscles were so flaccid she couldn't get herself to the surface let alone out of the pond. That's why she drowned."

Tom's eyes narrowed.

"But Kristin, muscle relaxants have to be administered very carefully or the patient stops breathing and then she wouldn't have breathed in debris. Plus, they have to be administered by injection. You couldn't just put it in somebody's coke. And they act very quickly. A matter of minutes."

No, everything pointed to some kind of drug-induced stupor. I knew how I'd felt when I'd awakened in the hospital to find I couldn't get my muscles to obey me. If I'd been in water, I would have drowned.

"Tom, it had to be some drug. Let me think. Suppose the murderer gives her a tranquilizer first—could something like that be put in a drink?"

"Sure, you could put Midazolam into juice or cocoa, or something with a strong enough taste to hide it, and that could work. Of course, mixing tranquilizers with muscle relaxants is itself dangerous."

"Come on. This is a murder. I doubt this guy cares about drug interactions. Unless that would have killed her on the spot. Would it?"

"Well, it depends on the dosages. With the tranquilizer itself you'd need a fair amount to make someone more than just woozy. How much did this student weigh do you think?"

"She was very short. No more than four feet, ten or eleven inches I'd say. And perhaps around ninety-eight pounds. Certainly no more than that."

"And you said she was Asian?"

"That's right. Korean."

"Asians on the whole are far more sensitive to all kinds of drugs than, for example, Anglo-Saxons. You have to be very careful to reduce the dose. There are even specific dosage tables for Asians. With a ninety-eight pound Asian woman you could get away with an oral tranquilizer in a drink. But then what?"

"Well, how long would the tranquilizer last?"

"No more than two hours to be safe."

Of course, that had been anything but "safe" for Ah-seong.

"But then when she's tranquilized, the murderer could inject her and she'd not struggle, right?" I drew my knees up under my chin and concentrated.

"Right. But cessation of breathing is a real risk." Tom leaned forward in his chair now, getting into it.

"But look, you gave me some kind of muscle relaxant and I wasn't in an iron lung. How come?"

We were near an answer, I could feel it.

"Well, it's monitoring the dosage carefully. And you could still move some, though it didn't feel like it to you I'm sure, but that was partially the beating your muscles had taken from cramping."

I got up and got a piece of paper and a pen out of my purse. I started writing up the times as best I knew them and thinking about the sequence and the administration of the drugs. If Ah-seong had been drugged at around 9:30 Monday evening, the perp could have left her groggy, maybe locked up someplace quiet, and come over to polish me off at around 10:00. Even having failed, and being (I hoped) injured in our struggle, he could get back before she was really with it again. Since the murderer was not exactly worried about the risks of drug addiction, a second dose of tranquilizer would be no problem. That could even have been an injection too. I frowned. These shots might have been seen on autopsy, but the murderer had not only access to drugs but seemingly expertise in administering them. The injections could have been between her toes or even under her fingernails, like addicts do to try to avoid those telltale tracks on their arms.

I went back to my calculations. So, tranquilizing Ah-seong again could have brought the time up to when the gates of the college would be locked, but before the bubbler would turn on. But how to get her into that pond breathing and then just obligingly stay there? There had to be some other drug like the muscle relaxant I'd had.

I turned back to Tom.

"Look. Clearly there are drugs that relax the muscles enough for drowning, but not stop breathing, even with some tranquilizers in her system. Think, Tom. I know you're used to saving lives, not taking them, but think like a murderer."

Tom frowned at me, but got up and went over to his computer. He sat down at the table and logged on. I waited a minute until he was scrolling and muttering before I went over and sat down next to him.

"What about Succinylcholine?"

"What about it?" What did he think, I routinely browsed drug websites?

"Well, it could work. Somebody who knew what they were doing and knew the dosages could carry a small woman to the pond, inject the drug directly into an inconspicuous place on the body and wait. A dose large enough to really impair the muscles from moving would cause her breathing to stop initially, but then it comes back one hundred percent in about a minute. That's not enough time to cause brain death. You can hold your breath for a minute, right?"

He looked over at me to see if I were following his reasoning.

I nodded, tense with the sense that we were getting closer.

"Then, if he'd slipped her under the water, she would have gone on breathing and inhaling water but not able to effectively move to get to the surface. She would certainly have drowned."

Tom bent over the screen again, scrolling and reading and making hmmm noises. Do they teach that noise in medical school?

"Here's something fascinating. Succinylcholine is metabolized almost immediately."

He looked up at me, pleased with his budding detective skills.

"What does that mean?"

"It means it would be undetectable on autopsy."

Oh, great. Another dead end in terms of getting hard evidence. The murderer was smart, I'd give him that.

I pulled my chair closer to the screen and Tom turned the computer so I could read it for myself. I read the first columns explaining Succinylcholine and how it worked, but didn't read up on side effects or long-term risks. That hadn't been Ah-seong's problem.

I sat back. It could have worked like that. And it sure confirmed my view of who murdered Ah-seong. But it got me no further toward actually proving it.

Unless the murderer was caught in the act of trying to kill again, we weren't going to be able to prove anything.

17

The Faust Idea. A little seamstress is seduced and plunged into despair: a great scholar of all the four Faculties is the evil doer. Surely that could not have happened without supernatural interference? No, of course not! Without the aid of the devil incarnate, the great scholar would never have achieved the deed.

FRIEDRICH NIETZSCHE, THE *WANDERER AND HIS SHADOW*

Early Monday morning found me breaking in to Frost's office. I was there by 6. I had begun to suspect that all the locks on our floor opened with the same key. I was about to test that theory.

I used my office key for Frost's door and it opened without a hitch. The building had obviously been designed in a more trusting era, a time now most Americans remember only dimly, if at all. Was there really a time when people didn't lock their doors? Depends on where the door was located, I guessed. In the Jim Crow south I imagined African Americans locked up their houses quite tightly. Of course, that rosy, distorted past in the minds of a segment of society is a product of desire. The privileged especially want to clean up the sins of history.

As I closed and locked the door behind me, I reflected that was probably the origin of the idea of a Garden of Eden. People do want to remember there was a perfect time and then blame somebody (often Eve) for screwing it up.

Well, this Eve didn't buy it.

I headed straight for the copy machine that was located in this office at the far wall, and I took out my cell phone. I had downloaded the instructions on how to change the time and date codes for our particular model of copy machine. I looked at my small screen. It said, 'First enter passcode.' I'd seen that when I'd first downloaded the instructions and I had a good idea what the password might be. If I guessed wrong, my little plan would be stopped in its tracks. I held my breath and typed in what I guessed was the password Frost used. The red went to green on the display and I was in.

The control panel of the copier was backlit and that was a plus since I dared not turn on any lights. I followed the instructions on my phone and the day and time stamps changed obediently.

Rats. The display also showed the machine was low on paper. I crossed to Frost's special supply closet, the one she guarded like Cerberus at the gates of hell, and snatched some more paper. I loaded it up in what I hoped was the right drawer, and the blinking of the 'low on paper' light went off. I took one additional blank piece of paper, put it under the lid, and typed in the number of copies I needed on the control panel. Then I pressed "Start" on the display and the machine obediently started to spit out 146 blank copies.

I watched the counter move silently forward, recording the copying of a book that wasn't there. It didn't matter. What I was aiming to do was to make my dear colleagues in the department believe a book had been copied on Friday during Frost's lunch hour. Because that is what the machine would store in its memory because I had, with the help of Google, effectively hacked it.

The rhythm of the machine was hypnotic, but I was too wired to let it soothe me. I was going to come back this morning and lie my head off. I would tell everyone I could find that on Friday I had made a copy of Ahseong Kim's book with all the underlinings and her notations. And that copy was still alive and well, carefully hidden in my office, still available for translation.

Well, spreading a whopper of a lie like that would brand me forever as a post-Kantian. Too bad. Kant and the other philosophers I'd liked so much were really wearing on me these days. I was edging closer and closer to the idea that truth and falsehood were much more intimately connected than those privileged dead white males had ever thought.

The humming continued. This was not one of the newer models of copier and it was taking a while. I looked nervously out the window and saw that the dawn had arrived. Then the light from the window fell on the picture that hung with full honors on the wall above Frost's desk. It was a ghastly painting of Elvis Presley on black velvet. Frost actually believed Elvis was still alive. This was by way of a shrine, and why I had guessed correctly that her password was "Elvis."

Henry and I had perpetrated a nasty but much deserved trick on old Frost at last year's holiday party. Of course, I mused, with the backlash the whole country was experiencing against "political correctness," it would probably go back to being a Christmas party this year.

What Henry and I had done was run narrow plastic tubing up the wall behind Frost's desk and we'd taped it to the back of Elvis's deep, dark eyes in the picture, making small slits in the pupils. The tubes were attached to a gallon of water hidden in the wastebasket in the corner. We had plugged a small pump into the outlet behind the desk. The party had been in full swing when Henry had sneaked over and turned on the pump. Our plan was then to exclaim at the miracle of a weeping Elvis. Unfortunately, we'd set the pump on too high a setting, and instead of weeping, Elvis had shot water out of his eyes across the room, hitting both Frost and Willie. Henry and I had been forced to confess after we'd rushed over to shut off the pump. Frost had been furious, and anything that upset Frost upset Grimes. We'd had to apologize abjectly and pay for the repairs to Elvis. But honestly, it had been worth it.

A beep from the machine startled me. I had my fake manuscript. I burgled a manila envelope from Frost's storehouse and then reversed my hacking of the copy machine. The display obediently changed to today's date, and I consulted my phone to get the exact right time.

I surveyed the room, trying to see if I'd disturbed anything that would give me away. I didn't see anything out of place, though Elvis gave me a sultry look. His eyes had never really gotten back to the right size since we'd had the picture fixed, but the bigger eyes worked for him.

Then I thought of the wrapper that had covered the extra paper I'd added to the machine. I grabbed it out of the wastebasket and stuck it in my waistband, under my coat. It wouldn't do to leave that around for Frost to find. Even the university cleaning services that came in the evening wouldn't leave such a big piece of trash behind. They'd leave the dirt and the grime, but they usually took the obvious trash.

I glanced back at the room from the door. Everything looked as it had when I'd entered. I hadn't turned on the lights, so all I had to do was lock the door behind me.

So I did.

* * * *

My next stop was the main library. In addition to the extraordinarily ugly architecture of this huge building, it occupied some of the most peculiar turf in the world. Not just space. The actual turf. This library had been built on the site of the old football stadium, where the famous "Monsters of the Midway" had been the terrors of college football until the president of the university had cut football down to size. But the old stadium had also been the location of the Manhattan Project, the frighteningly successful physics project that had been conducted secretly underneath the stadium during World War II. It had resulted in the production of the atomic bomb.

After the war, the university had dug up some of the dirt that had been the football field (and I'd always wondered if that was also to dig up any left over radiation) and trucked it a few blocks to cover a new field and eventually a new stadium.

But I didn't want to be seen exiting Myerson as the sun came up, and because of the Manhattan Project, I didn't have to. I went down the stairs to the basement and sought the door to the tunnel that connected us to the library basement. I could cross under the quad and get to the library basement without being seen. There was a whole network of tunnels that had been dug during the war research and they still existed. Oddly enough, most of them had not been closed off. The knowledgeable used them to walk under the main campus during the winter, cleverly avoiding the frozen surface above.

I trembled with anxiety as I started down the tunnel that led to the library. I would come out in an enclosed staircase below the library entrance. I knew my anxiety was due to the fact that behind a locked door where the tunnel met the library basement was the new student lounge and the rare book room beyond. I reached that spot and scrambled up the stairs as fast as my watery knees would let me to reach the main library entrance one flight up. I didn't like that rare book room, even behind a locked door.

Though it was only a little after 7, the library was open. The really wonderful thing about this institution is the pervasive assumption that there is never a time when people do not want and need to do academic research. With a small staff, the main library remains open until 2 in the morning and then reopens a scant four hours later. Since the time between midnight and dawn was often the only times I had free, I had had many occasions to silently praise those who thought a library existed for use. I thought so now.

I scanned my I.D. and went to the reading room tables and their ranks of computers. I wanted to do a computer search, but I didn't want to do it on my own office computer, nor did I feel comfortable borrowing Tom's. I'd left my own portable computer at my house. Yes, I'd picked up an Armani dress at home, and then forgotten to bring my own computer. Some academic I was.

I spent some time doing Internet searches for biographical material on several of my dear colleagues, but there was one in particular I was after and

I soon cut him out of the herd for deeper research. I cross-referenced previous places of residence with what local newspaper stories I could find from that same period. Not all local papers, of course, had back issues searchable online. I did a professional training search and found what I was sure would be there. Then I tried to get into a database for pharmaceutical licensing, but it was password protected and I doubted the password was "Elvis."

I searched for old issues of the university newspaper, and found to my astonishment that they were also not all uploaded. At least not as far back as I needed. I would have to go to the microfiche area if I wanted to look at those. Libraries can't store piles of newspapers, so they get photocopied and put on flat pieces of film. A whole Sunday *New York Times* can fit on a small space on a card.

The microfiche area was also in the basement. It made me really nervous to go back down the same stairs I'd used to go to the rare book room. Fortunately, the microfiche area was at the other side of the basement and I quickly scuttled over there. I located the cards for the years I needed in the old campus newspaper and set myself up at a contraption that let you read the teeny, tiny print on the film. It's kind of a metal scuba mask attached to a machine. The machine magnifies what's on the card and you view it through the mask.

It took some time, but I eventually found what I wanted. Actually, I found more than I had been looking for. I found that our murderer had murdered before, and I thought I had enough to show how he how he had acquired the expertise and the drugs needed for the earlier deaths to have been ruled accidental. I took copious notes and returned the microfiches to their files.

It was time to go see Alice Matthews. I dug out my cell phone and called her as I walked out of the library.

* * * *

By the time I reached the campus police station, it was noon and Matthews was waiting for me. She sat in her broken-down chair, leaning it precariously against the stained brown wall behind her. I sat down in front of her desk and started to pile conjecture upon conjecture.

She held up a hand to stop me and pulled open her drawer where she kept her cigarette stash. She lit up, but didn't bother to open the window to blow the smoke outside. She just inhaled, sighed and leaned back against the wall. But her warm brown eyes had turned a flat, dark bronze.

She waved a hand for me to continue.

I finished up my summary of what I suspected and then what I had found out online and in the old university newspapers. Alice glared, but it was past my shoulder. It wasn't me she was seeing now, it was a young woman student and her last weeks of life.

As I proposed the plan I had concocted for drawing the murderer out into the open, Matthews brought her chair back to the floor with a bang. She leaned forward over the desk toward me, her already snug uniform tightening across her chest.

As I wound down to my conclusion, she took a deep drag on her half-smoked cigarette, crushed it out in the metal box that contained the sand, slammed it closed and shoved it back into the drawer. She leaned even farther forward and her face was tight with anger.

"Man, you don't want too much do you? All you want is to fool this asshole into coming after you a second time, no, wait, a *third* time, to get a copy of the book, a copy which doesn't even exist, I take it, and you want me and some of my good friends here at the campus cop store to just happen by while you're getting murdered and arrest the guy before he finishes you off? Have I left anything out?"

"Nope. I think that about covers it. Except planning the timing and so forth."

Alice actually stood up. Now she was vibrating with rage.

"Planning? Oh, so you think this caper needs some planning? Oh, I'm so glad to hear you say that. I thought for a minute you were going off all half-cocked and no, no, here you are, doing some planning."

Alice banged her hand on the desk.

"What do you take me for, girl? An idiot?"

Alice had plainly not forgiven me for that episode with Kaiser and Edwin Porterman, though it still escaped me what exactly had pissed her off about that. Or did it? I had used her. Well, it had gotten the job done. I was prepared to do what it took to get the job done. Again. I slowly and deliberately looked over at the picture of her daughter. I waited until I was sure I knew she was registering what I was looking at.

"So, what's the alternative, Alice? You know damn well that repeat killers don't stop. Whose daughter will it be next? Some parents in Iowa who think a university in big, bad Chicago might be dangerous, but their daughter convinces them she'll stay on campus and not venture into the dangerous city? She'd be a perfect target. Or what about the minority scholarship student from our very own south side here? Will she be on her guard or will these ivy covered stone walls delude her into thinking this is a safe place? She could make the same mistake Ah-seong made. She might realize she was in danger and then turn to the wrong person for help, for counsel.

Maybe it will be a few years, Alice. It's been seven years since the last one, at least that I've been able to find out. Not much longer than that in the future and it could be your daughter. Does she want to go to college here, Alice?"

Alice had been looking at her daughter's photo while I spoke, but she turned to me and stomped around the desk, stopped in front of me, shaking with rage.

"You shut up. You just shut up. You think you're so smart, so cute with your educated accent and your cop language, but you don't know shit about anything and you sure don't know shit about being a cop."

And tears formed in the corner of her blazing eyes.

"You don't know shit."

Softer. Lower now. She turned and walked over to the dirty window of her office. She looked out at the students walking by and she swore creatively and at some length.

I was impressed. She might look like a kindergarten teacher but she swore like a seasoned cop. Vince couldn't have done better. But when she turned around, her eyes were still glistening.

I teared up too. Yeah, I was a shitty person sometimes. But I did know about being a cop. I couldn't seem to stop knowing.

I didn't wipe the tears from my eyes and neither did she. We just stayed where we were. Silent and with a gulf between us.

Finally she spoke.

"All right, Ginelli. But don't you give me that 'I'll plan' crap. I'll plan and you listen. And if you don't do everything I say the way I say it, when I say it, I swear to God if the perp doesn't get you, I'll kill you myself. You got that?"

"Yes ma'am," I said. I got it.

Alice went back around her desk and called up a map of the campus on her computer, turned the screen so I could see it too, and we got down to work. After about half an hour, she picked up the phone and called Mel Billman, her partner the night I had been mugged in the alley. Make that attacked with intent to kill.

Billman was quick about it. He came through the door in a matter of minutes. He was shorter than I remembered, but then I'd been sitting on the ground in the dark when I'd first gotten a glimpse of him. In the grimy light from Alice's office window, I could see he had straight dark hair, skin the color of copper and from the neck down he could be a contestant in a bodybuilding contest. Well good. This guy we were going after was dangerous. Mel nodded to Alice and then gave me the same glare she'd been giving me for the last hour.

I thought it would be wise to keep my mouth shut.

Alice filled Mel in while I listened. When he pulled up a chair so he could see the campus map on the screen, I knew we had him.

* * * *

I left Alice's office at about 3 in the afternoon and went to spread my lies around the campus.

I headed back to Myerson first and trudged up to our departmental floor. I pasted a smile on my face and opened the door to Frost's office. She was bent over her computer keyboard, her grey head swiveling rapidly from a handwritten document on her left to the screen.

"Ms. Frost," I said.

I kept the smile firmly in place as she turned to look at me, her papery skin even more slack than I remembered and her mouth pinched in a line. She just sat looking at me for a moment and I wondered for a second if she were ill. Then, with a shot of guilt, I wondered whether she'd figured out my dawn intrusion. But then she just nodded fractionally.

"I came by because I remembered I hadn't filled out the form in the copy log on Friday. I made a copy of a book while you were out at noon and I forgot to enter it in the written log."

Frost looked at me with more interest, her passion for written forms apparently distracting her from how I had gotten in to her office while she had been at lunch. I breathed a little more easily while she retrieved the notebook with the copy log forms from her desk. She silently handed it to me.

I wrote diligently in the lines provided, putting in Friday's date and my chosen time of 12:10, the ones I had electronically logged this morning, and then I put 146 pages and signed my name. I didn't know if anyone would actually check the digital log, but now I was covered both ways.

I handed the notebook back to her.

I continued in a conversational voice, though it was clearly going to be a one-sided conversation.

"I was in no shape to remember to do that after I was attacked in the book stacks Friday."

Then I lowered my voice conspiratorially and gave a chortle that sounded incredibly false to my ears.

"Whoever attacked me thought they were so smart."

God, I could never be an actress. But then Frost leaned forward, the better to hear what secret I had to share. Luckily Frost had virtually no human insight.

"Did you hear my office was burglarized and a book belonging to that dead student was taken?"

Frost nodded, seeming mesmerized.

"Well," I patted the fake copy in the manila envelope I had placed conspicuously under my arm, "I made a copy and I'm going to hide it really well in my office. Tonight when everybody's gone I'm going to work on translating the notes. I brought a Korean dictionary."

On top of the envelope containing the blank pages I had placed a Korean dictionary that I'd purchased not thirty minutes before.

This routine would not have fooled my kids, but Frost seemed to be buying it. I looked at her pinched and narrow face turned upward toward me with breathless anticipation. Her skinny nostrils were positively pulsating with the scent of gossip. Maybe it would work. I looked over at Elvis, but he was noncommittal.

I wiggled the fingers of my bad arm that were sticking out of the bandage and smiled a crocodile smile.

"Bye."

"Good-bye."

Good gad. Frost had said good-bye to me.

Excellent. In a very few minutes the news that I had made a copy of the mysterious book before it had been stolen would be all over the department. All over the university, actually.

As I opened the door to leave, I heard Frost lift the receiver of her phone.

* * * *

I walked down the hall to the faculty watering hole and pushed open the door. Donald and Adelaide were seated at opposite ends of the long table, each with a cup of coffee. I got myself a cup and pointedly ignored Donald and walked over to join Adelaide. I sat down and she paused in reading what looked like a student paper and asked me how I was doing. While I told her I was fine, I mentally prepared the lies I was going to tell her. I hated to do it to her, because of all my erstwhile colleagues, Adelaide was the one with whom I probably could have a friendship.

Well. Too bad. I opened my mouth and lied like a rug.

Out of the corner of my eye, I saw that Donald didn't raise his head while I was talking about copying the book, preparing to hide it, and then my planning to translate it tonight. I even patted the dictionary that I had placed on top of the envelope on the table and I could tell from the fact that his hand had stilled over the column of figures on the paper in front of him that he was listening.

Apart from getting a sign reading "Sitting Duck" and wearing it around my neck, I could do no more. I finished my coffee and went to wash my cup in the restroom across the hall. I prudently took the manila envelope with me. I didn't want any peaking while I was gone. I rinsed the cup and wondered if I'd laid it on too thick. When I put the cup back, I'd get another look at them, I thought.

I opened the door to the lounge, but in the minute it had taken me to clean my cup, both Adelaide and Donald had vanished.

* * * *

I went to my office to pretend to find a good hiding place for the ersatz book. But all I really needed to do was plant one more seed.

I got out my cell phone and called Myung Ha Kim.

18

The 'inner labyrinth', as Foucault imagines . . . suggests that behind the 'deceptive surfaces' of modern society lurks a human 'nature metamorphosized in depth by the powers of a counter-nature'. . . . 'A cage', the labyrinth 'makes of man a beast of desire'; 'a tomb', it 'weaves beneath states a counter-city'; a diabolically clever invention, it is designed to unleash 'all the volcanoes of madness'—threatening to 'destroy the oldest laws and pacts'.

JAMES MILLER, *THE PASSION OF MICHEL FOUCAULT*

As the sun was setting, I decided I was finished spreading my lies throughout the campus and I headed home to change. Home to the Rosemont house. I opened the door cautiously and turned off the alarm. As I walked through the front hall to go upstairs, I smelled dust. The house had that curious hollowness a dwelling emptied of people can get so quickly. A matter of days ago this space smelled of kids and dog and too much garlic. Now it was as impersonal as a vacant office.

I tried to shake off the abandoned feeling and hurried to don running shoes and loose fitting clothes I hoped would serve if it came to a physical struggle. Then I clambered up the sagging attic stairs and dug around in some boxes until I came up with my old body armor. I'd tossed all that reminded me of being a cop up here, except my gun. That I had turned in on the day I quit. Attics are like the unconscious of a house. Stuff you don't want to think about gets shoved into boxes and stored away, but it's never gone, never completely forgotten. God, I was in a weird mood. Shake it off, I told myself sternly. Just shake it off.

I took off my sweatshirt and shrugged into the vest and fastened the Velcro straps. This was a good one, a full tactical that should protect me even from a bullet. Our murderer hadn't shown any signs of liking firearms, but his attraction to knives and needles was enough for me. I wished briefly I still had my gun, though realistically I would never have kept it, even unloaded and locked, in a house with two curious boys. I put my sweatshirt back on and zipped it up. A little tight, but I could move.

As I walked back down the attic steps, the remembered feel of the body armor, instead of calming me down, wired me even more. As it rubbed against my chest, it brought back the very physical sensations of waiting, trussed up and tense, often in the cold and dark. The rough weave of the inner fabric rubbed against my breasts, literally arousing me for what was to come.

I picked up a wool hat and stowed my cell phone and my keys in my pants pockets. I checked my watch. Getting over here and finding the armor had taken some time. I needed to get going. I alarmed and locked the house.

Our plan, and yes, I had finally been allowed by Alice to contribute my thoughts, was simplicity itself. I was to take myself over to Myerson by 7 p.m. when it was dark and the vast majority of faculty and administrative personnel had left the campus. I would arrive at my office. Billman and Matthews would be already in the basement, having arrived by the tunnel. They would wait there until our prime suspect, someone who wanted to get Ah-seong's book and then kill me, entered. I would hit "send" on my cell phone, pre-dialed for the campus police emergency number. All I had to do was yell my location into the phone. Both Billman and Matthews would be monitoring for incoming calls on the emergency number, and would rush up the stairs. All nice and regular, like they had just happened to be close by. All I had to do was stay alive until they got to my office.

After I left the house, I quickly checked in with Alice Matthews on her cell, telling her I was heading to the campus. I stuck the phone back in my pocket.

I turned left and started walking down the street that led to the middle of campus. When I got closer, I turned right. A few of the remaining day toilers at the university trickled past me, heading home. They were walking quickly as night had fallen, conscious of the risks of city life after it was pitch dark. The grey stone of the main campus buildings in the distance held the night tightly, their shadows compounding the spreading ink. The ice pick winds from the west did not encourage pausing for conversation and in any case I saw no one I knew. By the time I reached the tennis courts at the edge of the quadrangle, the stream had petered out and I was alone on the sidewalk.

I was so intent on reaching my office on time, I was startled when a figure stepped out of the tall bushes that rimmed the courts. The figure grabbed my arm and I felt something poke my back. It was probably something sharp like the needle of a hypodermic, but the body armor kept the point away from me. I winced to feign pain and looked at him.

"Hello, Dr. Grimes, or, perhaps, since you've tried to kill me a few times, I think I'm entitled to call you Harold, don't you?"

Grimes grabbed for my other arm, the injured one, and gave it a painful shake. The arm he'd cut when he had sliced at me in the alley.

I lurched against him and felt his intake of breath.

"How're the ribs, Harold? I hope I broke at least one when I kicked you. You've been taking it easy at the office. Funny. I mistook that for grief at first."

Despite the pain in my arm, I tried to move away from the bushes toward the street and its streetlights, hopefully taking him with me. Stuck here in the shadows of the foliage, we were unlikely to attract attention. But even injured, he was a big guy and I was not dislodging him.

Grimes had not said anything to this point. When he felt me try to pull him, he moved to stand slightly to my left and behind me, holding my left hand with his left. His right hand must have the hypodermic needle in it and he was likely pointing it at my back. Then he spoke in my ear.

"You've been entirely too much trouble, Ginelli. Entirely too much. Now you're going to do as you're told for once, or I'm going to stick this needle in your back and you'll stop breathing in a matter of minutes."

I felt another poke and again I feigned wincing.

I spoke in what I hoped was a confident voice.

"No, no, Harold. That's the tranquilizer you've got in your syringe back there, isn't it? The drug you use to get your victims to lie down so you can pump them full of muscle relaxant. It's tough to manage dosages when somebody is struggling with you, isn't it?"

I turned my head so I could see at least part of his face. He registered surprise and then anger.

"Well, you've certainly improved your guessing lately. Too bad it won't help you all that much. Injected, this tranquilizer works very quickly. Then I'll carry you to the office and we'll finish there."

Confident voice, but the part of his face I could see was sweating. Good. This plan was not his first choice. Well, it wasn't my first choice for a plan either, for Christ's sake. Why couldn't he have waited until I got to Myerson?

"Carry me, Harold? Really? I weigh a whole lot more than Ah-seong Kim and with your broken ribs I don't think you could get me off the ground, let alone carry me."

I jerked away from him and tried to run.

He didn't completely lose his grip on my injured arm and he gave it a vicious tug.

"Maybe I can't carry you, but I can give you some more tranquilizer and you'll be very docile. Otherwise, I can make it is so you never use this arm again."

Another painful jerk.

"Now, we're going to walk together to your office and get this stupid copy you made of Kim's book. Where in heaven's name did you put it? I've already torn your office apart and I can't find it."

He jerked my arm again. I tried to wince convincingly but I was getting the hang of how he was pulling me and I just went with it. The squeezing was bad though. I could feel the stitches pulling out again. Tom was going to be pissed.

"Unless you lied about hiding it there?"

Well, Frost had certainly held up her end in this fiasco, or was it Willie? I thought it best to placate him.

"No, it's there. I hid it under the bottom shelf of one of the bookcases that's loose. On Henry's side, not mine."

I stammered out the lie with what I hoped he'd think was just nervousness. Of course there was no book copy hidden in my office. There was no point to hiding blank pages.

"Haruchi's side, really? Well he didn't seem to know it when I questioned him. Even tranquilized, he wasn't forthcoming about knowing where you'd hidden anything."

Despite the pain in my forearm, I lunged around to face him.

"What do you mean, when you questioned him? What did you do to Henry?"

In the shadows I could still see Grimes's face take on a twisted look of remembered pleasure. I had to keep in mind what a psychotic I was dealing with here. I had to stop thinking of him as the pompous, self-promoting academic leech and focus on the fact that he was a killer.

"When I opened the door to your office earlier, he was sitting there at the computer, working away. I sternly ordered him down to my office to discuss his, shall we say, extracurricular activities?"

He saw my look of surprise.

"Oh, yes. I know about his moonlighting at that place in the suburbs. Very bad of him. And now he has started working part-time for our computer center here. That was lax of them, not to check his contract. Quite the busy boy, your officemate. He was so conscious of his own guilt and I was so reassuring that he was actually grateful when I offered him some tea."

God. Henry. With a toddler and a pregnant wife. I had to get Grimes to the basement of Myerson, or better yet, get free of him and use my cell to call Matthews and Billman. I had no faith in Grimes's ability to judge adequate tranquilizer doses for Asians, despite his having been a pharmacist.

Yes, that's what I'd learned from my computer searches. I'd also read the obituary for Grimes's first wife who'd died years earlier in the small town where he'd been in practice. Accidental drowning. Like so many, academic religion was Grimes's second career. Or really third since he was also a murderer. I was hoping to give him a fourth career, in the penitentiary in Joliet.

I decided to keep him talking and then break away when his concentration lapsed.

"You used tea to give Ah-seong the first dose of tranquilizer too, didn't you?"

Grimes grimaced.

"Yes. Ginseng. Foul tasting beverage, but she'd given me a whole box of it when she started my class. Too polite to refuse when I offered her some. Just like your Henry. Far too polite."

He shook his perfectly coifed head, looking avuncular, like he was mentioning some minor faux pas.

"He's resting quietly, locked in my closet, waiting for us. The idea here is that you will both have a terrible accident with traces of alcohol and drugs in your bloodstreams. An affair with one's office mate, Ms. Ginelli. How tacky of you."

"Not nearly as tacky as murdering one's first wife, Harold."

He raised his eyebrows, but didn't comment.

"Was she a nurse too, Harold? Is that how you routinely get your drugs, or did you have a different source back then?"

I was trying to goad him, to force his attention on to how much I knew of his past, but he looked only mildly disgusted, not even upset.

"Sheila? Have a job? Are you kidding? No, I still had my license then. I've only let it lapse recently when they changed the re-certification requirements. No. I just needed her for her inheritance. And when she got it . . . " He shrugged.

"And now you have Dorothy get the drugs? That may have been a mistake. She seemed pretty upset when I saw her the day after you killed Ah-seong. She'll talk, you know."

I was grasping at anything to shake him, to get him riled, to force his concentration on to something else besides gripping my arm.

Grimes's face held a look of smug unconcern. It was sickening.

"I don't think Dorothy will say anything." He chuckled. "Her face is too swollen right now for her to want to venture out of the house. And she mumbles."

Great. Figured. He was a batterer too. Of course he was.

We'd been still standing in the shadows cast by the foliage around the tennis courts, but now he started walking, holding my arm even more tightly with his other hand in the middle of my back. From a distance we might have looked like lovers. What a ghastly thought.

He was hunching slightly as he walked, and his gait was uneven. Wait a minute.

"You're limping," I said, stopping to look down at his legs.

He jerked me forward, but I kept talking.

"Ah-seong kicked you, didn't she? You didn't get quite enough tran-quilizer into her before she realized what was happening. She'd come to you for help with her brother's pushing her around. After all, you teach 'Mar-riage and Family Ethics.'"

I fairly spat the words at him.

"So naturally she thought you'd help her and all you did was seduce her. Was it rape from the start, Harold, or did she try to refuse you Saturday night? You forced her and then you had to kill us both in case she'd told me anything. So what? Did you call her and say you were sorry and wanted to apologize? That she'd, what? Misunderstood and you really loved her? And then you fed her drugged tea. But she was smart. She was pre-med, did you know that? She read her own symptoms correctly and figured she'd been drugged. She started to struggle. You bastard . . . "

I wrenched with all my might and got my arm free of him. I kicked the same way Ah-seong had tried to do, for the kneecap. Grimes grabbed hold of my sweatshirt and tried to jam the needle into my chest. He swore when he felt the needle tip catch on the metal webbing of the body armor. He pulled his arm back and jabbed it into my forearm. I slapped it away and it crashed onto the concrete sidewalk. I stomped on it. But I could tell some had gotten in to me.

I turned and ran toward the nearest building. If I could just get far enough away from him, I could phone Mathews and Billman.

I ran up the steps and wrenched open the heavy doors. My injured arm was killing me and even now, the faster I moved, the more the tranquilizer would work its way into my bloodstream.

I got into the foyer and glanced around. What building was this? Oh, on the wall, a plaque. This was Fermi, the old physics building. I glanced around. No elevator. I looked at the stairs. Up or down? Down. To the tunnels.

I'd studied the campus maps with Matthews and Billman. Not only the surface ones, but also the tunnel system map that was available to the campus police. There was a tunnel from Fermi to the center of campus and there it connected with the tunnel that led to Myerson. If I could get to the tunnel system, I could lead Grimes directly to the basement of Myerson and they'd be waiting.

The door opened behind me and Grimes came in. I was extremely sorry to see that he had exchanged his needles and knives for a very business-like looking 38-special, what Smith and Wesson called the "personal defense weapon of choice" in their ads. I swung around the corner and took the stairs for the basement three at a time. It really helps to have long legs. By the time I reached the bottom, though, I was dizzy. The drug.

I heard a bang like a firecracker going off in a safe and realized Grimes was at the top of the stairs and he had fired down at me. In this marble-lined staircase, the reverberations were deafening. I turned and ran as fast as I could, which was increasingly slowly and yanked open the door to the entrance to the tunnel. I wondered vaguely why these things never seemed to be locked. Stupid. But good for me. I slammed the door behind me, but there was no way to lock it from the inside.

The tunnels are not fancy. They are cinderblock lined, with bare light bulbs hanging from wires every twenty-five feet. I figured I had less than a minute. I grabbed my cell phone out of my pocket and dialed the campus police number from memory. Our plan had blown up in my face, but I wasn't so woozy I couldn't remember the three digit emergency number for the campus police. I punched it in with sluggish fingers and pressed send. Nothing. Static.

I looked around. The tunnel was blocking the transmission. I glared at my screen. No bars. Crap. And on the other side of the door I could hear Grimes's heavy tread, coming after me.

I looked around for what I could use as a weapon. The cleaners use the entrances to the tunnels to store their pails and mops. Or they did in Myerson. A mop. Get a mop. Use the mop handle. My mind and my reflexes were slowing. I could barely force myself to focus on the problem.

Get away. You can't fight. That much swam up through the haze. Still . . . I grabbed a mop and swung it at the first hanging light bulb. I smashed it. Then I ran down the length of the tunnel, smashing the lights as I went. I made it to the first turn, an angle, not a sharp left, before I heard the sound of a gunshot. How many shots did a 38 have? Five. I thought. Five. Well.

That was two. Of course, methodical Grimes had probably brought more ammo.

I left the light at the corner alone. I wanted Grimes to be able to follow me. I just didn't want him to be able to kill me. I forced my rubbery legs to carry me down the spur of the tunnel, hoping it was the direction I wanted. Now I needed an opening to the surface to make the phone work. I'd seen some airshafts in other tunnels. Were there shafts in this one?

I smashed another five out of six light bulbs as I ran, leaving the tunnel in deep shadow but with enough light that Grimes could still follow me. I could hear him behind me, yelling my name and demanding that I stop. He really was crazy. Like I'd listen to him.

Wait. I felt a breeze on my face and I looked up. An airshaft. Would it be enough to get a signal. I looked at my phone. It was in my left hand. One good thing about the tranquilizer that Grimes had managed to get into me was I didn't feel so much pain in my arm. I wasn't really feeling much pain at all. I struggled to focus. Yes, that was one bar. I thought. Come on, Kristin. Focus.

I pressed 'redial' and the phone crackled to life. It rang and a voice distorted by static said, "What is your emergency?" I started to give my location and the phone cut off. A shot rang out, uncomfortably close. Time to break the light over my head.

I swung my broom handle and missed. Swung again. Missed. I could hear Grimes gaining on me. I grabbed the broom handle with both hands and swung at the light in frustration. I connected and the glass shattered. But my phone clattered to the floor.

Too dark to see where it had fallen. I groped around in the broken glass and felt myself get cut. I felt the cut vaguely, as though it were happening far away. I kept searching. I hoped I had one of those cell phones that could get hit with a golf ball and keep working. Of course, a shot from Grimes's 38 would be quite a tee shot. I giggled and realized the drug was affecting my emotions. I turned to search a little wider and my toe nudged the phone. I grabbed it. Then I had to find the broom.

It was like I was moving underwater, all my movements were so maddeningly slow. I could actually hear Grimes breathing. As I felt the broom handle touch my hand, he was too close for me to run. I grasped the handle at the end closest to the bristles and swung across the tunnel at mid-height as Grimes came charging up.

I felt the jar all the way up my arm. I heard a whoosh and thought I had connected with his mid-section and knocked the air out of him. I was tempted to try to get the gun, but I was so weakened and disoriented I needed to just get him to keep following me to Myerson.

I hung on to my trusty broom and my phone and took off again leaving Grimes swearing and groaning behind me. My. My. If the Dean could only hear our distinguished Chairperson now.

I reached a fork in the tunnels. One huge drawback of these tunnels is that they aren't labeled. Ordinarily I have a pretty good sense of direction, but drugged and injured and scared out of my mind, I ground to a halt. I tried to picture the map of the tunnels from where I had started out at Fermi relative to the location of Myerson. Myerson was west and slightly north of Fermi, so the left fork I'd taken had probably led to the center of the campus. So if I took this right hand tunnel . . .

A crack interrupted my logistical planning. Grimes was firing at me again. I jumped into the right-hand tunnel and broke the first six lights in my panic.

Then there were stairs on my right. What was this? I staggered up them before I could think it through, but a flat kind of cellar door kept me from exiting. I pushed on it. Locked.

I leaned close to the door and looked at the cell. Two bars. I had absorbed so much of the drug now that it took me three times to hit redial. Finally I heard a crackle and the connection. "What is your emergency?"

"This is Professor Ginelli. I'm in a tunnel under the main quad, probably the one that leads to Myerson. Dr. Grimes has a gun and he's trying to kill me."

If Grimes succeeded in shooting me, he would leave me there and get himself an alibi, probably with poor Dorothy swearing he'd never left the house. I wanted his name and "gun" to be recorded.

But there was no reply. Just static.

I almost screamed in frustration. But I hissed into the phone as loudly as I dared.

"Tunnel. Grimes trying to shoot me. Help!"

Then I heard Grimes reach the bottom of these stairs. I was trapped.

He was standing still, directly below me, but his head was cocked like he was listening. He didn't seem to see me. I held my breath and waited. If he moved on, I could get behind him and when I was far enough way, try to get him to chase me again. Again, optimally without killing me.

Despite my tranquilized state, I jumped when he addressed me. Apparently he did know where I was.

"Get down here, Ms. Ginelli, or I will shoot until I kill you."

Should I risk being quiet? Was it a bluff?

A shot missed me by inches and I screamed.

"I mean what I say. Come down here."

"All right," I said, "I'm coming."

I moved as slowly as I dared. It was like a dream state. The foggy feeling from the drug was getting much worse. Was it the pounding of my heart, circulating it through my limbs and up to my brain? Even drugged, though, I took the precaution of zigzagging as I came down, but that made me dizzier so I decided to go low, on my fanny for stability.

"Now!" screamed Grimes.

"Hang on, will you? That shot you gave me means I can't exactly dance down these stairs, you know."

As I scooted down to the bottom step, I was well below him and on the right side of the stairs. Grimes was facing me and this staircase, which meant he had his back to the tunnels. They were in shadow, but not completely black.

He was glaring down at me now, and that meant he couldn't see what was behind him, but I could. I could see Matthews and Billman hugging the far side of the right tunnel wall, their guns trained on Grimes's back.

I forced myself to not look at them and look up at Grimes as I stood up. I looked him in the eye and he calmly backhanded me with the gun in his hand and I rocked back on my heels and my shoulder hit the cinder block wall of the staircase. I wobbled and sat down on the first step and that's when I heard Matthews yell.

"Drop your weapon and put your hands up."

From my position below Grimes's belt, I could see him tensing and bringing his gun up. As he turned to fire at Matthews, I threw myself at his knees, chopping upward with my right hand to deflect the shot. He never got a shot off. The gun clattered to the floor.

Grimes went down like a sack of wet cement and the sound of his head hitting the concrete floor was something I will never forget as long as I live. It was like a hammer hitting a melon, a sharp tap and then a squish.

Grimes's legs went limp under me and I found myself floundering around, too drugged and disoriented to get off of them.

I felt arms around me, cradling me as much as actually trying to help me get off him. It was Alice. She dragged me away toward the right side tunnel and sat me on the floor. She sat down next to me, grasped my face with both hands and looked me square in the eyes.

"I told you if you didn't do what I said, I'd kill you myself."

She shook me very gently.

"Yeah, well, your plan was a complete bust, Officer."

We embraced each other and laughed hysterically.

While Alice had moved me over, Officer Billman had been bent over Grimes. He was now on his phone calling to get an ambulance, and glaring at the two of us. His look sobered Alice right away, but it took me a little longer to come back to my senses with the drug still coursing around in my veins.

It was the way Billman held himself as he looked down at Grimes that snapped me back into reality. I leaned on Alice and the wall and got myself upright. I went over and stood looking down at Grimes.

He was dead. The fall had cracked his skull. Blood and what might be brain matter made a spreading stain on the filthy floor.

In the distance we could hear the wail of the ambulance and the police cars as they made their way across the campus.

I hurriedly told Billman and Matthews about Henry Haruchi being drugged by Grimes and locked in his office closet. Billman looked furious, but he calmly told whomever he was talking to on the phone about the urgent need to send an ambulance and the police to rescue Henry.

I sat back down on the side of the stairs and leaned on the wall. I thought I saw Andrew Lee down the tunnel. He turned and left.

Since I was already hallucinating, I thought it would be okay to lose consciousness completely.

So I did.

19

For it is the wrong-doing of the opposing party which compels the wise to wage just wars; and this wrong-doing, even though it gave rise to no war, would still be a matter of human grief because it is human wrong-doing. Let every one, then, who thinks with pain on all these great evils, so horrible, so ruthless, acknowledge that this is misery. And if any one either endures or thinks of them without mental pain, this is a more miserable flight still, for they think themselves happy because they have lost human feeling.

AUGUSTINE, *THE CITY OF GOD*

I was back in another freezing cubicle in the emergency room. I hadn't lost consciousness for very long, apparently, but they'd immediately run some blood tests to figure out what Grimes had stuck into me. I was waiting to have somebody else come look at my cheek, which was swollen, it seemed to me at least, to the size of a large pumpkin.

Then there had been the little matter of sewing up my arm for the third time. A young man wearing a white coat with the words "Surgical Resident" sewn on a chest pocket had just been in. He consulted the computer and I guessed the blood tests were back because he gave me a topical anesthetic and efficiently stitched me up again.

And then I was alone. While I was shivering again, this time I was grateful for the solitude.

This was not the first time I'd killed someone. I'd shot a suspect when my partner and I had been called to a convenience store robbery that was still in progress when we'd screeched up in the patrol car. We'd gotten the call from just a block away.

As we'd gotten out of the car, I'd seen a guy in the doorway lift his gun to shoot back into the store. My response had been reflex, draw and shoot. Over in a second. I hadn't even hesitated. Though in truth I remembered I'd tried to aim low, hoping to stop the shooter without killing him, but he'd gone down on one knee as I'd discharged my weapon and I'd caught him in the right temple.

That guy had already killed the owner of the convenience store, a small Pakistani man whom I later learned left a wife and five kids. Grimes had killed, twice that we knew of, once that I suspected from my computer researches, and had attempted murder three times. At least. It didn't matter. The taking of a life is not something you dare shrug off with James Bond cool. That is the route to permanent numbness, the deadening of all human connection. And it was what I would walk on broken glass now to avoid. And so I did walk on the shards, going over and over it, back and forth, wondering if I could have avoided killing Grimes, letting myself feel that I had killed.

And it was worse than before. When the city police had arrived on the scene in the tunnel, I learned they had determined Grimes's gun had been empty. He'd used up his five shots and perhaps had not realized it. He had had other ammunition on him, but he had not reloaded. He couldn't have killed Alice or Mel. He would have been firing an empty gun.

So, yes, I'd killed him accidentally, but it had been unnecessary. I probed my conscience like Tom would probe a wound, to find hidden infection. Had I unconsciously been counting the shots? Did I know the gun was empty and I'd hit him that hard anyway? I didn't think so. As my weary mind circled back over and over it, I could not remember counting shots after the first three. The drug had taken care of my limited mathematical ability.

But it certainly didn't make me feel good to know it wasn't necessary. Yes, I had thought I'd been protecting life, but really I'd killed a man who was no immediate threat. I hadn't meant to kill him, and I was actually amazed that he had died from hitting the floor that way. But sometimes that was all it took. The human head, for all its bone, was actually quite fragile.

I sat on the table in the little cold cubicle that had very likely seen so much pain, so much misery and death and yet revealed none of it in its white on white sterility. I willed myself not to become like that room, showing nothing, feeling nothing. But the temptation to lay my head down and say, 'I'm innocent, it wasn't my fault' was so great, I trembled with the effort to hold on to human feeling. And what I said to myself after that is my business.

After a while, about several centuries it seemed, two men, one young and one older, came in, poked at my cheek and decided I needed an X-ray. More waiting.

I'd asked for Tom when I'd been brought in, but I was told he was in surgery and not available. I wanted to see Tom, though I didn't relish having to explain to him why I hadn't let him know what I had planned. The awful truth was it hadn't occurred to me, and if it had, I might have rejected the idea of telling him anyway. Too much like asking his permission. I didn't know, but it was food for thought.

The older doctor who'd ordered the X-ray came back and told me they were keeping me overnight for observation. With the insurance companies fighting every admission, I guess there might be cause for real concern so I agreed. Besides, there was no one home and even the antiseptic bustle of the hospital was better than the Rosemont house with no kids, no dog and no Carol and Giles. I'd called the Ginellis as soon as I'd been brought to the ER, and I'd told Vince a short version of what had happened. He didn't comment, he just said they'd bring the kids back tomorrow.

After the X-ray I was carted in a wheelchair up to a room. I obediently put on the gown they gave me and got into the bed. It was weird, but I felt a little closer to Tom in the hospital. I was going to have to think about that too. But not tonight.

Alice had ridden with me to the hospital, bless her, and I'd asked her to find out about Henry. She had been told he was going to be okay. He was apparently still very groggy from the tranquilizer Grimes had given him so they were keeping him overnight as well. His metabolism and the fact that Grimes had had plenty of time to give it to him orally in the dratted Ginseng tea and also give him a shot besides meant it had been a fairly close call. Alice was fairly pissed when she came back to me with that information and she was right. The problem was, she was not only pissed at Grimes, she was pissed at me for endangering him. I got it. I was pissed at me too.

I got back out of the bed and picked up the phone to check on him. Of course I could get no real information like Alice could, but I asked for Henry's room. It was on the same floor as where I was. I padded down there in the paper slippers they give you for free and opened the door.

Henry's face looked like it had been covered with a pale green epoxy and left to harden. It was a terrible color and frighteningly still. His wife was seated next to the bed, her head down on his outstretched hand. I realized they were both asleep. A blinking monitor cast a strobe light across the bed, bringing them in and out of focus. Or maybe it was the tears in my eyes. I shut the door as quietly as I could.

I went back to my room and got back into the bed.

Tom never came and I eventually fell asleep.

* * * *

In the morning I ate the watery eggs and dry toast they brought me and then got up and dressed in the baggy clothes I'd been brought in wearing. I didn't put on my body armor, though. Given my subsequent conversation with Henry, I think in retrospect I should have.

I headed back down the hall to Henry's room prepared to congratulate him on being alive. I also wanted to find out why he'd ducked me so consistently since Ah-seong's death. Had it just been the moonlighting?

I knocked and Henry's voice said 'come in.' He was in bed with his head elevated so he could reach the tray in front of him. So far it seemed he was avoiding the eggs and toast. And he certainly hadn't drunk the tea.

I'd come in all little Mary Sunshine and 'let bygones be bygones,' and I was met with a stony stare.

"Kristin."

That was it.

What was this? Was Henry blaming me for Grimes knocking him out?

"Henry. Glad to see you sitting up."

He gave me a flat stare.

I grabbed on to my fraying temper and tried to remember this guy had just about died. Since his wife seemed to have gone, I took the chair next to the bed and looked at him for a moment. Then I asked the question I wanted to ask, cold stare or no.

"Henry, why'd you run from me this past week? Why wouldn't you talk to me? Not that we'd have solved the case together, but what you knew about Ah-seong Kim could have been really helpful."

Henry lifted an eyebrow.

"The case? What case? What is it with you? What business was it of yours how I knew Ah-seong Kim, or where I was going or what I was doing?"

I couldn't believe it. I thought I'd known this guy.

"What business is it of anyone when someone is murdered?"

I was not succeeding in holding on to my temper.

Henry shuttered his face and turned it away from me. He made no reply.

I'd had absolutely no luck this past week waiting people out who wouldn't talk to me, but I tried it again. I just sat there in silence.

Finally Henry turned back to look at me, though he did not meet my eyes.

"You really have no idea the effect you have on people, do you? You run around butting into things, raking people over, showing no respect, no insight, no proportion.

"You know why I wouldn't talk to you? Because I couldn't trust you to respect the boundaries of privacy, to understand what I was doing and why and what it would mean to me and my family if you blurted it out to someone because you thought it might be necessary. I would be just a stepping-stone in your so-called case; I bet that's why Ah-seong wouldn't talk to you. You pushed her, didn't you? If you'd waited and tried to gain her trust, her respect, you might have been able to help her."

I leaned forward and spoke right in his face.

"If I'd waited to gain her respect, her trust, as you say, the result would have been just the same. She'd have been dead. Your 'take your time and give respect and just don't tread on me' approach doesn't get the job done, Henry. It's just an excuse. What did you do to gain her respect? Huh? Why didn't you notice she was bruised and upset? Why didn't you figure out Grimes was hitting on her and she wanted to break it off? You just tell me that."

Henry flushed and looked away again. I stood up. This was getting us nowhere fast.

Then Henry spoke quietly.

"I was too caught up in holding three jobs to notice her. You're right about that part. But I didn't trust you. That much is true. I'd felt pretty safe working at a convenience store in the suburbs, but moonlighting on campus was potential suicide. I didn't trust you. That's the bottom line. But I should have seen her."

He paused, looking grim.

"I did see it. A little. But I couldn't be bothered."

He covered his face with his hands.

Well, crap. A lot of us had failed Ah-seong.

It was true. I pushed. Too much, maybe. I could have tried to be less aggressive with Henry, but he needed to own his part too. And he was.

I told him we'd both got stuff to blame ourselves for, but we hadn't killed Ah-seong Kim. Grimes had. He was a dangerous sociopath and he'd been at the business of exploiting and raping and killing for a long time. I gave too long a speech, but eventually Henry lowered his hands. I touched the one closest to me, and then I left.

And I knew that what I'd thought was a friendship had been a lot less, and a big chunk of that was my fault.

* * * *

I got back to my room to find, joy of joys, that Kaiser and his minion were waiting for me. This was shaping up to be quite a day. Karl was fairly drooling over the possibility of charging me with murder.

"So, why'd you off the guy?" he started. Icabod was already writing.

I looked at him and said I would say nothing without benefit of counsel.

While Karl literally shouted questions at me, I sat down in a chair by the window, took out my cell phone and called an old college roommate who was an attorney with a large, downtown law firm. Anna was good. She was so good she was going to make crab cakes out of Kaiser for even attempting this. Thank God she picked right up and I think she could hear the almost panic in my voice, and probably Kaiser's screamed questions in the background. She promised to hurry right over and cautioned me to say nothing until she got there. I gave her my room number and disconnected.

I knew Anna would come. I knew she would be great. But I was terrified down to my socks. It is the way of abusers. They know just what will scare you and make you feel powerless.

* * * *

Anna had come and gone, telling Kaiser that unless he was prepared to charge me then and there that we'd set a time to meet him downtown after her client had recovered from her injuries. She met him glare for glare. Anna wasn't a tall woman, but she worked out and her compact body fit very nicely into her St. John suit. Her sleek blond hair was short and trim as she was, and it made a shiny helmet on her head. She was decorated, as she always was, with an abundance of exquisite jewelry designed to intimidate. She intimidated Kaiser. It was a big relief.

She gave him her card and he and Icabod departed. I hugged her and she hustled off to pile up her billable hours.

I sat down in a chair and waited to be discharged. Tom still hadn't put in an appearance. With all the emotional turmoil of the last eighteen hours I was beginning to read a lot into his absence. I looked up quickly when the door opened, expecting it was finally Tom. Astonishingly, it was Dr. Andrew Lee dragging Myung Ha Kim by the arm.

Lee carefully shut the door and literally positioned Myung Ha in front of me, but toward the center of the room. In the room, but not too close.

One other thing I'd learned from Alice Matthews last night was that I'd hadn't hallucinated seeing Lee in the tunnel. Apparently Lee had been walking by the cellar door exit where I'd tried to contact the campus police with my cell phone and he'd heard my desperate message. He'd whipped out his own phone and made the call for me.

Matthews and Billman had been only about a hundred feet away and had, as Alice had said they would, been monitoring all calls to the campus emergency number. I'd been right about the direction of that tunnel. It was the one that connected to the basement of Myerson where they were waiting. All they'd had to do was enter the tunnel and walk a short way, and they saw Grimes pointing a gun at someone in that staircase. Hence their timely arrival.

In fact, I might owe my life to Andrew Lee. It was an uncomfortable feeling.

Based on my previous conversation with Henry, I decided not to jump right in with questions, but see where Lee wanted to take the conversation. Well, that and the fact that I was flabbergasted and had no idea what to say anyway.

Lee stood next to Myung Ha. He'd let go of the young man's arm, but he spoke to me.

"I have explained to Mr. Kim that you are responsible for searching for and finding his sister's killer when others would not believe she had not killed herself. Mr. Kim is leaving for Korea today to accompany his sister's body to their home, and I wished for him to thank you for the service you have rendered his sister and his family."

I looked at Myung Ha. His young face was struggling between pain and stoicism. I could acknowledge his grief at the death of his sister, but I felt he should feel pain for his disregard of her own interests and concerns. He should feel guilt because of his own mistreatment of her. And now he could not conveniently blame me, so those chickens were coming home to roost. But there was so much pain etched there that I could not find it in my heart to refuse to hear what he had to say. He did not invent his social system, even as I had not invented mine. We were both products of cultures that could make us feel we were in the right, even when that could very well be untrue.

He said thank you to me in both English and Korean, and I held out my hand to shake his. He bent slightly at the waist but did not shake my hand. Then he looked up at Lee. Lee told him to go wait in the hall.

Andrew Lee remained standing.

"I have encouraged Mr. Kim to seek counseling before he returns to the university. His treatment of his own sister and his own anger need to be examined thoroughly. He feels very strongly the need to maintain the family dignity since the death of his father, but he has taken the wrong path to accomplish this."

I regarded Lee for a moment and then realized it was my turn.

"I must also say thank you. I know it was you who called the police when you heard me trying to reach them from the tunnel. It seems I owe you my life and I am grateful."

Lee looked appalled.

"No, certainly not. I did what was necessary, what anyone would have done."

So he didn't want my gratitude. Well, I could see how he would regard me as a ticking bomb and wish to distance himself from what had occurred. He certainly deserved me to give him that if that's what he wanted.

"Yes, certainly. And Officers Matthews and Billman directly saved my life. It's true."

He may have been a stuffed shirt in a lot of ways, but he was no fool. He twisted the corner of his mouth in an ironic half-smile. Then he bowed slightly and was gone.

My head was swimming from these encounters and still no Tom.

Suddenly it didn't matter. The door burst open and the boys ran into the room followed by Natalie. Vince plodded in behind them, smelling of beer and cigarettes. Natalie smelled like her gardenia perfume, and she wore a lot of it, and that mingled with Vince's smell and was topped off by a nice dollop of kid sweat and chocolate ice cream. I drank in the smells like someone who was dehydrated. And I was. These bundles of energy and life were life's fluid. They were my connection to the planet.

The kids nestled in as close to me as they could with me sitting in a chair. I could see them trying to be careful of me, but craving the closeness. I felt anchored to life, tied down like a hot-air balloon that would drift away into the upper stratosphere and be destroyed without these anchors. Mike gently patted my cheek where it was bruised and swollen and I let myself go completely into the circle of their love.

After a few minutes, I looked up to see Natalie simultaneously beaming and crying, and Vince's small eyes lasering into mine. Despite the faded check shirt that was too small for him, he looked like he was in uniform.

"Nice work, kid. You're a helluva cop for an egg-head."

We smiled at each other while Natalie scolded him for using such language in front of the children.

She'd not been to kindergarten lately, I assumed.

20

Philosophy "regains its speech and gets a grip on itself only on its borders and limits."

Michel Foucault, in James Miller, *The Passion of Michel Foucault*

It was now the beginning of December. The weeks since Grimes's death had been horrendous.

Kaiser had continued to be determined to see me charged with murder and I'd had to appear many times downtown to answer questions. But never without Anna. We'd met with Kaiser, other police detectives, and even the Assistant U.S. Attorney.

Anna had been a center of sanity for me, her sleek suited form a needle pointing due north when the compass of the rest of my life had been gyrating wildly. Alice Matthews, Mel Billman, Henry Haruchi and even poor Professor Lee had been questioned. Finally the AUSA had agreed Grimes's death was accidental.

The newspapers had a field day. This was a real life "Thelma and Louise" avenging woman story. Sometimes I was called "The Philosopher Cop," but the Hollywood tag line was the most popular.

Dorothy Grimes had been charged as an accessory before the fact in the murder of Ah-seong Kim. I'd told Anna about Grimes battering Dorothy and we'd gotten one of Anna's partners to defend her. I would testify to both Grimes's admission of battering her, and Dorothy's condition when she'd come to the office after Ah-seong's death. Even Frost was willing to testify that she'd heard Dorothy yelling at Grimes in his office.

Combined with the suspicion that Grimes had killed his first wife, Sheila, that made his threats to Dorothy all that much more credible.

Dorothy was lucky Grimes had died. I would not have been surprised if she hadn't already been scheduled for a fatal accident in the creepy brain of Harold Grimes. Anna said her colleague had hopes that the charges against Dorothy might even be dismissed.

The Department of Philosophy and Religion had been in some turmoil, to put it mildly. The university brought in a shrink to work with Grimes's students who were understandably upset to find they had been taking their ethics classes from a sex-harassing rapist and murderer. Of course, they'd probably learned more about the difficulties of doing ethics in the twenty-first century than most undergraduates, but nobody but me saw it that way.

The shrink had even met with my students for a few sessions. They were a little shaken and unsure how to deal with me. I thought he'd been helpful, if only in the official acknowledgement that it was okay to be upset with me. That took place during the two-week medical leave I had taken to get plastic surgery on my arm and recover my own mental balance, at least a little.

But there were personal issues that were also terrible for me. Giles had not been able to look me in the eye when we had all convened back at the Rosemont house. After several days of this, I cornered him when we were alone in the kitchen. Carol had taken the boys to the park.

"Giles?"

He visibly jumped, but he did not turn from the stove where he was preparing dinner. His narrow shoulders under his tee shirt bunched with tension. I felt very much at a loss as to how to deal with this.

"Giles," I said softly. "I need to know what's bothering you. We live in the same house and we should try to work out our problems, try to talk about them, anyway. I'm willing to answer any questions you might have."

I paused and took a deep breath.

"Do you think I killed that man on purpose?"

There. I'd gotten what I thought was at least part of the problem out in the open.

Giles didn't turn and he spoke so softly I had to lean toward him a little to hear.

"You have a violent spirit, Mrs. Gin." Giles always shortened my name. "It troubles me."

He continued to be turned away from me and I could see his back and shoulder muscles clench even tighter.

Well, if truth be told, and this was a good time for truth, it had troubled me too. Was still troubling me. I owed it to Giles to tell him that. But Henry hadn't been wrong about my rushing into things, crashing past other people instead of listening to them.

"Giles, what should I do about the violent spirit?"

He was so astonished by my question that he dropped the spoon on the stovetop, scattering black beans and splashing sauce across the surface. Fastidious Giles didn't seem to even notice. He turned and looked straight at me. I realized this was perhaps the first time we'd really looked at each other since we'd met.

"You want to know from me what to do?"

His voice was soft and wondering, no longer tight and forced.

"Yes. I think you're right. I feel that in myself some. Maybe you and I could talk more, about what you think and how we can restore peace not only between you and me but to our house?"

I gave him a slow smile and held out my hand. He took it in both of his and grasped it warmly rather than shaking it.

"I will help with this. I will think what is best and we will talk."

As he turned back to the stove and began carefully wiping up the spill, I felt empty but also curiously free. It was the first decent moment I'd had in weeks. I wished Henry and I were still sharing an office, and that we were still speaking.

But that had been another blow. Henry had quit the department and he was working for the Computing Sciences department full time now. He'd left without a personal word, not even a note.

I did have a violent spirit. Was that better than the closed off automaton I'd been? I'd let a genie out a bottle and the genie had come out pretty weird, pretty erratic. I'd alienated Henry, Giles, and it seemed, also Tom.

Tom had not gotten in touch since the day of Grimes's death. I was by now fairly angry about this, and my violent spirit was generally raging internally about it. These past weeks had been the worst in my life since Marco had been killed. Tom's silence had really hurt at first, and then all the other crises had driven it to the back of my mind, though not back far enough, and not late at night. I'd settled on anger and it was working to keep the hurt at bay. But wasn't that what Giles was saying to me? I clearly had a lot to think about.

On the plus side, I did have a job for next semester if I wanted it. In fact, one of the only humorous things that had happened in these last horrible weeks had been the interview with Dean Wooster after I'd been cleared of any wrongdoing in Grimes's death. I suppose it was only efficient to wait to talk to me until it was clear I wasn't going to be charged with murder. If I were being prosecuted for killing Grimes, then the question of my continued employment would be moot. Or I guessed it would have. Murdering one's boss is usually cause for dismissal.

The Dean's secretary had called and I'd been invited to meet him at his office. When I arrived I was ushered, perhaps even hustled, through the door. The Dean was ordinarily a smoothie. He was tall, certainly several inches over six feet, with a full head of hair greying in a distinguished fashion. He favored double-breasted suits with the kind of geometric ties that are designed to convey that the power suit can barely contain this young, go-getter. He kind of reminded me of Richard Gere in his pre-Zen period.

But on this day, and even though I was there at his request, Dean Wooster was visibly sweating. There was a small, moist line across his upper lip and his hands were cold when he greeted me with a handshake. And he only gave me the tips of his fingers, probably afraid I'd flip him over my shoulder if I got a decent grip on him.

Then he'd quickly retreated behind his desk.

Well, I'd killed the Chair of my department. Maybe I should inspire a little fear in the Dean.

The meeting went as swiftly as he could manage it. He spoke rapidly and in a monotone. The university was sorry for Grimes's behavior, he thanked me for my efforts to expose him, and if I would just kindly refrain from holding the institution itself liable, would I like to continue on as an instructor.

I told him I had no interest in suing, though that had distressed Anna. And yes, I would like to continue teaching. But I had two conditions.

As I uttered the word 'conditions,' his eyebrows had flown up to meet his blow-dried hair. After I had explained what I wanted, and his eyebrows came down slightly, he said that should 'be no problem' and he would have a new contract for me shortly.

I smiled sweetly and said that would be fine. The Dean shuddered and said a terse good-bye.

* * * *

And so I was walking across the campus on this December day, headed to another faculty meeting. Adelaide had been made Chairperson of the department. It was just Adelaide, Hercules, Donald and me these days, since Grimes was dead and Henry had left. We had a lot of issues to discuss, not the least of them three faculty searches to begin. That had been one of my conditions to the Dean. Philosophy and Religion would get to keep the positions that had been vacated, and add one more. I was mildly looking forward to the meeting, or at least not dreading it.

Suddenly I spotted Tom walking toward me across the quadrangle and he was accompanied by a woman. I tensed. No. As they got closer, I saw the person with him was a young, tall and gangly girl. A relative? A daughter? Tom saw me too and headed in my direction. As we came up to each other, I concluded the latter. Their eyes were identical, except hers were turning hostile as Tom stopped to speak with me.

"Kristin. I'd like you to meet my daughter Kelly. Kelly, this is my friend Kristin."

I must have looked surprised by his describing me as a 'friend,' and my expression was not lost on Tom. He looked very embarrassed.

I stuck out my hand.

"Hi, Kelly."

Kelly looked at my hand and mumbled what I thought was a greeting.

Tom's look of embarrassment was replaced with parental resignation, a look I had had occasion to manifest myself.

"We were just on our way to the computer center. Kelly, why don't you go on ahead and I'll catch up?"

He looked at her like she was a volcano registering significant seismic activity. I knew that feeling too. Even approaching seven, the boys in a bad mood could make me very leery in front of other adults.

Kelly sneered quite effectively and slouched off. I guessed she was about 13, and she was almost my height. Poor kid. I remembered it well.

Tom watched me watch her.

I turned back to him and waited. The daughter had been a buffer for a few minutes, but I was unwilling to bridge the awkwardness now. I just stood there and waited.

Tom looked back at me for half a minute. Then he spoke in a subdued voice.

"My ex-wife died in a car accident the same evening your department chair died. I was on a plane to New York by 7 that next morning. I had to take some bereavement leave time, and my life since then has been dealing with that, moving Kelly here and trying to help her, and me, get through it. With all you were going through, I didn't think we'd be any help to each other."

I was literally speechless. I was so prepared to reject any excuse as inadequate or made up that his simple statement set me right back on my heels. I should have trusted my instincts about him. I should have called. I should have done something when I didn't hear from him. Well, I thought. I'll trust my instincts now.

I didn't say anything. I just leaned forward and let my head rest on his chest for a few minutes. Then I pulled back and looked up. Tom's disbelieving smile was good enough for me. I smiled back.

We started to move a little closer to each other when a shrill voice rang out over the quad.

"Daaad!

Kelly was not willing to let her father be alone with this strange woman. I wondered if she'd seen me rest my head on his chest.

I gave Tom a wry look.

"This is going to be rough, isn't it? I bet she hates herself and everybody around her right now. I can only imagine what getting her together with my boys will be like."

Tom visibly trembled.

"Let's not even think about doing that right now. Let's get to know us again. I'll call you tonight."

The hideous "Daaad!" rang out again.

"Late. I'll call you very late."

He surreptitiously touched my hand and was gone, loping toward the smoldering bundle of teen waiting at the far end of the quad.

Despite the awful prospect of this angry teenager and twin six-year-old boys, I was momentarily happy. Then I remembered Tom and Kelly's tragedy and grieved for them. It is so hard to achieve happiness and it is so ephemeral.

I trudged on to the faculty meeting.

* * * *

As I got up to the office floor, Adelaide was just coming out of Frost's office. Frost. I wondered how she was taking her great leader's demise. I'd scuttled in and out of the office to teach my classes after I'd been cleared, and her door had always been shut. I'd not ventured in.

I walked up to Adelaide and saw a young woman I didn't recognize occupying Frost's chair. Probably a temp. And then I saw Elvis was gone.

Adelaide turned to me and said kindly, "Come on down to my office before the meeting. I have some good coffee in a thermos. You look like death on a plate."

I grimaced and acknowledged that the last few weeks had taken a toll on my youthful good looks. Adelaide chuckled briefly, but then sobered and I followed her in silence to her office.

Her office was now Grimes's old office, of course. I knew she'd moved in here, but with all that had been going on, I hadn't stopped by. It was sort of eerie. I wondered how it felt to Adelaide to be occupying the office of her old nemesis, and him a dead and buried murderer at that.

She went over to a side table that I thought was new, and she poured me coffee from one of those good, stainless steel thermoses. She handed me a cup, and gestured to me to sit on a couch that was also new. God only knew what Grimes had gotten up to on the old couch. I was glad she'd gotten rid of it. I would have been happy if it could have been burned in a bonfire in the center of the campus, perhaps as a centerpiece of a Take Back the Night rally.

She'd also made a nice grouping of chairs on either side of the new couch, and placed a colorful rug on the floor in front of the couch. The desk had been pushed back along the far wall, almost into the turret affair that was there. All in all it looked sufficiently different not to be too weird. Of course, that's why she'd done it.

I sat on the couch and she sat beside me. Her customary flowing garb was an unrelieved dark blue. I wondered about whether she was grieving. Odd.

Then Adelaide turned a pale but determined face toward me and I slowly realized how wrong I was. Again. She harrumphed and began with deliberation.

"I want you to know some history. You deserve to know it. You need to know why I hated Harold."

I started to speak, to say it wasn't necessary, but she held up a hand.

"No, just let me get through this, okay?"

I nodded.

"I've thought about saying this to you and I want to say it. Maybe I even need to say it, since I've never told anybody.

"Harold and I joined the department within a year of each other. He was here when I came and married. I'd was twenty-five and I'd always been heavy. I'd buried myself in my books and I'd told myself I didn't care that guys looked at me and looked away. But I did care. And the more I cared, the more I ate."

Christ. This was awful. I hoped she knew what she was doing telling me this. She was my new boss, after all.

"Well, Harold came on to me. At first subtly, and then more strongly. I had no knowledge of that sort of thing. None. And it was decades ago. Who talked about that stuff, harassment and victimization and you know? Well, I let it go pretty far one day, or I didn't resist enough or something and he just climbed on me and stuck it into me. I was a virgin. It hurt like hell."

She turned her head a little, but I could seen a few tears forming. They didn't fall. They just sat there on the top of her cheeks like tiny pools. Such little tears for such an immense wrong. But I suspected they'd had sisters over the years. Many sisters.

"I didn't tell anybody. I had to take a leave. They called it a 'nervous breakdown.' Whatever. I was lucky I still had a job to come back to, given the attitudes.

"Well, maybe he did me a favor. I became a feminist after that and that's what helped me. I joined the National Organization for Women, and I volunteered at the women's center here. It helped, you know?"

I nodded. I knew.

"I've always hated the bastard, but I never suspected, I swear I never suspected what he did, battering Dorothy or, God, coming on to students."

She looked agonized.

"Stupid, stupid, stupid. I, of all people, should have known. How could I not have seen it?"

How much harm these abusers do. It's like a toxic waste spill, contaminating everything as it ripples outward from the first violent act.

I grasped Adelaide's trembling hands and leaned toward her.

"He was good, Adelaide. He was really good at it. He fooled a lot of people for a long time. And he traumatized you so badly, you didn't even like to think about him, did you? And you had to work with him. Why wouldn't you just block him out? That's simple survival.

"Never blame yourself for what it takes to survive. Place the blame where it belongs. On Grimes and whatever forces in our world enable and protect him and guys like him from discovery. But don't blame yourself. If you do, he still wins."

Her large hands felt old in mine, frail and weak. I longed to hug her, but her innate dignity restrained me. That and the fact that we had to continue to work together. Better not push it. I let go of her hands, and sat back and waited.

She used the back of one hand to dash the little pools of tears away and she straightened up.

"Damn right we can't him win."

I knew it was an act and so did she. That's okay. Acts are necessary sometimes. Reality is not all it's cracked up to be.

I stood to leave.

"I'll see you at the meeting."

She nodded absently, but then suddenly barked, "Yep. We have a department to build."

Yes, we did. Maybe I should have told her my other condition I'd forced the Dean to agree to, but it didn't seem like the right time.

* * * *

We were back in the conference room and the ghosts had increased, some of them actual ghosts, like Grimes. Hercules looked even smaller and wirier than ever. He'd gone to France right after Grimes had been buried and had only returned last week. He was the only one in the room when I arrived, and he greeted me normally. Interesting guy.

Donald walked in behind me. He still looked sheepish when I was around. It was appropriate. He was a sheep. He'd followed Grimes like a little lamb. Donald had admitted to the cops that it had been Grimes who had urged him to call and turn Edwin over to them. And he'd never even questioned why. He'd have fit right in in occupied France. I didn't know if Hercules knew this, but I wouldn't like to be looked at the way Hercules looked at Donald these days.

Adelaide came in briskly and called the meeting to order.

She announced that our first order of business was to form search committees for the three vacant positions in the department.

Now was the moment. I cleared my throat and spoke.

"Actually, we need to fill three and a half positions."

"Why?"

Adelaide was back in form. Blunt and in charge. Our previous conversation might never have happened.

"Because I negotiated a half-time leave with the Dean at full pay for at least two years. I plan to consult with the Campus Police Department. They have agreed. And I will use that work as part of my dissertation research."

The news silenced the room very effectively.

Adelaide regarded me gravely from the head of the table. Then she smiled.

"Ducky, you are not the run of the mill colleague, that's for damn sure. Not at all. Go get'em."

Hercules didn't blink and Donald looked sick.

Things were getting back to normal in Philosophy and Religion.

* * * *

When I left the meeting, night had already fallen. In December, in the Grey City, light was disappearing by mid-afternoon and now it was nearly pitch dark. As I walked across the campus toward home, I felt the two sides of my life slide into a whole. I deliberately walked where I knew the tunnels ran beneath me, crisscrossing under the surface of the main campus. Underneath these gothic edifices that framed this space and formed the public face of the university, a complex structure of power and privilege lurked, a subterranean support for the supposedly objective knowledge above.

I had decided to change the topic of my dissertation. Radically change it. I was going to write a post-modernist interpretation of higher education as a complex network of power, knowledge, and institutionalized violence. And what better way to research that than to see all the layers, to track how the academic and policing power structures collided, colluded and worked together to suppress the buried knowledge beneath.